DAWN HUSTED

GIRL

GONE

GHOST

Also by Dawn Husted

Safe

Touch of Darkness

Scythe of Darkness

ACKNOWLEDGMENTS

The world would be a terrible place without editors who correct all the grammar mistakes. Huge thanks to my editor, Kelly Hopkins, for not only correcting mistakes, but also challenging my writing in each and every sentence. Without you, my books would never be reader worthy.

Thank you to my critique partners who offered advice and read my work in one form or another: Barb Hopkins, Julie Ferguson, Molly Blaisdell, Liz Mertz, and Kathy Whitehead. Also to my proofreaders: Sasha Chihak, Candilynn Fite, Laura Francis, Chauma Smith Guss, and Liz Mertz. Your keen eyes helped shape and revise *Girl Gone Ghost*.

For Mawmaw

ONE

Yes, Brenham—a town in the birthplace of Texas—had a serial killer. My best friend's body was discovered nine weeks ago.

Holding Magnolia's obituary in my hand, I couldn't peel my eyes away from her heart-shaped face. My eyes watered. The newspaper clipping encompassed her mesmerizing smile and all the years we spent growing up together. Why did she have to die? I kicked my shiny green pompoms into the corner of my room. One of my cheerleading medals fell off the bedroom wall, onto Kaylee's fluffy black and white tail. My border collie growled and her back stiffened, hair raising along her spine.

"They're only pompoms," I muttered as I bent to pick up the medal. *What's the matter?* The sea green ribbon attached to the medal had formed a perfect M on the carpet. Bending over, a chill wafted over my back and up my neck. The air conditioning hummed on above my head.

Kaylee showed her teeth at the corner. I waved my hand at her. "Stop it. Sit. What's gotten into you?" I hung the gold medal back on the nail next to dozens of others. My fingers had crinkled the top edge of the clipping. *Dang it.*

I grabbed my copy of *East of Eden* off my desk and stuck the clipping between the pages to flatten it again— and put the obit away one last time. A familiar pang squeezed my chest, and I wiped a tear from my cheek with the back of my hand. I couldn't focus on Magnolia anymore. I needed to let her go. She was gone and she wasn't coming back. Opening my dresser drawer, I slid the novel inside. It rested beside my half of our friendship necklace, the same one I had removed two days after her death.

My phone buzzed with a text from my boyfriend, Chris Jenkins. *Just pulled up.*

In the reflection of the dresser mirror, an outline of our high school's mascot stared at me with wide-eyes and a green, roaring mouth. I remembered the day Magnolia helped me place the cub sticker on the wall—the same day we made the cheerleading squad our freshman year, three years ago. Closing the drawer, I breathed the memory of Magnolia in and out for the last time.

The doorbell rang. I turned my light off and rushed to let Chris inside. We were having dinner tonight—like it was another normal Saturday night with my family.

Opening the front door, Chris walked in and winked. "Hey, babe." His arms slid around my waist and squeezed. I laced my fingers through his. He smelled woodsy.

I glanced into the kitchen. Mom grabbed food from the island in the middle and placed the bowl on the dining table.

"Sonora, fill the glasses," she said. Chris released my hands.

"Where have you been? I thought you'd be here fifteen minutes ago?" I asked him.

"Sonora, did you hear me? Fill the glasses, all the way to the top."

I hated filling glasses with ice, and she knew it. The cold icky cubes sounded like freshly painted fingernails scraping the hood of my Taurus.

Mom's pristine hair swayed on her poised shoulders as she hung her apron on the hook.

Chris followed me and grabbed the glasses off the kitchen island and handed them to me one by one, winking at me with his dreamy, dark chocolate eyes.

"Make that one half-full," he whispered to me as he grinned.

I stuck my chin out to mimic her, "Mom likes the 'hot tea to melt the cubes with perfection.'" I laughed and smiled at Chris but filled each cup as requested.

Here we were, having dinner, like normal. But my senior year was on the brink of spiraling out of control—I could sense it. Who had killed Magnolia? Why? Dad turned off the jazz music playing in the background and shooed my border collie, Kaylee, into my room. "In you go. No begging at the table," he told her as he shut the door. Dad turned back to the long wooden table. Behind him, vintage racks displaying antique spoons hung on the navy blue wall. We held hands as he sat. "Who wants to say grace? Chris?"

I squeezed Chris's fingers, prompting him to speak.

"Sure, Mr. Stewart," Chris replied, closing his eyes and bowing his head.

"Bless this food and help Brenham High win the game Friday."

"Amen," Dad said, loosening his tie from around his neck. He wasn't the football type, but that didn't stop him from cheering for the team.

"Sonora, can you grab the sour cream please?" Mom asked. Scooting my chair back, I ambled into the kitchen, past my brother's empty seat. I missed Bram. Why did he have to move out? I yanked on the door and studied the contents. Containers of yogurt, butter, and assorted Tupperware blocked the view. I reached for the sour cream behind leftovers of questionable age. An eerie dampness floated over my arms. Something smelled old and rotten as if seafood had been left to spoil. I rubbed my nose, shaking the horrid odor off, and shut the door. "Mom, you need to clean the fridge," I said, entering the dining room.

"Sonora, don't be ridiculous. The fridge is spotless," she replied, waving my insane notion off as usual. I grimaced. Why did she have to use my name in every sentence? Why? I handed her the container and sat next to Chris, wriggling the moldy smell from my nose. Beneath the table, he casually crossed his ankle over mine.

"So Chris, are you starting on Friday?" My father passed him the green beans from the middle of the table.

"Yes, sir, Coach wouldn't have it any other way." Chris plopped a serving onto his plate, passing the blue bowl to me next. "And Sonora will be cheering from the sidelines." He winked and nudged my side. I was the cheerleader dating the star football player.

"How do you like the new coach?" my dad asked.

Chris nodded, focused on the food.

Dad wasn't about to ask deeper questions about football. His professor brain didn't allow much time for sports, but he knew the town had hired a new coach. Everyone in a small town knows when that sort of thing happens.

"Sonora, how's the dance committee coming along?" Mom asked as I took a bite.

My fork froze in midair. "Fine," I replied, not exactly feeling in the mood to talk about the Fall Fling. I wanted to stop thinking about Magnolia, but it was hard. I guess Mom found it easy to forget my dead, best friend.

The horrid smell rushed around me. The same fishy smell as before. *Weird. Where was it coming from?* I leaned over to Chris and sniffed.

"Did you just smell me?" he whispered out the corner of his mouth.

I shook my head, playing it off. His cologne was distinct, rosewood and lemon, his hair astutely angled. He was perfect. My boyfriend wasn't the rancid haddock source. I glanced over at Mom's flawless makeup and Dad's impeccably ironed shirt. Nope. Not them either.

The smell became overwhelming. How did nobody else notice it? I sucked in a breath. It had to be from outside. Chris shoveled mashed potatoes into his face. Dad dipped into the dinner rolls, unaware.

Ugh. I coughed, and an errant bean lodged in my throat. I coughed again, trying to knock the lump lose, but it remained in place.

Then I couldn't cough.

Trying to take a deep breath, the slimy, healthy vegetable obstructed my airway. I tried to cough. Choking! No air in. No air out.

I frantically gestured to my throat. My eyes widened.

Chris dropped his fork. It clanked against his plate. "Sonora?" Jumping up, he yanked me from my seat and knocked my chair out of the way with his foot. Wrapping his arms around my stomach, he thrust inward and upward violently. My ribs throbbed. My lungs begged for air. Nothing.

"God, do something!" My mom yelled, panicked.

Wait. Mom never panics. Her voice wavered in and out.

"C'mon! Breathe!" Chris clasped his hands around my waist, but I could barely feel them. *Stay conscious.* Bright neon spots flickered in my vision, and the table clouded out of focus. Was this what Magnolia experienced when she died?

He yanked inward AGAIN.

Nothing happened.

"Sonora!" Dad's voice echoed.

My legs wobbled, my stance weakening. Chris thrust his fists into my stomach once more. I hunched over from the force, and the green bean dislodged, skittering across the table.

Inhaling an enormous mouthful of oxygen, life breathed back into my limbs. Weak, I slapped my palms against the table in effort to stay upright. The placemat slipped off the edge, and my plate of food plummeted to the floor—over my new Gucci flora flats.

"Sonora," my mom said again, sounding less worried and more annoyed by the mess.

Would you please stop? I wanted to scream at her but didn't. Months ago, I'd had a mental breakdown from stress, and ever since, it was like Mom couldn't repeat my name enough.

I hung my head as the table slowly stopped spinning. It was as if I'd finished a string of back handsprings at a pep rally, and my brain hadn't caught up with my eyes.

Chris's panicked hand rested on my back.

The room became solid once more, but something was different.

In the corner, behind my dad—stood a ghostly corpse, one silvery eyeball hung from its socket. The ghost paled in comparison against the dark blue walls.

I shook my head and squeezed my eyes shut. *I must be seeing things.* Oxygen starvation did things to a person. I breathed in steadily and looked once more.

The corpse had moved closer. A worm slithered in the hollow place behind the droopy eye. Water ran from its hair and dress, collecting in a silvery pool at its feet. Her drenched white dress sucked to her body, turning the dress a shade of slippery peach. Golden hair hung like sodden pompoms down both sides of a haggard face.

My legs buckled and my right elbow slammed against the table as I collapsed to the floor.

"Sonora!" Chris yelled, dropping next to me, shaking my shoulder. "What's wrong?"

Four feet away, she peered at me with one glossy eye above swollen cheeks. Her wet face resembled a purple water balloon about to pop. Her eyes and nose a permanent shade of bruise.

The tiny shimmer of a friendship necklace, a gold locket in the shape of half-a-heart, dangled around her translucent neck.

It can't be.

I plunged backward, away from Chris. Away from everybody. Away from HER! My spine skinned the edge of the wooden chair, and the pain held me upright. This couldn't be real. She couldn't be real.

Magnolia had been my best friend—nine weeks ago, her body washed ashore on Brushy Creek's swampy banks. She had been murdered by the Creekside Killer.

This wasn't *any* corpse. It was Magnolia. I'd known her my entire life. I hadn't seen her dead before, but I'd recognize that necklace anywhere.

In a blur, her ghostly form rushed toward me.

TWO

My feet slipped in the mud. The short vague form attacked me, shoving my upper body backward and sideways at the same time. Who pushed me? My right shoulder turned involuntarily, and I tripped and fell. My heart raced as I plummeted toward rushing water. My face slammed into rocks. Blood gushed down my throat, bone crackling in my ears. Broken nose. Clumps of mud clogged my throat. I could hear nothing except for the clap of waves. And then I couldn't even hear that.

I lurched forward out of a deep sleep, catching my breath, the vision vivid.

Kaylee growled at the foot of my bed. I rubbed a hand against her fur for comfort.

It'd been thirteen days since Magnolia Ackerman first haunted me in the dining room. Thirteen days tattered with nightmares playing like a broken movie reel. Thirteen days with little sleep. I still had no idea why.

A knock jolted the other side of my door.

"Yes?" I mumbled with my eyes closed.

"Sonora. You've been asleep all afternoon, get up. Remember, I have to be early. You need to drive yourself," Mom spoke, remarks of tardiness hidden between her words.

"I know this." I'd only been asleep for an hour, not all afternoon.

"You have your dress?" She tapped the door again. "Open up."

I whipped my legs from under my covers and stumbled past the footboard. I swallowed, anticipating Magnolia to make an appearance before I unlocked the knob. But she didn't.

Mom walked past and yanked the blackout curtains open. "Your room's a mess," she said. Dim light melted over my floor. Two pieces of clothing on the floor didn't constitute a mess.

I sat on the edge of my bed. Mom took her typical not-going-anywhere stance, arms crossed over her chest. I glanced at my alarm clock. It was half past four. I still had time. Sort of.

With a huff, she marched over and plucked my yellow skirt off the carpet. She peered in my closet, pulling out the teal dress she had bought me weeks ago when planning the fundraiser.

"You have your shoes and dress. Everything's ready. Don't be late." She nodded, looking around my teenage wasteland one more time. "And you look terrible."

"Thanks, Mom." I hadn't been sleeping well at night, so I took a nap during the day, but the nightmares didn't stay away like I had hoped.

After taking a shower and blow-drying my hair, it didn't take long to finish getting ready. I twisted my red hair into a side-bun. Dangly earrings tickled my neck. I wiggled my toes, the strappy shoes a little snug. Staring at myself in the mirror, I was my old-self, the Sonora who didn't see ghosts, or spirits, or whatever Google described Magnolia as. I called her My Worst Nightmare. And nothing kept her at bay, not salt, not iron, not anything. The tips and tricks for reigning in the undead on the ghost hunter blogs were of no help to me.

I grabbed the car keys and studded wristlet off my dresser. Kaylee jumped on my bed but remained inside my bedroom, as if to guard it in my absence. I wished I was riding with Chris or his twin brother, Cooper, but they'd woken up sick and weren't going. Maybe I should've faked being sick? I shook my head. No, Mom would've seen straight through that lie.

Besides, getting out of the house might be nice—a little peace from the hauntings. Although, attending a fundraiser, one where Magnolia was the focus, wasn't appealing for so many reasons.

Outside, the cool September breeze flowed over my legs, neither hot nor cold. Texas would get cooler from this day forward, a break from the sweltering, summer heat. In the flowerbed, a wooden cutout of a cheerleader megaphone poked above two sage bushes. My first name painted in white above the smaller lettering, *Brenham ISD*.

My family's house was located in a small, quaint neighborhood, about a fifteen-minute drive from Mag's home. I paused beneath the gigantic magnolia tree canopied over my yard and gazed up at the periwinkle sky. Streams of clouds striped across the vivid blue where the moon had yet to make its appearance. With every fiber of my being, I resisted climbing into my pearly-white Taurus and leaving this moment of peace. The fundraiser for Magnolia's family had to be held in the Majestic Hotel—

the only space with a ballroom large enough to hold the crowd. I texted Rosa, my new best friend, and asked if she planned on attending. Was I the only one in our small group planning to be there?

The tree's dark green leaves shushed together in the breeze. I missed the huge white blossoms of springtime. My body hurt knowing I'd never enjoy them again with Magnolia at my side. We used to sit on my front porch and gather the large fallen leaves. When we were ten, I climbed the tree too high. Mags didn't hesitate and quickly scaled the branches to help me down. We laughed all afternoon.

I climbed into my car and headed into town. A few lefts and rights, it didn't take long to reach the parking lot of the Majestic. The rectangular building towered into the sky with a blanket of windows. I parked behind a ragged Honda Accord, as my phone beeped with a familiar melody. I knew who messaged me before I even looked. *You're late,* Mom texted. Rosa hadn't replied yet. Being new to town, she hadn't known Magnolia well, but I still hoped for her to make an appearance. I wanted at least one friend to hang out with.

You can do this, I thought. I licked my lips and inched the rearview mirror down to check my lipstick. My heart sped up a little. Would going to the fundraiser make things worse? What if Magnolia ended up visiting me more because of it? But she'd never haunted me out of the confines of my own house.

I had barely opened my door when a car flew around the curb, parking in the space next to me and nearly severing my lower leg in the process. Loud Metallica vibrated my eardrums. I jerked the door close, hitting my shin. *Ouch!*

The engine turned off and so did the music. The old, rusty, two-door Firebird looked like it had been hand-painted by a can of dull black spray paint, the rims too. Beneath the black exterior, faint colors of red remained. I knew whose car it was.

Fellow senior classman, Lachlan Granger, stepped out—not paying any attention to me. He had moved here when he was younger—from Australia or New Zealand or from one of those countries on the other side of the globe. But his accent prevailed, mixed with a Texan twang.

"Hey!" I shouted, opening my door more. My back hugged the edge of the frame as I slipped carefully out the small space between our cars.

His eyes darted over to mine, and instead of apologizing, he shrugged his shoulders and turned around.

"Hey," I said, louder. "Emo! You nearly killed me!"

He didn't stop, but instead, tromped toward the entrance like he had somewhere to be. Was he headed to the fundraiser? Lachlan Granger, the boy who didn't care about anyone, was going to a cultured event overflowing with locals?

"Whatever," I mumbled.

I bent over and snatched my wristlet off the front seat.

A large sign with Magnolia's picture sat inside the floral entrance to the ballroom. Magnolia had been the only high school girl murdered, and she was the focus of tonight's fundraiser. Behind Magnolia's, another frame glimmered, a collage of the other victims, six college girls. Proceeds from the fundraiser would be reserved for information that led to the killer's arrest.

I opened the door to distant voices and music clamoring from inside the ballroom area. The sweet smell of dark chocolate and fruit-filled pastries wafted past my nose. A voice cut into thin air. "I don't want—" said one sharply.

I peeked around the corner surprised to find Lachlan arguing with his father at the end of the long hall. His dad had been assigned as the lead detective to the case. Why wasn't Magnolia haunting him instead of me? Detective Granger might be able to do something for her. I strained to hear their conversation as groups of small-town swanky people passed on my right. My fingers palmed the slick, pearly wallpaper. I leaned in, listening closer.

A black t-shirt hugged Lachlan's chest, above black jeans and black boots. Not exactly high-class fundraiser attire. Lachlan's jaw tensed and he stepped away from his father. His eyes flickered in my direction.

I snapped up, behind the corner, hiding, when a fishy odor permeated the space. My shoulders seized. *Oh no!*

Magnolia lingered inches from my face. I thought ghosts hovered above the ground, but no, not Magnolia. She stood, eyeing me with her one red-rimmed, silvery eye. The other rolled across her cheek.

She'd never haunted me outside my house before. Why now? My back straightened as she took a jagged step closer. Her grotesque nose nearly touched the tip of mine. My stomach rolled. I couldn't breathe.

I covered my nose, trying to block the smell. Her translucent hand reached forward, touching my fingers.

"Find my killer," she said in a raspy voice—speaking for the first time. FOR THE FIRST TIME. The mucky flavor of creek water and the bitterness of iron inched up my throat. Was that blood or mud I tasted?

I crumbled to the floor, smacking my knees on the hard layer of maroon carpet. I might as well have fallen on cement. A piercing pang shot up my thighs, spreading to my hips.

Why didn't she wait until I was in the middle of the ballroom where she could *really* make a fool of me? Catching my breath, a faint voice sounded from my left.

The steps closed in. Mr. Granger leaned down and grabbed my upper arms, bracing my elbow to help me stand. "Are you alright?" he asked in a concerned voice.

A crowd had gathered, and someone said, "Get her dad, hurry." Someone else added, "She's as crazy as Janice Miller."

Decades ago, Janice was a teenager who spoke to imaginary friends and had been made fun of for years.

Now much older, she lived alone in a rundown shack in the middle of town and was rumored a psychic. Kids egged her house on a routine basis.

"No, it's okay," I hissed through clenched teeth, still on the floor. I didn't need my parents to think I'd gone mental again.

Magnolia flickered in and out of soppy form. *Go away, Mags!* I shut my eyes. *I don't see her. I don't see her.*

I opened my eyes. Magnolia's head shook violently and then she disappeared. *Leave me alone!* Why would she do this to me? The next time she appeared, I would let her have it. Tell her to stay away!

Mr. Granger's other hand graced my back as he lifted me.

"Are you alright?" he asked again.

Behind him, Lachlan trudged past in thick boots. A visible vein throbbed across his neck, and his eyes narrowed as he shook his head at me. "We were talking. Way to interrupt," he murmured with a sliver of an accent.

Magnolia wanted me to find her killer? *How am I supposed to do that?* I could get killed too! Was the killer here—at the fundraiser? I tensed at the thought.

"I'm fine, really," I assured Mr. Granger. Lachlan stood off to the side of the small crowd. "My heel snagged on the carpet and I tripped."

"Are you sure?" Mr. Granger asked.

I took a step away and brushed the tips of my dress down. "Really."

My dad emerged from the set of ballroom doors, bursting through as if there had been a classroom emergency. "Sonora," he said, rushing toward me with his hands frantically in the air. "Someone said you fainted?"

Mr. Granger casually let my dad take the lead.

The crowd broke up and exited the scene. I drew a deep breath through my nose.

"Where's mom?" I asked, wondering why she hadn't rushed out behind him. He looked down at the reddish skin on my knees. His eyebrows arched as if questioning what happened. "I tripped, nothing more than that. Promise."

He breathed out and slowly smiled. "Okay. Well, if you say so. It's about to start, she couldn't leave. Let's find our table, okay?"

My knees hurt a bit as we walked.

Dad opened the door. I swallowed a pea-size ball of fear as we entered the ballroom. Was the Creekside Killer inside? Was he one of the people in the crowd? Why else would Magnolia appear, for the first time ever, outside of my house?

To my left, a video of Magnolia danced across the screen on the stage—a snapshot of the two of us cheering at a football game flipped by. I froze. A lady in front looked over her shoulder at me. Was anyone else looking at me? I had already caused one scene, maybe they waited for me to cause another. I peeled my attention away from the footage and glanced around. Faces of a hundred people dotted the room. Two unfamiliar men in sharp black suits and earbuds cased the back. *Were they FBI, or hotel staff?*

Mom approached the microphone as the music from the video faded. Not wishing to bring more notice to myself, I took my seat as did everyone else.

"Let me first express my gratitude to those here tonight. All donations will be handed to Brenham PD." As mom spoke, I noticed the empty chairs around the table next to ours. A little vanilla card on top read *Ackerman Reserved.* Where was Magnolia's dad? Surely he came, right?

"We must find whoever did this to our beloved Magnolia Ackerman. Like so many of us, she was born and raised here in this beautiful town." Mom's voice hitched for a moment, as if about to cry. "I, for one, can't sleep, knowing that whoever did this is still out there." Her hand rested over her heart as she inhaled. "But tonight isn't about tears, tonight is a celebration of this young lady's life, as well as all the others."

Was the killer celebrating with us? I shuddered at the thought.

THREE

The bell rang after Calculus.

I sauntered to lunch. Rosa grabbed my arm, pulling me forward. She was perkier than ever as if all my energy had been absorbed into her. "Wake up, Sonora," she said, shaking my elbow. "We're halfway through Monday already. You didn't even say anything about my new shorts." She stopped walking and stuck her leg out for me to notice. Her tight blue jean shorts had been hemmed two inches above the acceptable dress-code. How did she get away with it?

"Sorry. I'm in zombie mode." Someone had stuffed my brain full of cotton. I suspected Magnolia. Rosa tugged me forward.

Chris followed alongside, playing Candy Crush on his phone. They sat down at our permanent cafeteria table, and I plopped on the seat across from Rosa.

"What's for lunch today?" Rosa wondered.

"Smells like pizza," Chris said, his eyes glued to his new high score. "You want something, hon?"

I shook my head. I wasn't hungry. Food, the last thing on my mind.

"Hey, you working tonight?" Rosa asked me, blowing a neon yellow bubble between her lips before sticking her gum beneath the table.

"That's so gross," I murmured, slightly envious of her blasé attitude. I pulled out an avocado sandwich I had no intentions of eating.

Cooper, Chris's twin, joined with his new girlfriend, Angela, at his side. "What's gross?" Cooper asked. "Your lunch? 'Cause avocado is pretty gross."

I shook my head. "Nothing."

The two of them didn't look like twins. Chris was a stocky football player, lacking a neck, and Cooper was tall and lean, perfect for the basketball team. If they played the year right, they were both headed for scholarships.

Cooper continued speaking. "Looks like mushy green crap."

Angela, with pink tipped nails, kissed his hand before releasing it to go to the lunch line. He watched her walk away, and a solemn expression flashed over his face for a moment. Was he thinking about Mags? It would've been her eighteenth birthday today—October 1st.

I leaned over and whispered to him. "Magnolia?"

He tilted his head, shrugging his shoulders to his ears.

"We promised not to talk about her anymore," Rosa answered for him. *How did she overhear me?* The fundraiser was the most her name had been mentioned in weeks.

"Is that why you didn't come Saturday?"

"Saturday?" Cooper questioned, assuming I spoke to him. Chris didn't say anything, still focused on his game, not having left for the lunch line yet.

"Yes, the fundraiser," I reminded them.

"No, I had other important things," Rosa said. She did whatever she wanted. A hardcore rebel who didn't adhere to acceptable behavior. A fundraiser probably seemed too acceptable for her.

"Oh yeah, stupid stomach virus. Remember?" Cooper added.

"Ew." Rosa scrunched her freckly face and stuck her tongue out in disgust. "No more sad or gross talk, okay?"

"Fine," I replied. She and I had made a pact after Magnolia's funeral, though it was more her than me. Talking about Magnolia only led to 'super uncomfortable thoughts'—making it harder to *move on*. But now I dealt with her ghost. Nothing about *that* was comfortable.

Rosa leaned forward, her cat-lined eyes intent on mine. "So? Are you working?"

"No, I'm not working tonight," I said, finally answering her prior question. I took a bite of my sandwich and forced it down, placating Rosa with a wide grin. "Tomorrow." The bite was a lump in my throat, and I chugged half my water, flashing back to when I choked for real. Chris glanced at me and then went back to playing on his phone.

I wanted to leave Magnolia behind, like my friends had. Not in a bad, forget you kind of way, but more in a way that allowed my life to resume normalcy. But lately, she hadn't left me much choice.

A shift in the atmosphere turned my attention to the other end of the bright cafeteria. In the distance, on the other side of the large room, I spotted Magnolia. I froze in the middle of another bite. Avocado smooshed against my teeth.

Magnolia—at school. My luck dwindled faster than a Friday night at an away game.

Her sopping clothes would have left puddles on the floor if she were real. Her one-eye gaze locked with mine.

I couldn't look away.

A high-pitched "find my killer" rang in my head as her mouth opened. I shoved my hands against my ears, dropping my sandwich to the ground. *Leave me alone!*

Then as quickly as she had appeared, she left. *Did she hear me?*

"Sonora," Chris whispered across the table. "What's wrong?"

I closed my eyes and rubbed my head. Magnolia's voice started as a whisper and then grew louder. "Find my killer!" The shrill warning vibrated between my temples. If I didn't find her killer, would she ever stop haunting me?

"Stop bothering me!" I yelled. *Go away! Leave me alone, especially at school, in front of my friends.* If I couldn't hold it together, she'd ruin everything. I had cheer competition coming, Fall Fling ahead, I didn't *need* this sort of attention. Not now. Not after the fundraiser fiasco.

"Geez," Chris replied with his hands defensively in the air. "It's only a fight. Nothing to freak about."

The expression on Rosa's and Cooper's face brought me back to reality.

"Huh?" I replied. Nobody else at the tables seemed to have noticed my outburst.

Chants bounced off the cafeteria walls, echoing in the large room. Afraid to see Magnolia again, I squinted toward the commotion.

In the same spot where she had been, Lachlan Granger towered over a student who lay with his back on the ground, holding his jaw. Dear Gawd, what had the druggie done now? This was the second time Magnolia appeared when Lachlan was near and asked me to *help her.* Why?

Vice Principal Fox waved Lachlan over and stabbed his finger in the air toward the office. A release of boos filled the cafeteria. Students that had gathered subsequently dispersed like oil as more teachers approached.

μ

For the rest of the day, I couldn't stop thinking about Lachlan—the menacing way he stood over the student he'd hit. Did Magnolia want me to ask *him* for help?

Focus, I chided myself. Cheer practice now, ghosts later. My hands gripped both sides of the flyer's waist. I pushed upward from behind, not paying much attention. The girl's ankle rested in the base's hands. In the air, she grabbed the tip of her cheerleading shoe and maneuvered into a scorpion position.

"Ready?" the lead base hollered, giving the flyer a countdown.

Without warning, the flyer's ankle twisted. Not reacting fast enough—too sleepy for fast reflexes—I moved late to catch her back. Her elbow knocked me in the nose as she hurtled toward the gym floor. She would've hit her head if it weren't for the bases catching the brunt of her weight.

I grabbed my nose and leaned down to help her up with my other hand. "Sorry, Jessica." I winced, my nose hurting. She was fine, my nose not so much.

The bell rang.

"Tomorrow, bring water, we run the track," Coach Gold warned.

Rosa sat in the bleachers, biting her nails, waiting for me.

I grabbed my water bottle and jogged over to her. "Hey, I need to do something. Catch you later, okay?" I said.

She rolled her eyes. "No, not okay."

"I'll call you, promise. Got to hurry." I rushed out of the gym before she could ask why. My nose tingled, not as bad as Magnolia's had from my murder-ish dreams. At least there wasn't any blood.

In the sunny parking lot surrounded by freshly cut fields, I spotted Lachlan walking to his car. Students scattered everywhere.

I swung my head both ways, searching for any friends that might notice me talking to him. I didn't see Cooper or Angela—or Chris.

The breeze swished through my hair as I nearly stepped on a goldfinch hopping across the path. Approaching Lachlan, I glanced around once more as I jerked my hand toward his shoulder. He turned before I made contact.

His blue eyes were bright, contrasting with the color of his dark hair. The narrowing of his gaze gave me pause.

It was the same look he'd given me at the fundraiser when my untimely *episode* interrupted his argument with his father. Maybe this was a bad idea?

Half of me wanted to spin around, run the opposite direction, pretend like I'd made a mistake. But everyone in school knew everyone, and it was too late to pretend.

Biting my lip, I looped my thumbs through the straps of my backpack.

Not too far away, my car was parked. My escape, I thought.

"What?" he said flatly, securing his wavy hair behind his head. A black freckle adorned his neck. The same neck that had pulsed with rage days before. Did he remember that it was me, the one he had ignored in the parking lot at the fundraiser?

I straightened my shoulders and cleared my throat. "I need your help."

Without missing a beat, he said. "I don't sell."

His words took me aback. "What …"

"If you need something to keep you focused, talk to Ethan." His jaw clenched, and he cocked his head to the side as if wanting me to leave.

Keep me focused—did he think I needed pills to stay awake? Were the bags under my eyes worse than I thought? Of course, why else would I be here talking to *him*? But that's not what I needed. I shook my head. "No." I paused. "You are so irritating," I mumbled under my breath.

"What did you just say?" His eyes narrowed.

"Nothing. Can you come to B's Steakhouse tomorrow night?" The words flew out funny and sounded like I asked him on a date. My determination waned.

He crossed his arms. "Trying to set me up or something? Did my dad put you up to this?"

This conversation wasn't going the way I planned. "No. And why would your dad put me up to anything?" I swallowed. "I'm working. Come at eight. Okay?"

"Twenty, and I'll be there, Queen Sonora," he muttered, sticking out his hand, palm side up.

"Twenty what? And don't call me that." *Queen Sonora?*

He rolled his neck and lowered his hand. "Do-o-llars," he mouthed, emphasizing the *o* with an Australian *r* sound.

"You want money?" I didn't have much cash, not any extra that I wanted to give *him* anyway.

He shook his head. "Whatever. Not my problem then."

"Fine," I said louder. I wanted to ask him for his help to find Magnolia's killer. He was the son of the lead detective, maybe he had info I could use, clearly Magnolia thought so—*I think.* "I'll buy you dinner and give you twenty, extortionist. Just be there okay?" Then I walked away without giving him another chance to request more. Plus, if I lingered too long with Lachlan, it'd be all over school by morning. Gossip spread faster than mono between freshmen.

I headed straight to my car.

Did I make the right move? I sat in the driver's seat, my hands on the wheel. Had it sounded like I asked him on a date? I hoped not. But it was a little late to retract the offer now. And for many reasons, I wasn't comfortable talking to him in front of my friends. The two of us meeting at work, on a slow day of the week, was the safest way to chat without nosey onlookers.

μ

At home, the whitewashed wooden door leading into the kitchen was one of those built with a spring that automatically swung shut. I caught the door before it slammed and brought attention to my arrival. The updated cabinets and deep mahogany floors stretched from the living room, all the way into the dining room. The remodel had been a gift from Dad last year. Copper pots dangled from decorative hooks above the island in the middle of the kitchen; one of the pots had been a Mother's Day gift from Bram.

I might as well have been the only child since Bram hadn't visited in over a year. My heart hurt thinking of him. My parents' relationship with my older brother was *strained* ever since he quit college and moved in with his girlfriend. Which meant I hadn't seen him much either. It was strange and rude, even when I called him, he didn't pick up or return my calls.

A bunch of envelopes sat stacked on the granite countertop next to the sink. One envelope remained open with the bill neatly unfolded. The header labeled St. Joseph Psychiatric Hospital—where my parents had placed

Grandpa. My hands shook, looking at the name of that place. Would I be committed next?

I grabbed a glass from the cabinet and filled it with water, attempting to cool my nerves. What if I wound up there too? What if this ghost business never ended? As if on cue, Magnolia appeared. Her dank fishy odor thickened. Her eyeball hung over her cheek and dripped translucent water over the mail.

The door to my parents' room opened, and Mom strolled out. I jumped and shoved the envelope beneath other bills, sweat streaming down my forehead. Go away, I thought to her. My fingers trembled.

Magnolia didn't leave.

Mom rubbed lotion on her hands. "Sonora, how was school?" she asked. "What's that awful smell?"

Crossing the kitchen, she walked through Magnolia's ghostly form. My eyes widened and I sucked in a breath. Mom thumbed a button on the new stainless steel oven. Her auburn bangs perfectly lined her chic eyebrows. Her silky hair hung in a pristine ponytail. My hair was fiery red, like my dad's.

Mom was gorgeous, in a forty-year-old way. No matter what time of day, she dressed as if the mayor might stop by. During her senior year, she was Brenham's Senior Maifest Royalty. I, on the other hand, lacked her grace— or at least it started to seem like that.

"Is that a stain on your sweater?" she tsked, darting over to examine it closer. Magnolia moved toward me. I stepped to the side, not wanting her to touch my arm. Not wishing to know what it felt like.

Glancing down, I fidgeted with my sweater, tugging it from Mom's hands. Between her OCD and Magnolia's presence, I was suffocating.

"Only a water spot, Mom." I smiled, trying to keep my hands from trembling, and yanked my shirt from her grabby fingers.

She reached over the island, grabbed a pan, and filled it with water.

"School's fine." I eyed the mail on the counter, refusing to look at Magnolia.

"Just fine?" She placed the pan on the stove and slipped an apron over her head.

"Isn't it a little early to eat dinner?" Magnolia's ghost dissolved; my eye twitched as she disappeared. I rubbed my eyelid, trying to get it to stop.

"Dad skipped lunch today. He'll be home from work soon," she answered, facing away. She poured a bag of rice into the pan and turned on the stove.

"Rice again?" For the second night in a row. *I'd starve on her diet if I didn't have a job at B's.* "Bram hated rice, and you never made *him* eat it." I looked around the kitchen, scared that Magnolia might come back. Please stay away!

"Sonora." Mom's voice was steely, her way of putting an end to the Bram conversation. "It's a different kind of rice," she assured. She and dad never talked about him, as if I was an only child now. I sort of wanted to force her to say his name, but I let it go.

I spun around, attempting to the leave the kitchen, but she said from behind, "Sonora." Her tone halted me. "I've made an appointment for you, with Dr. Sylvia."

I swallowed. Dr. Sylvia was the therapist that my parents forced me to see whenever I wasn't acting the way they wanted—and she didn't work or live in town.

"Sonora, I've noticed you're not sleeping lately. I'm worried about your grades. I think she can help. Okay?"

I didn't smile and hurried off to my room, a place much less sterile. A place where I didn't have to hide my fear.

Tossing my backpack on the carpet, I sank into the soft, cream-colored comforter on my bed.

Was I going crazy? I was only seeing one ghost. That couldn't constitute the need for medical intervention, right?

FOUR

Dinner was a bland mix of rice, red beans, and cornbread. The parental conversations not much better. I ate quickly and decided to take Kaylee outside. I placed the harness around her, snapped the blue leash on, and walked down my driveway. The weather had already dropped ten degrees, and the cool breeze felt nice, not as humid.

"Hey," a girl's voice hollered from across the street.

As fate would have it, I was about to be caught in the Angela trap. Or what Rosa and I liked to call, La Trampa Angela. Spinning around toward her voice, I moaned inwardly.

Kaylee's leash twisted around my knees, and I rotated to unwind it.

I didn't want to deal with the girlfriend of my boyfriend's twin right now. I wanted to be alone—no ghosts, and more importantly, no Angela. Reaching the end of the driveway, I turned left, trying to ignore her. I was walking my dog *by myself.* I needed space away from Mom, away from school … away from Magnolia. But the sidewalk was on the other side of the street, directly in front of Angela's house.

I despised Angela's tacky fall décor. A leafy wreath with sunflowers and a large ribbon hung on the green door, pumpkins lined the porch, and an outline of a raven stuck out from the bushes.

Deciding to take the street instead of the sidewalk, Angela jogged up to me with a wide grin. Her colorful leggings hugged her perfect, fit body.

"Oh. Hi," I muttered through a forced smile, pretending not to have noticed her at first. I'd never get away now. Stepping around her, I brushed past her shoulder and headed across the street, to the sidewalk.

Cooper liked her, but I didn't. What did he see in her? When senior year started, she'd shown up to school with a completely different persona. From freshman to junior year, she wore the same blue jeans and t-shirt every day. Her hair had always been a mess that nested on top of her head, and the glasses she wore were too big for her face. Then wham, the first day of twelfth grade, a cute skirt hugged her hips, her glasses went sayonara, and her dark hair had been straightened. She'd even dyed a strip pink, and it actually complimented her skin. Most notably, she had caught Cooper's eye. In my opinion, she was the reason Magnolia and Cooper never got back together prior to Mag's death. If the two had been dating, Magnolia wouldn't have been alone *that* night.

"Going for a walk?" Angela asked, pacing next to me since I didn't stop. Her bare toes pushed off the cement. Even her nails were shiny pink, matching her strip of hair. She tried hard to fit into our group.

"Yep, that's what it looks like." My voice trailed off, unenthusiastically. Magnolia had made fun of Angela once during her ugly duckling phase, and Angela had overheard. Now, it was like Angela was shoving her new persona in dead Magnolia's face by dating her ex—my boyfriend's brother.

Yuck, years from now, we could be future sisters-in-law. I shuddered at the nauseating thought.

"Mind if I join?" she asked.

I could never put my finger on it, but I didn't trust her. Her father was the head basketball coach at the local junior college. But I had a sinister feeling she dated

Cooper merely as a distraction for something much bigger. I didn't know what exactly. Or maybe that's why Cooper dated *her*? For her father's basketball connections?

Rosa didn't like her either. She thought Angela was an annoying tick that wanted to suck the life from everyone around her.

I finally slowed my pace. Kaylee's leash yanked my elbow. "Where's Cooper? Shouldn't you be at his house or something?" Chris had left for evening football practice.

She swiped her hand through the air. "He's working on a history project, boring stuff."

I stared at her as she bounced from foot to foot. "I really want to walk alone, if you don't mind." Being polite to someone that I didn't like was too much work, but for Chris, I'd try. "Sort of a meditation thing," I hinted, hoping she'd leave. I began walking away.

Her steps lagged behind.

"Of course, I understand," she yelled.

I continued forward, but I didn't hear her footsteps padding in the opposite direction. Was she standing there all creepy-like, watching me?

Squeezing the leash, I turned around. Yep, she hadn't moved an inch. I folded my arms with the leash in hand.

Something obviously was on Angela's mind. I heard the echo of Rosa's voice: *La Trampa.*

"What is it, Angela?"

She licked her lips. "You and Lachlan, something happening there?" Was she spying on me?

"Why were y'all talking in the lot?"

She *had* been spying. My heart pounded. Had she told Chris? If Chris found out, he wouldn't be happy. Lachlan and Chris had a major history. They were best friends until an argument in the eighth grade. They fought over a girl who ended up not liking either one of them. But *that* day in the middle of PE, their friendship unraveled. Noses were broken. From then on, they refused to acknowledge the other existed. The whole thing had become an old fuse that I didn't care to light.

I straightened my shoulders and looked Angela square in the eyes. "He wanted my help with school work."

Angela's eyes narrowed.

"You don't have any classes with him," she countered. She tucked the pink stripe of hair behind her ear.

She was nosier than Pinocchio.

"Not any *this* year," I corrected. He and I had been in the same classes a few times over the past couple of years, but I never said more than two words to him until now.

She tilted her head, watching me. My hands began to sweat as she walked forward.

"Would you mind keeping this between you and me?" I asked. Chris and I were in a good place, I didn't feel like arguing over something as stupid as an ancient rivalry with Lachlan. I had enough on my Sonora plate with supernatural hauntings by my dead best friend.

"So did you help him?" She leaned in, continuing in a lower voice. "Or worse, buy one of his more *lucrative* products?" Her eyebrows arched. Nobody was outside or in close proximity of overhearing.

I stepped back and shook my head sharply. Blood rushed to my cheeks. Now she accused me of being a junkie! "Course not." If rumors spread that I was buying anything, I could be kicked off the squad. Everyone knew that the emo crowd didn't hang out drinking sodas and eating non-pot brownies. For cheerleader sake, I didn't need to be associated with that group.

With one hand on her hip, she smiled. "A guy like him only means trouble."

"Between us. Okay?" I didn't want to answer more questions—from anyone. I needed the gossip train stopped here, especially if I wanted to hold my spot on the squad for the competition.

She leaned forward and scrunched her shoulders. "It'll be our secret," she whispered with a tight smile.

Now Angela and I had a secret. Only *friends* kept secrets. We weren't friends, just two people who had no choice in dating twins.

"Since we're sharing secrets, Cooper would kill me if I told you—"

"—What?"

"It's not something he wants to talk about, but do you know why Magnolia texted him the night before she, well, died?"

My attention took a U-turn. I perked up. "What text?"

She shrugged. "The word *sorry*. That was it. No explanation, nothing."

What did Mags have to be sorry about? "Cooper never told me that." Why wouldn't he have told me? "Do the police know?" I asked.

She nodded. "They questioned him about it, after searching her phone, but he didn't know why. It's not like they were dating anymore."

"True," I said.

Magnolia and Cooper had broken up a month before her death. Angela didn't exactly break them up, but Cooper and Magnolia were meant to be together. And they would have worked their problems out if Angela hadn't beautifully wormed herself in. Magnolia had her issues, but she and Cooper were destined.

"It's bothering him, which means it's bothering us, and well, I hate that. I was hoping you'd know why, but I guess you don't." She paused. "Look, I'll keep that secret about Lachlan for you, if you don't tell Cooper I mentioned anything. Deal?"

Kaylee tugged, and my body jerked to the side. "Fine." Kaylee barked, and a cold hand graced my shoulder. I turned around, but nobody was there.

"You know, Sonora, this was lovely. We should talk more often."

I turned back around, my stomach recoiling at her suggestion.

"Bye-ee." Angela waved as she skipped back up the path that led to her front door.

Why wouldn't Cooper have told me about the text himself? Why was it such a secret?

My thoughts wandered as we trailed over the three-mile stretch of sidewalk circling our neighborhood. Why would Angela think I knew anything? I didn't like thinking about it, but Magnolia's and my friendship had been on rocky ground too before her death. I turned the corner as the sidewalk veered behind fences. Truth be told, I felt guilty about ignoring her calls. Could I have prevented her murder?

Damn Angela for pouring salt in open wounds.

What did Cooper ever see in her? Months ago, we were the Royal Flushes—Magnolia and Cooper—and Sonora and Chris. But now Magnolia was gone, and Angela took her place but didn't fit in. It'd be great if Cooper would date Rosa. But Rosa wasn't interested.

My friendship with Rosa became tighter after Magnolia's death. I was lucky to have her.

I hesitated near the spot where the sidewalk disappeared into a thicket of trees. Magnolia and I used to run through them when we were kids. I gripped the sweaty leash. Why had I walked this direction?

If it'd been dark, I wouldn't have attempted to walk alone. But Kaylee was with me, and she'd never let anyone—especially the Creekside Killer—lay one killer finger on me. None of the victims lived in this neighborhood, and all but Magnolia lived near campus. Wherever he hunted, I believed I was safe here.

"Come on," I said to her, bending over and petting her neck. Her soft black ears perked.

Picking up speed, I walked into a tunnel-like path of trees that canopied the sidewalk.

The sunlight scattered across the trail like a kaleidoscope, dispersing light through long branches. Goosebumps prickled my neck. A thick branch hung close to the path. Magnolia and I use to race to see who could slap it first.

The shade from the trees lay across my skin like an unwanted blanket of gloom. It invited fear—or a ghost—that I was desperately trying to keep at bay. Warily, I sniffed the air. Nothing smelled of rotten fish. Would Magnolia haunt me here?

Seconds in, a shuffle to my left startled me. I froze. A tan furry rabbit hopped out of the bushes and stopped. Its little nose twitched as it ate a piece of grass. Kaylee yanked my arm, ripping her leash from my hand as she darted after it. "No!" I stepped on the tail end of the leash in time before she disappeared into the thorny thicket.

As I relaxed, a familiar odor surrounded me. *Magnolia.* Bending over slowly, I grabbed the leash. My heart raced and my legs weakened. Snapping upward, I sped toward the sunlight at the end of the path, running from the scent.

The moment the warm sunset touched my shoulders, I hunched over with my hands on my knees and panted. Kaylee too. These past weeks, my emotions ran close to the surface, as if Magnolia's feelings had been frozen inside of me. The memories of her last moments released flesh-eating insects into my dilapidating soul. Her fear before she fell into rushing water tasted like a dirty nickel. My own mind held captive by her death.

"Nothing will happen. I'm just out for a walk, that's it." I turned back toward the shadowy path and glanced up.

Our branch hung over the path. "Mags, I'll help," I said into the breeze, my thoughts turning back to the day Magnolia had been found.

The police had discovered her body on the shores of Bushy Creek, but nobody knew how she got there. As much as I didn't want to think about how or why she died, I needed to find her killer or she might never leave me alone. And when and if I did find the killer, I'd inevitably know *how* she died. Was her death deliberate and premeditated? Or was her death hasty and unexpected— right place, right time?

"I can do this, Mags," I said looking forward to the dim path beneath the trees. I wanted to push myself. I didn't want to be afraid.

The shadow from a long branch mimicked a giant bony finger, beckoning me inside.

Lachlan. His face leapt into my mind. If anyone had backdoor access to the case, it would be the son of the lead detective. But what if Lachlan thought I was crazy? What if Chris found out? Or worse, what if my parents found out? They'd admit me to the psychiatric hospital for sure.

But I needed his help; Magnolia had made that much clear. One foot in front of the other, I moved back toward home, hoping Magnolia wouldn't appear. And she didn't.

FIVE

Conversations bounced off the walls and customers filled every seat. The waiting area behind the hostess station jammed to capacity. B's Steakhouse was packed more than usual.

I grabbed a fry from the plate and hunched down, staying out of sight from Tracy, the manager. "These are the bomb," Rosa said with a mouthful of fries, cheesy strings hung over her bottom lip.

Chris ignored us while he played Candy Crush. I didn't realize they'd be visiting me at work so late—and stupid me had scheduled Lachlan to meet soon. But I still had an hour before he'd be here.

Three appetizers and half-eaten entrees splayed out across the table. I took another fry and dipped it in her ranch, starving. "We need to shop soon," she muttered.

Fall Fling was a month away.

"Uhuh," I shook my head, agreeing with her. "You have a date?"

Chris looked up from his game, as if to say something, but then he continued tapping the screen.

"Maybe." She winked. "We only have a couple weeks left. It'll be here before we know it." She nudged Chris in the arm, rolling her eyes. "Put it down. You're obsessed."

He didn't look over.

Rosa eyed me.

"Chris, you really *are* obsessed," I said, reiterating her.

Chris glanced up for a second. "Contrary to popular belief, the male species can do two things at once." His thumbs tapped the screen again.

Rosa stuffed another fry in her mouth.

"Yeah? What about football players? That's two for two, a dumb jock *and* male," I said.

"Probably the same thing they say about cheerleaders," he replied, not looking up from his phone.

Rosa and I rolled our eyes.

"So what were *we* talking about then?" I asked him.

Chris eyed the basket and grabbed an onion ring. "How much better these taste than your fries." As he spoke, a piece of onion flew from his mouth, landing in the middle of the table.

"No, you idiot," Rosa scolded.

"Fall Fling …" I said.

He was on his phone more than normal, playing games. Sometimes that annoyed me, but I loved him.

Over Chris's shoulder, Lachlan walked in. I swallowed a fry quickly, nearly choking. I sucked in a breath—he was early.

I slapped my chest, coughing. "I gotta get back to work." The words tumbled out fast and I rushed over to the hostess.

Lachlan's eyes met mine as I approached the front.

"Hey Joanna, can you stick him in Rob's section?" I motioned at Lachlan.

A smile painted her face. "Sure," she said.

That was too easy. Joanna didn't like me—probably had something to do with spilling a Coke on her my first day on the job. But maybe she had finally moved on.

I immediately entered the kitchen to grab more rolls for one of my tables. When I returned, Lachlan was seated at the booth directly behind Rosa and Chris—in *my* section.

"Dammit," I whispered, clutching the basket of rolls.

Stalling as long as possible, I circled a few more tables and refilled drinks. A bald man shoved my hand away from his full drink as I tried to grab it for a refill.

I couldn't wait any longer, afraid that Lachlan might leave. If his eyes had been needles, my face would contain a thousand tiny holes.

Rosa and Chris looked like they were about to go. Rosa placed her phone in her purse, and he shoved his in his pocket.

I motioned with my finger in the air, asking Lachlan from across the room for another minute.

I sauntered over to Rosa, casually, as if I wasn't hiding anything. "See you later," I said. She scooched out of the booth and gave me a hug.

Chris leaned in and gave me a kiss. His lips felt warm and perfect, but I pulled away, hoping to get him out the door. "Are you okay?" he asked, leaning away to gauge my response.

I pulled out my pad of guest checks. "Of course, simply need to get back to work. This place is crazy."

My eyes met Rosa's and I smiled. Was she suspicious?

"See y'all later," I said, a little too cheerfully.

Chris opened his mouth. "If something was wrong, you'd tell me, right?"

I laughed halfheartedly. "Course, babe," I paused. "Really."

"Whatever, later," Rosa replied.

Chris squinted, rubbing his brow. "Okay." He kissed me once more before turning around to leave. I watched their backs until they pushed open the front door. Other customers shifted into view.

Our table was still full of food. Cold, but food nonetheless.

The busboy reached over to stack their plates in his plastic tub. Without hesitating, I grabbed a half-eaten basket of chicken tenders before he added it to his tub of dirty dishes.

Taking four steps to the side, I placed the basket on Lachlan's table.

SIX

"What can I get you to drink? I asked nonchalantly. I'd narrowly avoided a Chris/Lachlan encounter.

Lachlan eyed the half-eaten plate and scrunched his face. "Not that."

So much for him eating the food without questioning where it came from.

I let out a frustrated breath. "This isn't for you." I shoved a chicken tender in my mouth, playing the plate of food off as being for me.

He leaned back, propped his elbows on the table and thrummed his fingers on the edge. "What's good here?" he asked, grabbing the menu and opening it slowly, taking his sweet time like he hadn't been here many times before. B's was located in the quaint downtown square and had been open since before I was born. Everyone in town, every passerby through town, had eaten here at least once.

"Well, you've got prime rib and the Ft. Worth Ribeye"—without thinking, I had named the most expensive items on the menu—"but my fav is B's All American Burger. Or you could go with one of the appetizers, a meal by itself."

"Whatever shall I order, Queen Sonora"—he closed the menu and smiled—"I'll take the prime rib ... and a Coke."

I clenched my teeth. "Great choice." He ordered the most expensive item. My fault. "Why do you insist on calling me that?"

"What? Queen?" He looked me up and down. "Name fits you."

"I don't like it." I narrowed my eyes, shoved another tender in my mouth, and walked away to place the order in the computer.

Why did I ask him here? I decided to serve a few more tables before approaching him again. Would he help me? I hadn't told Rosa or Chris yet, and never intended to either, so inviting Lachlan into my secret felt reckless. But it also meant there was little to lose in regards to friendship. Can't lose something we never had. His and my exchanges would stay strictly ghost business.

As soon as his food was ready, I brought it to him. The plate thudded against the table as I set it down hard.

Tracy eyed my section of the room, observing servers and customers. I remained standing long enough for her eyes to skitter away.

Sitting down, I hunched over, ducking my head beneath the wooden seatback to talk.

Across from me, Lachlan ducked his head too, mocking me.

"Cute," I said flatly.

He tooled the tiny white bowl on his plate, next to the red meat. Melted butter sat on top of the luscious pink center. "I need some horseradish. Not this wimpy kind mixed with sour cream." His gaze rose to mine, and he looked over his shoulder. "Should I ask Tracy for help?"

Why was he being so annoying, especially when he's getting free food and didn't even know what favor I was about to ask him? I squinted, wanting to spit in his horseradish. "Fine," I said. "Be right back."

He smiled. I could tell he enjoyed this.

When I returned, I slapped the bowl of horseradish next to his plate, a little spilled over the sides. "Happy?" I asked.

"Very." He grinned.

"Can we get down to business, or do you need a refill?"

He tapped his glass, Coke bubbles fizzing to the top. "I *think* I'm fine."

"I wasn't really asking."

Lachlan cut the meat and forked a big piece in the bowl. A glob of spiciness coated the slice.

"That's too much," I warned.

He brushed my comment off and placed the bite on his tongue. Instantly, wet coughs escaped his lips as he covered his mouth.

I laughed. I'd done the same thing once before—intense horseradish burn—like my nose was on fire. "That's what you get for being an ass," I said.

Lachlan didn't look amused as he chugged a large sip of Coke.

I bit my lip and decided to ask him now, or I never would. "I need your help," I blurted, searching for Tracy to make sure she hadn't spotted me sitting on the job.

He dipped another piece of red meat in the small bowl, this time more sparingly.

Asking for his help wasn't high on my list of to-dos.

He took another bite. "What do you need?" He phrased it more as a statement rather than a question.

"Well...," I paused. "Your father is one of the investigators on Magnolia's case, right?"

He tilted his chin to the side, his gaze wary. "Yes, head. Why?"

"I need you to find out some information for me. Like suspects and stuff."

He let out an arrogant laugh and dropped his fork loudly. It clanged against the side of the plate. "You're kidding. That's why you asked me here? Why I waited over an hour?"

I shook my head, suddenly wishing I hadn't stopped him in the parking lot yesterday.

Lachlan held up his hands. "I can't help you, and even if I could, I wouldn't help you. The feds are breathing down his throat for answers. No way am I getting in the middle of that."

Feeling humiliated by his smugness, all I could think of was Magnolia and how she may never leave me alone. I couldn't go on like that. I refused to go on like that.

I straightened my shoulders, not minding if the tip of my head moved into Tracy's view. Looking Lachlan directly in the eyes, I leaned closer and said, "No, I'm not kidding. Now, will you help me or not?"

His hands balled into loose fists on either side of his plate, and he studied me.

He grabbed his glass and took a sip, all the while not averting his gaze.

"No," he reiterated, licking his lips and leaning against the back of the seat.

A sharp breath caught in my throat. "What? Please."

"That's my answer." He began eating again. "You can leave now. Would've saved you some money if you had asked earlier. Then again, glad you didn't. This is delish." He winked and shooed me away with a flick of his hand.

"If you want money," I started. There had to be something he wanted that he'd be willing to trade information for.

"It's not the money." He paused. "I don't have access to my dad's files. Nor do I want access."

"I don't believe that. You had to have heard something, anything that could help."

"First, I don't want to help you. And second, Cliff and I have an agreement. He doesn't stick his nose in my business if I stay out of his way and don't get into trouble."

Didn't you get in trouble at school just the other day? "Cliff," I repeated.

"My dad," he corrected.

"You're on a first name basis with your dad?"

"No." He acted as if his answer was explanation enough.

"Fine. Whatever." I didn't have anything else to say, and I'd wasted fifteen dollars on prime rib. "If you change your mind—"

"I won't," he finished chewing.

I thought about grabbing his glass and pouring it over his head, but I didn't. Tracy hadn't noticed my absence yet, but she would if Coke was suddenly all over the booth and the floor.

Now, what would I do?

"Do you mind?" he asked, gesturing with his eyebrows for me to leave.

I exhaled, defeated.

The only other idea I had come up with was to talk to Magnolia's father, but I really didn't want to. I hadn't been over to her house for months.

"Fine," I said to him, sliding out of the cushy seat. "If you change your mind—"

"—I won't."

SEVEN

I stared at the tall building as I meandered from under the overhang of the parking garage. The morning light was bright, it was ten minutes until noon. I gulped my fear and moved forward behind Mom. After having asked Lachlan for help, I was no further into the investigation. Mags still haunted me and I wasn't getting any sleep.

Pulling my phone from my purse, it beeped with a text from Chris: *Feel better.*

He thought I was missing school due to sickness. But I wasn't sick.

"Come on, Sonora," my mom said, moving toward the glass entrance. A large, sturdy sign in the grassy knoll read *Cypress Enclave.*

My palms were sweaty. A group of men in suits eyed me as they passed. I fidgeted with my fingers. Were they looking at *me?* Did they know who I was? Everyone in the world was connected by six degrees of separation. They could be the cousin or aunt or sister of a friend of mine.

I approached the doors and stepped inside the building. Dr. Sylvia's office was situated on the fourth floor. I glanced up at the ceiling as if I had x-ray vision and could see the doctor waiting, holding a notepad with my name on it. I walked with small steps toward the elevator, one foot inches in front of the other. My knees wobbled.

I shouldn't worry that anyone I know may have seen me, but I did.

Going to a therapist was more uncomfortable than tripping in front on the field at a pep rally. Sitting in her office in the comfy chairs wasn't the problem. Talking to "a professional" about my issues made me feel different, abnormal, like I had been born on another planet and placed on Earth as a joke. No one I knew went to a shrink. At least no one admitted to it. What if she put me on meds? What if I had to go to the nurse and take them? Everyone would know. I didn't want my brain messed with. Worse, my parents were fine with shoving a loved one in a mental facility if the mood called for it.

The elevator reeked of strong floral perfume. My hazy reflection stared back from the metallic walls as I contemplated my future.

My grandpa lived in a psych hospital. It's only a matter of time before I met the same fate—since I saw dead people. Was medication such a bad thing if it made Magnolia leave me the hell alone?

Seconds later, the elevator doors opened. I hesitated, not wanting to exit.

"Sonora, if you don't hurry it up, the doors will close again." My mom stepped out. I released my grip on the railing. "Sonora." Mom snapped her fingers.

I shuffled into the hallway. My body on autopilot; my legs moved but didn't feel like *my* legs. I wanted to rush back to the car, drive the hour and a half home, act like everything was fine. Mom pulled open the maroon door, revealing the large waiting room that smelled like old paper. My hand reached up to prop the door open so I could walk in, but it didn't feel like *my* hand. My body moved forward without my consent.

Mom signed-in at the front desk. Only one other patient sat in the waiting room watching a child play on the floor. A little boy, too old to be playing with such toys, rammed a Tonka truck into a pile of magazines. When he turned to look at me, he beamed. He didn't mind being here as much as I did. I smiled back. Why did I smile? Dull needles did somersaults in my stomach, and I wrapped my arms around myself.

The door across opened. "Sonora Stewart," called a lanky man with a goatee. The plastered smile drained from my face.

"It will be fine," Mom whispered, placing her hand on my back as I stood from my seat.

The assistant ushered me down the dimly lit hallway to the office. Dr. Sylvia sat in an oversized, comfy leather chair. Her assistant shut the door behind us.

"How have you been?" she asked. She crossed her legs and clasped her hands with ease. Her kind, almond-shaped eyes helped calm me. Natural light shone through the plate glass window to our left, bathing the room in sunshine.

I sat on the couch across from her. Her office wasn't anything like the movies, not sterile or stuffy, but the room still gave me the willies. A Galileo thermometer sat atop the desk behind her, along with a silver nameplate and other organized knickknacks. Audio speakers hung on brackets in the top corners of the room. Last session, light classical music strummed in the background.

"I'm good." I squirmed in my seat, my knees bounced.

Dr. Sylvia observed my restless legs. A candle burned on a small table in the corner, and her office smelled of lavender. By no means did she look as nervous as I felt.

A few minutes into the awkward silence, she pulled out a large gray cloth and unfolded it between us. The top side was painted with Checker lines. "Well, tell me about school, or about your family. How are you doing?" She organized oversized wooden checker pieces, giving me the white ones.

I licked my lips and breathed in the cloying lavender. "School's fine. Having some trouble in one of my classes, but I'm working hard to bring the grade up."

"Are you and Chris still together?" She grabbed a mint out of a glass jar next to her and handed me a piece. I took the candy, popping it in my mouth. My chapped lips burned from the essential oils.

"Chris?" I said.

"Yes, last time, you shared that the two of you weren't communicating well."

I laughed inwardly, forgetting the last time I had spoken to her was five months ago when Chris had refused to answer some of my texts and calls. I'd thought he cheated on me, but he hadn't, his phone was out-of-service while he and his family were away on vacation.

"Chris and I are great. In fact, couldn't be better. Fall Fling is coming up." Odd. Sitting here in her office, the dance didn't seem as important anymore. It was hard to be excited between being haunted and being tired. "Everything's good." I leaned over and grabbed a white checker.

Dr. Sylvia moved a black checker diagonally. "Your mom told me you haven't been sleeping well."

There it was, the real reason I was here. Mom.

"That's true," I answered shortly. I prodded a checker forward, opposite hers.

"Would you like to talk about Bram?"

My neck tightened, I wasn't expecting her to ask about him. Bram's leaving home was more of a family situation, and if she wanted to help, she should talk to my mom and dad—not me.

"You know," Dr. Sylvia started, as she moved another black piece, "it's okay to be sad about him."

I avoided looking at her, and responded by jumping over two black checkers and removing them from the board. *Why is she asking about Bram?* Dr. Sylvia had no clue what really bothered me. It was as if she grasped at straws, so I tossed her a juicy one.

She moved another checker forward.

"It's not him, it's my friend Magnolia's death." I jumped another one of hers. Was she letting me win?

"Good play," she replied, reaching for the notes on her side table. "Magnolia, yes, I remember her. But I haven't talked to you since her death. Her story was all over the news. How have you been dealing with it? Is that why you're not sleeping?"

Yes, and no. No way did I want to tell her about the ghost, anything that would flag me as a crazy. So I thought of something else, the truth, but far away from Ghostville. "Before she died, I wasn't exactly what you would call a *good* friend."

Dr. Sylvia nodded and leaned back, flipping through her notes. "Her mom died in a car wreck. The head-on collision"

I shrugged.

"I'm sure that was tough on your friendship." She paused, gauging my reaction with narrow eyes. "How had she dealt with the passing of her mother? A tragedy for all involved."

Was I crossing a line? It was weird talking about how my dead best friend dealt with the death of her mom. But it kept the focus off of me, so I went with it. "Not well—she dropped out of cheerleading." I leaned over and moved another checker piece, jumping two of hers.

"Sonora, sit back and relax for a second."

I exhaled and crossed my arms, ready to go through the motions. The faster we got this session over with, the better.

"A loss of that magnitude has a profound effect on a child, no matter the age. The fact that the two of you were working through a difficult time in your friendship, which is understandable given the circumstances, doesn't mean you should feel guilty about her passing."

"Her murder," I corrected.

Dr. Sylvia uncrossed her legs. "Is that why you've been losing sleep?" She found a way to circle the conversation back to me again. Damn, she was good at this.

I unfolded my arms and moved another checker piece out of turn to give me time to consider my answer. With my hand in motion, my body seized and my back tightened. Suddenly, the speakers in her room blasted on. A Rag'n'Bone Man song blared. Dr. Sylvia jumped from her seat, shoving her palms against her ears. With a contorted look on her face, she rushed over and began tapping furiously on her iPad.

The song was the same one that had played on my phone whenever Mag's called before she died. It was *her* song. The notes dug into my spine and squeezed each vertebra with a pair of icy pliers. I tried lifting my arm, but it hurt! I swallowed. The only part of me that could move was my eyes.

"Sonora?" Dr. Sylvia shouted over the music that finally shut off, leaving a ringing in my ears.

Magnolia withered into view, between me and the doc. My breathing halted, the sensation of water rushed through my lungs. I was drowning! I coughed. Pain fired through my torso like a pinball machine.

I stared. Magnolia didn't say a word. She lingered between us, her legs cut off by the checkered cloth she stood in.

It took all my strength to move my fist upward to my chest, attempting to beat the water pressure away. Attempting to cough it out. Was she trying to kill me? Was she *that* mad at me for the way things ended?

Dr. Sylvia flew across the table, through Magnolia's form. She grabbed my shoulders and shook me. "Sonora, what's wrong? You're turning blue!" Water filled my lungs, forcing out the air.

Frantically, she leaned me forward and slapped my back.

Above her, Magnolia floated, her eye drifting near her nose.

Ten seconds later, Magnolia faded away. Air. Sweet air flowed up my nose. I gagged. Panted. My body slouched forward, against Dr. Sylvia's stomach. Checkers tinkled to the floor.

"Sonora, what was that? No more mints for you."

I dry heaved into a trash can. Did she think I had been choking?

"Are you okay?" she asked, flustered with pasty cheeks.

A fishy smell prevailed in the room, replacing the scent of the candle no longer burning. Dr. Sylvia crinkled her nose but said nothing.

"I'm fine," I blurted, my sweat-soaked shirt turning icy. "Get away from me!" I yelled at Magnolia who was no longer there. Dr. Sylvia flinched at my abrasiveness, her hands flung up as if to block the verbal blow.

I corrected my tone. "Sorry. The mint," I offered as a way of explaining my near-death experience. "I'm tired. My mom's right, I haven't been sleeping well."

After composing herself, she sat back down with wide eyes. "I know your mom doesn't want you taking anything stronger than vitamins for sleep. But sometimes, talk therapy and vitamins can only help so much. Sleep deprivation messes with mood swings and your overall health. Okay?" Her chest rose and fell, like she'd run a sprint. She rubbed her trembling hands together.

I swallowed and ran my fingers through my disheveled red hair. I didn't need meds. I needed an exorcism.

"I know you're only trying to help, but really, I'm fine. I'll be fine," I assured her. If only I could find

Magnolia's killer, my life could go back to normal. "Are we done?"

"For today," she replied. "But let's schedule another session soon."

Not if I can help it.

Dr. Sylvia escorted me out of her office and into the waiting room. Mom looked up from reading a book, and her eyebrows rose. I smiled casually as I approached her. "All good, ready to go," I said and nudged her arm. Dr. Sylvia followed from behind.

"Let's meet again in three weeks?" Dr. Sylvia requested, not letting me escape easily. "My assistant will email you to schedule a time."

EIGHT

The roaring sound of the lunchroom dulled into distant echoes. The avocado slipped out the edges of my sandwich. I hung my head and closed my eyes wanting nothing more than to doze. Two more nights of sleepless terror from Magnolia had taken their toll on my psyche. The vitamins and melatonin tablets hadn't helped a bit.

I inhaled deeply and squinted, trying to pull myself awake, out of the trance.

An image of another ghost, of a college guy wearing horns on his decapitated head, flashed behind my eyelids. I shook the image off. I was starting to have hallucinations of people that weren't even there.

A tap on my shoulder snapped me back to reality.

"Say something…" Cooper whispered sharply in my ear.

"What?" I raised my head.

Lachlan sat across from me, in the seat Chris normally sat in if he hadn't had left campus for lunch. Why hadn't I simply gone with him? Rosa wasn't at lunch either. Where was she when I needed her the most?

Lachlan's glare focused on me.

I leaned over to Cooper. "What's *he* doing here?" I asked. I had an idea of what Lachlan may want to talk about—Mags. But that wasn't a subject I wanted to approach here at the table, in front of my friends.

Angela leaned forward and pursed her lips, making her cheekbones look perfect. She had promised to keep our secret. She better.

"I don't know," Cooper muttered. "He's talking to *you.*"

I quickly glanced at Lachlan, our eyes met. Stalling, I looked down at my food and picked at my bread. What was I to say? Dusting bread crumbs off my fingers, my eyes flickered to his. "Look, I don't know what you want or why you're here." My tone was a bit too harsh. A pain of regret stabbed me inside.

Lachlan's cheeks reddened and the vein in his neck throbbed. Cooper and Angela snickered. "What are *you* laughing at," Lachlan raged at Cooper. He slapped his palms on the table, eyeballing me before abruptly pushing off with his hands to leave.

I took a bite of avocado, utterly repulsed by what had happened. However open-minded Lachlan may have been, he wouldn't be anymore.

"Did you have to laugh?" I snapped at Angela.

"It was kind of funny," Cooper said, defending her. "His nose still looks crooked from when Chris wiped the floor with him in the eighth grade. And, why would he be talking to us?

The question lingered in the air for an awkward moment. I shrugged. "I don't know. Your guess is as good as mine."

"Well, *I* do," Angela butted in.

I grimaced, ready to blurt to Cooper what Angela had confided in me about the text.

But what if Angela shared my secret as well?

Cooper probably wouldn't buy my stupid lie about Lachlan asking for help with homework. What if the whole school found out about Mags and deemed me a crazy person? My head felt funny and my vision spun.

If my parents found out, they'd instantly commit me, distancing themselves from their *troubled* daughter like they had my grandfather.

"He has a crush on her," Angela finally answered.

At those words, the spinning stopped. Why would she lie for me?

Cooper burst into laughter. "Lachlan? That guy doesn't like *anyone*, especially not Sonora." He managed to speak between belly laughs and fell out of his seat. Ugh. He was like an annoying cousin no one wanted to sit next to at Thanksgiving. "Wait until Chris hears this one."

Coolly, I rewrapped the remnants of my sandwich. "I didn't realize the thought of Lachlan having a crush on me was so incredibly funny."

I forced a smile and pretended to be unbothered by his stupid antics while searching the cafeteria for Lachlan. Where had he gone?

I gathered my lunch and shoved it into my small bag.

"I need to run to my car for my Chem book. See y'all later," I said, and then darted out the cafeteria, leaving Cooper's mocking laughter behind.

Outside, passing parked cars, I walked toward the football field. I had a hunch Lachlan and his friends might be beneath the bleachers having a last minute smoke before the bell rang. I hoped he'd be there now. The football practice field and bleachers sat empty. I pushed the turnstile at the entrance to the field. The metal arms creaked as they rotated. I shook the door on the side of the concession stand. Locked tight.

Squeezing the loops of my backpack, I sauntered down the track toward the opening beneath the bleachers.

Magnolia appeared in front of me. I halted and stepped around her. "I don't have time for you right now," I muttered. For the first time, her presence didn't startle me; I was on a mission to end all this.

The sun shined through the stands. The gold light cast long shadows on the brick walls lining the bathrooms.

"Hello?" I hollered. The fishy odor approached. I spun around, but Magnolia was gone.

Nothing. No reply from Lachlan. My voice only echoed.

Something clanked further below the bleachers, and I halted my steps.

"Anyone there?" I leaned forward, examining the space from afar, but couldn't see much.

I moved closer to the noise.

Glancing around the edge of the brick walls, nobody hid on the other side of the bathrooms either.

Lachlan wasn't here.

I didn't have his phone number. Unless I saw him in the halls or caught him in the parking lot after school again, I wasn't sure how to get ahold of him. And neither of those options appealed to me anyway. Both led to more friends having the chance to accidentally observe us talking.

μ

"Go home," Tracy, my manager, urged. She held a salad plate filled with mashed potatoes—instead of dressing. Right then, I stumbled, and my hand knocked a drink off the table next to me.

Magnolia's ghost flittered into view. The rancid smell overtook the kitchen, like someone forgot to empty the lobster tank. I covered my nose. It was hard to smell her over the food, but I could. My hands trembled as her droopy eye slid back and forth.

"I still have an hour left on my shift," I shakily replied. In an hour, I'd be a puddle on the floor.

"We can handle it. Go home." Her words were harsh. I'd never been sent home from work before. I was one step away from going home for good. Magnolia menacingly closed the distance. I turned to leave and as soon as I reached the doors, I sprinted toward my car.

In the dark lot, I held my keys, splicing them out between my trembling fingers. Whoever killed Magnolia and those other girls still roamed free. Until I found him, my life was over.

Lachlan. Would he ever talk to me again?

As soon as I shut the door to my car, I locked it and grabbed my phone. I tilted the rearview mirror, smelling Magnolia, but she wasn't in my back seat or next to me.

Where was she? Not here. My shoulders relaxed.

I tapped on the Internet app, wanting to find Lachlan's address. I thumbed his name in, and as the phone searched, it lost signal. "Damn phone." It had problems at inopportune times. I shook it and clicked the circular button at the bottom, slapping the face against my palm as if I could force it to work. The musty odor worsened in my car. I reached into my purse, pulled out a tissue, and shoved pieces of it up my nose.

"Is this you?" I yelled at Magnolia, who I couldn't see. Was she causing my phone to glitch? "You're only making this harder."

Not giving up, I removed the battery and waited a few seconds before holding down the power button again. "You're the one that wanted me to talk to him."

A minute later, my phone lit up and the smell vanished.

Lachlan's address wasn't hard to find.

With a flick of my hand, I tossed my phone on the passenger seat.

I leaned forward to look in the rearview mirror, and then slammed on the breaks—jerking my head backward. A bearded ghost wearing clothes from another era loitered behind my trunk, a large knife in his hands, the blade reflecting an invisible sunlight.

I screamed and my arms shook as my fingers tightened around the wheel. Hallucinations—that's all this was. Lack of sleep. What if it was her fault? What if she opened some portal or hole or something? What if other ghosts followed her through?

Without wasting more time, I released my foot off the pedal and accelerated out of the parking lot, heading to Lachlan's.

Beads of sweat gathered on my forehead every time I glanced in the rearview. I wiped my palms on my shirt so I could grip the wheel better.

Turned out, Lachlan lived ten minutes away from my house.

The stars barely dotted the sky, the full moon bright as I rolled up to his address.

The front of his house, a narrow one-story with chocolate shutters, sat among others of similar size. I grabbed my phone to check the address again but unfortunately, I had no signal. Stupid phone. A tall street lamp on the corner lit the house.

The numbers on the mailbox, 3849, seemed correct with what I remembered.

A bitter taste coated my tongue and the fishy odor filled my car again.

I reached my hand between the seats and found an old stick of gum. If I was going to confront Lachlan and *apologize*, minty breath would help.

My eyes flitted back and forth between the two cars parked in the driveway as I second-guessed the address before stepping out.

The rubber soles of my shoes crunched against the pea-gravel path curving from the road to the front door.

Approaching, I raised my hand to knock but stopped. What if this was the wrong house?

Taking a few steps back, I rubbed my neck, thinking.

Beyond the door, faint music played. Lots of drums and screaming guitars. From my brief run-in with Lachlan at the fundraiser, I knew Lachlan was fond of loud music. I turned around and followed the origin of the heavy metal to a side window.

I examined the area for neighbors before carefully inching my eyes above the brick edge of the window.

The room was empty, clearly belonging to someone that liked the color red. The rich carmine walls and bold black furniture screamed guy's room.

Abstract art hung on the walls, along with two portraits painted of the same woman. Bold and large, taking up an entire wall. Usually, a guy's room contained Sports Illustrated posters and muscly car gadgets. *Something* along those lines. At least Chris's did.

A new heavy metal song blared from the speakers in the corners.

A door opened to the right, and a half-naked Lachlan walked out with a towel around his waist, another slung over his head. Steam tumbled from behind him.

I swallowed. He pulled the blue towel off his head and draped it around his neck. It was definitely Lachlan. He looked hot and shiny beneath those emo clothes.

Headlights flashed behind me as a neighbor pulled into a driveway.

Lachlan's head tipped to the side, and his brows raised as his eyes fell on me.

Shit. I dropped to the ground, forgetting that he could see me.

With humiliation, my heart raced. Slowly, I straightened my legs.

Lachlan's torso blocked the entire window.

I winced and mouthed, "Hi"—adding a little side-wave.

"What are you doing?" he said. His voice was muffled by the glass barrier, but I could still understand him.

"I need to talk to you." My lips moved exaggeratingly as if *he* couldn't hear *me*.

He pointed at his ear. "What?"

"I. Need. To. Talk. To. You," I said louder.

"Still can't hear you."

The neighbor looked curiously at my stalkerish behavior. Blood rushed to my cheeks.

Lachlan grinned ear to ear, seemingly entertained. My gaze dropped to his nice washboard stomach.

I shook my head, attempting to rid the image of his body from my thoughts.

With more control, I pressed my lips together and narrowed my eyes.

He managed to stop laughing for a second to unlock the window. He slid it open and leaned out.

"You couldn't have done that earlier?" I asked, unamused by him not opening the window sooner.

"What's the fun in that?"

"Whatever. Can I come in?" I didn't wait for him to reply and shoved him backward so I could climb inside. Off balance, his towel nearly dropped as I swung my leg over. My eyes remained forward, but I stole a quick glance.

NINE

Averting my attention to the art displayed on the wall, I crossed my arms. "Can you put a shirt on?" I suggested. "Pants would be nice too."

"Queen Sonora." Lachlan bowed with his arms out. "Please, come right in and tell me what to do in my own room." He tightened his towel and grabbed a wrinkled t-shirt off his bed.

"Don't call me that." I marched over and straightened a spot on his rumpled black comforter before sitting down. "What did you want to tell me at lunch?"

As if I hadn't spoken, he moseyed over to his dresser and tugged on a pair of boxers beneath his towel.

"Did you hear me?" I asked, with his back facing me.

His room smelled like the interior of an old car with a hint of fresh soap. He combed his fingers through his wet hair. "Yeah, I heard ya."

"And?"

"Am I supposed to show you the same politeness that you showed me in front of your friends?" The word 'politeness' was awkward on his lips.

I stood up, letting out a long, slow sigh. "I'm sorry." My voice cracked a bit with a soreness in my lungs. Those words didn't come easily, but I needed him on my side. And I *had* acted like a total bitch, which I didn't particularly like about myself. But I didn't want this part of my life mixing with that part of my life. "You wouldn't understand."

His head tilted. "That's an apology?"

"Will you help me or not?" I asked.

A second later, he held out his hand. "Money talks."

"Money, again?"

"If you want to hear what I have to say, and you do. Believe me. Then you'll pay for it." His stance didn't falter.

"Fine. How much?" I grunted.

"Fifty."

A wisp of annoyance escaped my lips. "Ten," I countered.

"Twenty," he rebutted.

My neck stiffened. "Fine. Twenty." I smiled inwardly, because I would've gladly offered forty. Twenty dollars to discover whatever information he had obtained would be worth it. Especially if that meant Magnolia would leave me alone sooner rather than later.

He stalked over to a built-in desk in a nook in the back of his room. Above the desk, hung a bookshelf filled with an array of colorful books. Who was this guy? Paintings, red walls, washboard abs? I would've never thought he, druggie squad leader and all-black wearing emo, would be one to read books.

As Lachlan opened a drawer, I noticed a tin cup holding a bunch of paintbrushes. Paintbrushes?

"Did you paint these?" I asked. The art reminded me of my brother, he loved abstract.

Lachlan closed the drawer and turned around with a manila folder by his side.

"Yeah." He paused, waiting for me to pay attention. "Here's what I've got. And I should really charge you more. It's worth it."

"You mean, *you* painted these," I said, not replying to his money remark. Two painted portraits of a woman mirrored each other on the wall behind me. The smeared black and abyss blue strokes around her angular face warmed me with despair. I rubbed my itchy throat, wanting to turn away. But I couldn't. She was beautiful, but sad. Her eyes depicted vibrant as Lachlan's. Who was she?

"That's what I said." He walked over and shoved the folder in my hands.

I peeled my focus away from the wall and opened the folder. It was filled with a bunch of scanned copies— or snapshots or something. The pictures were off-centered and a little blurry. "How did you get this?"

"My dad."

"He let you have these?" I was appalled and simultaneously grateful.

"Course not." Lachlan made a how-dumb-do-I-look face.

I waited for him to explain. "Well?"

"You're very irritating."

"Only when I need to be," I replied.

A hint of a smile tugged at the corner of his lips. "Like I said before, these are worth way more than twenty dollars."

I snapped the folder shut and held it behind my back. "How did you get these?"

"He brought a box of work home. When he was busy, I snapped some pics of the info with my phone."

I guess that's why they looked like snapshots because they actually were.

"You said a box. How much more is there?"

"A lot. But that's all the info I could get."

I opened the folder back up. The first few pages held details of where the bodies were found and the manners they were disposed of. Bile inched up my throat, and I averted my eyes and closed it again.

"Deal's a deal," I said under my breath. I chewed on my minty gum of which I was grateful for right about then. "Thanks."

"Wow. A thanks from Queen Sonora. Whatever shall I do?" He bowed deeply.

"Stop that," I hissed. The gratefulness I had felt quickly disappeared. "You're a punk."

He shrugged his shoulders. "A richer punk now thanks to you." And he held out his hand.

I winced. "Look. I don't have the money on me."

His hand fell to his side, and his eyes narrowed.

"But I'll bring it tomorrow."

Behind me, the lights from his neighbor's driveway shined in his window.

"Why do you need this stuff anyway?" he asked.

Because I see ghosts, but I wasn't about to let that slip, even if I'd seen his impeccable abs. "Just feel that I owe it to Magnolia."

He stepped closer to me, half an arm's length away. My breathing hitched. He smelled of Irish Spring soap, and I inhaled deeply. A knock jolted his door.

"Here." He quickly grabbed a pen off his desk and jotted down his cell number on the folder.

"Lachlan," a man's voice resonated.

"Yeah, dad?"

"Move your car or the keys are mine. And whose car is in our driveway?"

"You better go," he said, unfazed by his dad's threat.

I turned around and climbed out the open window. Leaning back in, I whispered, "This stays between us, okay?"

He nodded, but I suspected he didn't want word getting out about what he had done for me any more than

I did. Before I darted from the window, a metallic glimmer beneath the bed caught my eye.

It was a bracelet with dotted specs of diamonds curving to the middle to a larger emerald. I'd seen that bracelet a million times before. It had been Magnolia's. Why was it under Lachlan's bed? Before I could ask, Lachlan shooed me away. I scurried to my car, not wanting his father to spot me with the folder, my head filled with more questions.

I pulled out of the driveway, parked across the street, and flipped open the folder, scanning the notes made by Detective Granger. Spreading a few images out beside each other, my stomach turned at the site of the corpses. I swallowed. The dead girls looked way worse than the ones in the movies. I needed more space, more light, and more time. Seeing Magnolia's corpse, a sinking feeling settled over me and I snapped the folder shut.

TEN

Coach Gold motioned for me. "I need to talk to you. Alone."

After running drills the last twenty minutes of practice, sweat streamed down my neck. I grabbed a green towel and wiped my forehead.

I shrugged and nodded. Now what? The rest of the squad headed off to the locker room with nervous looks in my direction.

I walked over, shaking my shirt to fan my wet stomach with cooler air. She motioned for me to have a seat on the bleachers.

"I'm sorry to do this, but my hands are tied. School rules. You're benched for the next few weeks until your Calculus grades are up. I received a notice today and your parents will receive one too, if they haven't already.

Instead of coming to practice, you'll finish homework and study for tests in my classroom."

"You can't do this! The competition is in six weeks! If I can't practice, I'll be out."

Coach shook her head. "I'm sorry, Sonora. You're the best backspot we have."

My eyes dropped to the red tape that crisscrossed the gymnasium floor. I had an inkling that this could happen, but I never thought it actually would. I mean, it's cheerleading. Nobody's been tossed off the squad before—not in their senior year.

"I'll talk to Mr. Jones about my grades. I'll get this fixed."

"Failing a class is a big deal." My heart dropped between my ankles. "Is everything alright? You haven't been yourself lately." She paused. "What's going on?"

What was I supposed to say? I leaned back a little, adding space between us. "Magnolia's death. It's hard. You know?" Short answers were all I could muster. A lump of despair inched up my throat, the kind of lump that cropped up before tears. I stood, rooted in place, unable to take one more ounce of bad news.

She placed a hand on my shoulder. I didn't like it. "Do you want to speak to Mrs. Chenault?" she asked.

I shrugged her hand away, and my eyes snapped up to hers. The last thing I needed was to talk to the school counselor. There's nothing she'd be able to do for me anyway. And seeing ghosts isn't exactly "routine behavior." There's probably nothing in her handbook for that.

I shook my head. "I'm fine. Promise."

Coach Gold squinted and rubbed her elbow. "No practice, okay? Do your homework, get your grades up, you'll be back on the squad in no time."

"Right," I answered. What would Mom and Dad say when they found out? Heat warmed my cheeks. Tears edged the rim of my eyes. Before Coach took notice, I retreated from the gym.

My life was spiraling out of control.

Rosa wasn't waiting in the gym, but she'd probably be here soon. To dodge her, I skipped showering and headed straight to my locker. I didn't want to talk to anyone. Who cared if I stank before going to work. I didn't, not anymore. Nothing mattered anymore.

I grabbed my backpack and headed to my car. If I wasn't a cheerleader, then who was I? It might sound stupid to someone else, but I put years and years into this squad, into the friends and teammates. And now all of it was on the brink of being lost.

Sitting in the front seat, thick tears fell from the tip of my nose. I was done. Nationals were coming soon. If I was benched, then I wouldn't be allowed to take part. The squad would suffer.

My chest throbbed. To stop the pain, I pushed the tip of my thumb hard against my sternum.

How would I find a killer that not even the cops could find?

I grabbed the wheel for support and squeezed, digging my nails into the rubbery texture.

Watching students chatting in the overcast parking lot fueled me. I spotted Lachlan in my rearview mirror. He climbed into his Firebird. For a brief moment, I remembered his nice abs and sexy accent but shook the pleasant thoughts away. I still owed him twenty dollars and an interrogation about Magnolia's bracelet. Beneath the passenger seat sat the folder he'd given me. I opened it.

Placing the open folder on the seat, I reached for my phone, but the screen froze—again.

I thumbed the home button and nothing happened.

I beat the back of it against my palm, and then finally, it unfroze.

I dialed work.

Tracy answered. "Hi, this is Sonora." I fake coughed twice before speaking. "I'm sick and can't come in." I sniffed deeply, trying to appear audibly ill as possible.

"This is your second mark." She paused. "Next time, it'll be your last," she warned.

Bitch.

After I hung up, I pulled out of the school's lot and headed straight to Magnolia's house. I'd put this off long enough. Lachlan had given me the photos, but if I truly wanted to increase my odds of discovering the killer, I *had* to speak to Mr. Ackerman—Magnolia's father. Maybe he knew something I didn't.

Being benched from the squad fanned my determination to do whatever I needed to get Magnolia out of my life.

My phone beeped in my purse with a new message. Keeping my eyes on the road, I reached for it and glanced down.

What are you doing tonight? Rosa texted.

I mulled it over before replying. *Nothing. Why?* I typed back.

Wanna hang? Friends forever. That was our mantra, even though we'd only been friends for a few months.

Whenever Rosa wanted to hang, that was code for let's talk *now*, drama class 101. Sometimes she was a bit overboard in that department. Drama was Rosa's middle name, or it should've been.

I welcomed the gossip, but I had somewhere else I needed to be first.

Sure. Gotta do something, text me on your way.

Mr. Ackerman still lived in the same house. For months after the crash stole Magnolia's mom, she and her dad received enough food for an apocalypse. Before the crumbling of our small group, we used to sit in her kitchen. We'd label containers with expiration dates and pile them in her freezer. My favorite was a tub of homemade strawberry ice cream; she and I finished that off in one night while we cried together.

I turned left onto Sycamore, a long and windy street. It wasn't five o'clock yet. Would Magnolia's dad be home from work?

They lived at the end of a cul-de-sac. I hadn't seen him since Magnolia's funeral. How would he take me showing up on his doorstep?

Next to his home, there was a blue sign with the words *Yard of the Month* stuck in a neighbor's lot. Overgrown rose bushes and knee-tall weeds decorated Mr. Ackerman's yard. The flowers on either side of his mailbox had wilted beyond the point of no return, black and dead.

If this was the outside of the house, what did the inside look like?

If he wasn't home, then I could at least say I tried. Would that placate Mags enough? I contemplated the best approach. What would I say to him? In the distance, beyond his roof, a surge of gray clouds rimmed the blue horizon.

With trepidation, I turned off the ignition and the radio faded. *Please don't be home.*

The garage was shut. The blinds closed.

I padded up to the front porch.

As I reached the door, I covered my face with my hands. Something smelled rotten.

In the corner, Tupperware and glass platters topped with foil had been stacked on top of one another. Tiny gnats buzzed all around. I swatted at them as they tried entering my nostrils.

Breathing through my mouth, I shielded my face with my hand and rang the doorbell.

Five minutes later, after swatting flies and not getting an answer, I decided to come back another time.

As I spun around, Magnolia's grotesque ghost froze me in place. I hadn't smelled her over the rotten scent lingering from the spoiled food. No wonder so many flies buzzed my head.

I swallowed. With stiffening shoulders, I turned to face the door again, not looking at Magnolia. I could *feel* her behind me with every hair on my neck. A thick fishy taste coated my tongue.

Seconds passed. I knocked again.

When nobody answered, I exhaled. A gnat flew in my mouth and I yacked, spitting it out on the weathered welcome mat.

"See Mags?" I looked over my shoulder cautiously, but she had already disappeared. The tension in my back released.

Was she inside? Was I not the only one she haunted?

I rang the doorbell again to prove a point that nobody was home.

Nothing.

Turning around again, a creak from the door halted me mid-stride off the porch.

My eyes slid over the smelly food and up to the tiny crack in the door. It was open, but nobody hovered in view of the opening.

"What now?" I asked myself.

My brain screamed to run, but I leaned forward toward the shadowy crack. I pushed it open. The metal hinges whined as I peered around the edge of the door inside. "Hello?" I asked in a high-pitched voice.

A glimpse of her dad emerged from the right as he crossed beneath the archway of a hall. Coldness skittered over my shoulders like tiny needles prickling my skin. "Mr. Ackerman?" I whispered, not wanting him to actually hear me. I eyed the metal threshold on the ground, a barrier between the porch and the inside of the house. The tips of my shoes paused between safety outside and the unknown inside.

The shadowy living room filled the space directly in front of the door. Dreary light shined through the bay windows on the far wall and the curtains were drawn tight. A blanket on the couch and the remote on the coffee table the only signs of life.

"It's now or never," I whispered.

My knees shook as I crossed the threshold and shut the door. The moment it closed, the hairs on my arms stood. I reached back to open it. I yanked on the doorknob, but the door wouldn't budge.

I squeezed my car keys in my right hand, giving me something to hold onto.

Easing toward the hall, I called for him. "Mr. Ackerman?"

Approaching the archway, I placed my hand on the wall and leaned around the corner for a better view of the master bedroom. I'd been in this house countless times and knew the layout with my eyes closed.

His bedroom door was wide open, but the room was too dark to see inside. The hallway not much brighter.

I repeated his name, creeping closer to his bedroom. The soles of my shoes stuck to the filthy carpet with each step.

My eyes adjusted as the distance lessened. A few more feet.

In the sunless room, the ceiling fan rattled like a bearing had come loose. Twisted blankets piled on top of the bed.

"Mr. Ackerman?"

Behind me, the faint sound of labored breathing ripped the air from my lungs. My body tensed with fear.

I turned slowly.

Mr. Ackerman stood right behind me, his head hung down and his eyes trained on the floor. He looked half alive and as if he hadn't slept in months. He looked worse than me.

I stumbled, and my keys fell from my grasp.

Without taking my eyes off of him, I braced myself on the wall and bent over to pick them up.

Mr. Ackerman's hair was half a foot longer than usual and oily. His overall frame frailer. He'd lost a ton of weight. I almost didn't recognize the feeble-looking man as Magnolia's father, as if all his toned muscles dissipated into thin air. A vile smell of sweat mixed with sour fruit wafted off his clothes, like he hadn't bathed in weeks. Had he been like this before Magnolia's death?

I stepped back to get away from the stench. It was worse than Magnolia's ghost, worse than the front porch.

"Mr. Ackerman. You scared me," I said, brandishing a wavering smile, cupping my hand over my nose.

His eyes flittered back and forth between me and the unkempt room—I was standing in his way.

"Let me make you some coffee. Okay?" I said, hoping he'd take me up on the offer rather than falling into despair. I needed him to talk, not crash into a more perilous, useless state.

He mumbled something that I didn't understand and then spun around. I took his response as a yes. I'd never seen him without a cup of coffee in his hand or wearing a suit and tie. But when I stopped returning Magnolia's calls, I hadn't visited her either. How many weeks had their home been deteriorating before her death?

With weak knees, I followed him into the kitchen.

Unlike the living room, the kitchen was like his bedroom—a gigantic mold fest. Old dishes piled high in both sides of the sink, along with more flies.

I opened the pantry, it was bare. What did he eat? His small frame was a testament to all the weight he'd lost.

The only thing in the pantry was a tin box of raspberry tea—Magnolia's favorite. I didn't much care for it. She liked a lot of things that I didn't: fried eggs, pistachios, orangey drinks, broccoli, SpaghettiOs.

I searched the cramped counters and then the fridge. Opening the fridge was a giant mistake. Rotten fruit had leaked yellowish innards on the shelves, and uncapped milk reeked. I slammed it closed.

There wasn't any coffee, so I settled on making expired tea. I'd never made this kind of tea before, but it didn't seem that much different than the sweet tea Mom made.

Placing a berry bag in the coffee pot, I added water and flipped on the switch.

My mouth felt dry.

There weren't any clean cups, but there was soap.

I washed two mugs, air drying them by swinging each back and forth, and wiped the handles with my shirt.

I poured us both a cup. Steam hovered from the lid.

At the table, the silence lasted forever.

The fear I felt when I entered the house had gradually dissipated, replaced by solemnness. Mr. Ackerman was all alone.

In the same manner, as if I were babysitting a four-year-old, I placed the mug in front of his hands. "Drink this, it'll make you feel better."

He took a sip, then another. Light slowly seeped into his eyes and he stared at my face like he hadn't noticed me before.

My heart thumped against my ribs, and then I asked the first question. "Do you know who killed your daughter?"

ELEVEN

My question was blunt and to the point. I assumed I knew the answer—that Mr. Ackerman didn't know who killed his daughter. But I needed to start off with a bang, jostle him from his barely-functioning persona. Plus, there was a small chance that he *did* know.

His hands remained clasped around the hot mug and his eyes widened. "No." His solid gaze met mine before he asked, "You?"

Surprised and taken aback by the rebuttal, I shook my head. "Course not." If I had any idea, I would've gone to the police already. I wanted to put Magnolia in my rearview more than anyone.

The mug was too hot and I placed it on the sticky mahogany table.

He gazed out the window as a set of chimes riddled with shimmery dragonflies clinked in the wind. Thick clouds blocked half the sunlight. A storm?

"Do you know if the cops have any new suspects?" I asked.

He stared at the musical dragonflies, letting a minute pass. "There was one," he said in a low voice. "The man didn't have an alibi, but they never told me who he was…." His voice trailed off.

"Anything else? Anything you do know?" He had to know *something*.

The chimes rhythmically punctuated the silence.

"Do you mind if I look in her room?"

Without emotion, he turned around and jutted his chin in the direction of the hallway.

Watching him, my heart sank. He had nobody. No wife, no daughter. Magnolia didn't have siblings, which is why we were so close in the beginning. That is until she became too hard to be around, dreary all the time, snappy and unhappy. Before long, she stopped hanging around the group, like she had another life and didn't need us anymore.

"Thanks," I said quietly, scooching back from the table.

He didn't budge.

Her room was the last one on the right, directly down the hall from her parents'. Wait. Her dad's.

The solid white door was closed. A pink sign with her name painted in green hung in the middle. I placed my hand on the wooden grooves, remembering good times of sneaking into the kitchen for midnight snacks. Then I wrapped my fingers around the handle and stepped inside.

All her furniture, her posters, her stuffed animals, hadn't been moved. The blankets on her bed were messy, as if someone had recently slept in them, as if Mags would be home any second. And the carpet was much cleaner in here than in the rest of the house.

Taylor Swift posters covered the wall. The zebra-print curtains her mom had made her—which Magnolia hated—hung above her window.

I shut the door, needing some privacy in case Mr. Ackerman decided to join me.

I sneezed as I shoved open the curtains. Dust motes sprinkled the air in the musty room.

"Magnolia?" I said. "You here?" For the first time, I hoped she'd come through, give me some sort of sign as to what I was looking for.

I closed my eyes. "Magnolia," I whispered a second time. Maybe this telepathy thing worked both ways and she'd come if I concentrated hard enough.

I opened my eyes, but she was nowhere. I didn't feel or smell her either.

I sat on the edge of the cushiony bed where we'd shared so many secrets. It felt so wrong, being here without her. "Why did you have to die?" I closed my eyes, breathing in the room.

Rubbing the zebra printed comforter, the softness beneath my hands, I laid back. My body relaxed and the silence soothed me. "I miss you."

Sitting up, I looked around. "If I were you, where would I hide something I didn't want others to find?" The blue-distressed side table next to her bed contained two drawers. I pulled on the glossy knob, opening the top drawer. Piles of birthday cards from years past lay inside. Flipping through the pile and not opening them, I found the last one I had given her. An orange tabby cat, singing into a microphone, covered the front of the card. I laughed quietly. Mags loved that one.

I opened a few, not really wanting to read them. All the salutations were from her parents or friends I recognized.

Stuffing them back inside, I searched the bottom drawer. Pens and pencils scattered the edges, on top of more papers and pictures. The pictures were nothing I hadn't seen before.

I opened the pocket door of her closet. Shoes lined the carpet, and a black shirt sat twisted and wrinkled in the center. Running my hand along the walls, there were no hidden compartments.

What was I missing? My gut told me to come here, Magnolia all but forced me inside, there had to be *something*.

I let out a huff and turned around, thinking.

Her book bag hung on a chair in the corner. It was exactly like mine, except hers was purple and mine a honey gold. I marched over, opened it, pulling out a binder and two notebooks. As I flitted through them, a blue piece of paper fell onto the ground.

It was a receipt for last spring's Carwash fundraiser. The last get together she had attended before dropping the squad later in the year, right after her mother died.

I lifted the mattress and patted inside, but nothing had been hidden beneath.

The receipt fell out of my pocket. When I bent over to pick it up, a metallic sheen caught my eye, underneath the distressed side-table.

I reached between the grooves along the bottom edge and pulled out dust bunnies along with a small, silvery shaded journal embossed with mauve jewels. In all the times I'd been to her room, I'd never seen this before.

I wanted to open it. Guilt toyed with me. But this was what I was looking for, right?

Afraid that Mr. Ackerman might catch me with it, I stuffed the journal down the back of my athletic shorts.

Leaving her room, I walked back toward the kitchen. He was still sitting at the table, not having moved a bit. I stopped halfway and turned toward the front door, wanting to leave. Then I stopped. "Can I get you something to eat?" I said loud enough for him to hear.

He stood. Without uttering a single word, he brushed past me and into the hallway. I took that as my signal to exit. So I did.

I shouldn't have taken the journal, especially if it could help the investigation, but also because it was probably something her dad would want. Something personal of his dead daughter's.

I brushed aside the cloud of flies as I dashed down the brick steps. The sun peeked through the clouds. The ground wasn't wet. The storm had passed right over without raining.

I hurried to my car and pulled out the journal and placed it on top of the folder Lachlan had given … or I had bought. I still needed to pay him.

The whole way home, I couldn't think of anything else besides the secrets hidden inside her sparkling journal. The sunshine reflected off the jewels in the passenger seat. Colorful sparkles danced on the ceiling. What had Magnolia written? Why was it hidden?

At home, I ran to my room, bypassing Mom. We'd have to talk about cheerleading and my grades, but I wanted to hold off as long as possible if she let me.

Not two seconds after locking my door, I received another text from Rosa. *On my way.*

I didn't have much time.

Kaylee held a tennis ball in her mouth, and she nudged my arm. "Not now," I said.

Sorry, Magnolia, but I have to, I thought. Reading her inner thoughts seemed wrong. What if she haunted me more for doing it?

I opened the bejeweled journal.

TWELVE

Tuesday, January 3

It's been three days since you died. I didn't even get to say goodbye. I love you, Mom. I don't think he can handle it. I can't. Your ugly coffee mug is still on the counter, waiting for you. It feels like everything is supposed to stop, the world should cease turning, but people keep dropping by and saying how they're so sorry! Sonora came over today, pretending like everything was okay, like nothing irrevocably changed forever. She even made me laugh. She's handling this better than me. Dad's friends ask how I'm doing and assure that you're in a better place. But what does that even mean? It's not like they know anything for sure. I can't stop crying.

Dried watermarks blurred the ink on the pages. A pain swelled in the back of my throat. I wanted to call Bram and tell him how much I loved him. He should come home and make everything all right.

I flipped forward a few weeks.

Wednesday, February 15

Cooper doesn't understand. How could he? I don't even know what's wrong with me. I'm super happy one moment and then the next, it's like my body slammed into a brick wall and spit out a cripple. A cripple that nobody can see but me. Nobody sees the pain I walk with every day. Not even him. He wants to help, but he can't. Even Sonora is backing away.

Pages later, I saw my name again, but I couldn't bring myself to read what she'd written. Not yet.

Rosa walked in. I hadn't even heard the doorbell ring. Snapping the journal shut and wiping my face with the back of my hand, I pretended to yawn. I didn't want her to know what I'd been reading, what I'd stolen and why. I wasn't ready to reveal what was happening.

Rosa lingered in the doorway, staring down at her phone. I shoved the journal beneath my bed, out of view.

"Sonora, you have no idea. Tyler is a gigantic a-hole."

I laughed awkwardly and little too long. She cocked her head and squinted. "You okay?" she asked.

It was hard lying to my new best friend. "Who's Tyler?"

She exhaled. "Tyler Minzelli of course."

I knew who Minzelli was.

"Wait, didn't you have a crush on him in the seventh grade?" she asked, changing the subject.

"I thought he moved." I hadn't thought about him in years. "Besides, how do you know that?" This would be Rosa's first full year at the school.

She slouched in a disappointed manner. "He lives ten minutes from here. BFFs are supposed to *know* these things." She paused. "Wait, you don't still like him, do you?"

I raised both hands, halting her question. "No. He's *all* yours."

She dropped her purse to the floor; the same Michael Kors brand as mine but yellow and more vibrant. I wanted that color too, but Mom bought me a black one. Plopping down cross-legged, Rosa turned to face me. "Why are we sitting on the ground?"

She leaned back against the bed, in front of where I'd hidden the journal.

Her left hand graced the sparkly edges with her fingertips.

I sprang up and moved to my bed, hoping she'd follow.

She rolled her eyes. "What are you doing?"

"The floor hurts my back." I shrugged.

"Whatever, grandma …." She moved to the bed. Slouching across from me, Rosa hugged one of my pillows.

Thank God, I thought. I didn't need her finding the journal, leading to bothersome questions.

"Now tell me what happened," I said.

"Well, you know how the Fall Fling is coming?" she started.

"Yeah, how could I forget?"

"He's actually thinking about going with someone else."

I sat forward, confused. "I didn't even know y'all were together? When did this happen?"

"Last month."

"Why didn't you tell me?"

"He wanted to keep it a secret," she paused, "and I sort of liked the rush of hiding it and all. Hiding in the bathrooms, making out in the back of the theater. He's such a good kisser!" For a split second, she closed her eyes, as if toiling through the memories. Then tears welled and exploded down her cheeks, like they'd been locked behind a broken dam.

Watching her cry made me jealous. Jealous? How could I be jealous of Rosa?

I should be holding her. Comforting her. Telling her everything would be okay like a good friend should do. But instead, I sat there. I hadn't told her about cheerleading yet, and the guilt for not doing so tugged at my stomach. We told each other everything—at least I thought so until she hooked up with Tyler and didn't say anything.

Finally, I reached forward and wrapped my arms around her shoulders. "Rosa. Boys are dumb, they want something one minute, and the next, they don't. It has nothing to do with you, he's probably already changed his mind by now."

"We were like Romeo and Juliet—destined." She cried. "Minus the dead part."

I let go of her and she leaned back against the headboard. She threw her phone down on the comforter between us. "Read for yourself."

I picked up her phone and typed her password. The screen unlocked.

I thumbed the message icon and Tyler's name was at the top. It didn't take long to find the text; he was asking someone else to the dance. He didn't even have the guts to state who that someone else was. How was he planning to go to our school's dance if he didn't attend our school?

Rosa's nose was shiny. Mascara streaked her cheeks like wet paint in the rain.

"To hell with him," I said. "You'll find another date. I'm sure of it."

"No, I won't. And I don't *want* anyone else. I want *him*," she choked.

"I can't believe he didn't tell you in person."

"He tried. I mean. After B's the other night, I went over to his place, got the feeling something was off. I hoped I was wrong. I wasn't." Her shoulders shook with more sobs.

"Then that's what we'll do."

Heaves of breath caught between her tears. "What's what we'll do?"

"Convince him he's a fool."

"Huh?"

"If you start hanging all over someone else, he'll change his mind. He'll think he's an idiot for ever suggesting the idea of going with another."

The corner of her mouth rose ever so slightly. It was nice having girl talk. Magnolia and I used to do it all the time, but when she died, a hole replaced our chats. Rosa filled it. Nobody could ever take Mag's place exactly, but Rosa came close.

"It'll work. Promise. Everyone always wants what they can't have. Boys aren't any different," I said.

"You really think so?"

"I know so."

But who was I to talk? The only image that came to mind right now was one of Lachlan in a towel. I cleared my throat. I should be thinking about Chris, not him.

"By the way, I'm off the squad." I paused. "Well, at least until my grades are better."

"That wench!" Rosa said without hesitating. Her tears stopped. "The nerve of her." Her fist pounded the bed and she threw her phone at my dresser, missing the mirror by centimeters.

I flinched, not expecting Rosa to get angry so fast. Her emotions raced from zero to one hundred easily, but it felt good to have someone in my corner.

"I'll show her," she said.

I laughed and walked over to grab her phone. A hairline crack had sliced across the bottom of the screen.

Her being upset at my expense made me smile.

I handed the phone to her. "I'll get my grades up soon, cheering in no time."

The atmosphere shifted. Rosa squealed. "I know exactly who would make him jealous."

"Who?"

"Tyler. I have to figure out how to get him to notice."

I chuckled. "I don't think you'll have a problem with that." I envied her outgoing, I-don't-care-what-others-think attitude. When there was something she wanted, nobody stood in her way.

"Be right back, need to use your bathroom."

A knock sounded from the other side of my door. Rosa paused with her hand on the doorknob.

"Sonora? Are you okay? I heard a banging noise," Mom asked.

Rosa winced, knowing she was the cause.

"Yes, Mom, just an accident," I said. Would she use this moment to discuss me flunking Calculus?

Footsteps sounded as Mom walked away, relief sank over me.

Rosa left the room. When she returned, the smudged mascara had been washed off her freshly polished face.

"I have to go. But I'll call you laterz," she chirped.

"Okay."

As soon as she disappeared out the door, I reached for the journal—and another knock sounded. "Sonora," Mom said.

Languidly, I answered. "Yes?"

Mom and dad walked through without waiting. "I received an email and a phone call from the school. Do you have something to say?" I raised my eyes at dad for help, but he remained solid and supportive at Mom's side. His arms crossed.

"I know, I'm sorry," I said.

She sighed with a stony expression. "Coach Gold informed me that you're off the squad."

I nodded, feeling completely defeated yet once again. "I'm working on it. Promise."

"Do I need to schedule an appointment sooner with Dr. Sylvia?"

I raised my hands up in defense. "Give me two weeks. I don't need to talk to her every time there's a hiccup in my life."

"That's what she's there for, Sonora. It's nothing to be ashamed of. Don't be like your grandpa. He lived in denial for years before accepting help," Dad finally spoke.

My back went rigid. "I'm not Pawpaw. I'm a teenager. Kids fail classes all the time."

"Not you," he replied.

"Give me time. I can turn this around, I know I can," I pleaded. "Trust me."

Mom and Dad made eye contact with each other. "Okay," Mom said. "Two weeks."

THIRTEEN

I woke up, unable to sleep.

In the dark kitchen, I grabbed a glass of water. A gigantic teal clock hung on the truffle colored walls, recently painted months ago. It was the middle of the night, I needed to be quiet.

Sipping on the cold smoothness, visions of Magnolia's death flashed through my mind. Horrific visions filled with the bitter taste of terror.

My heart thumped in my ears.

Kaylee growled in the far off distance; I was somewhere else. My hand tightened, white-knuckling the glass. I couldn't stop Magnolia from invading my mind.

My arms jerked, and my eyes rolled upward.

Barely able to speak, I choked out, "Stop."

Kaylee's cold nose nudged my left hand.

My chest relaxed and I panted for oxygen. The kitchen shadows closed in. I placed my glass in the sink, no longer thirsty.

Retreating to my bedroom, I could feel Magnolia growing stronger. But how? Why?

I rotated the handle of my bedroom door and pushed it open with one swift motion, afraid to walk inside. My leg muscles twitched.

I motioned for Kaylee to trot inside, ahead of me. She stopped growling. That *had* to be a good sign.

Peering into the darkness, I reached in with my right hand and switched on the lights. Feeling a tad safer, I tiptoed forward.

My eyes danced around the room. Magnolia wasn't anywhere.

My shoulders relaxed. The tension in my neck melted until I spotted my closed closet door. I didn't remember shutting it before bed. One last place to check: my closet. I swallowed and inched closer to the white door.

"One."

Two.

Three.

"Now." I flung the door open and released a breath when I saw that it was empty.

From a hiding spot beneath my dresser, I pulled out the folder of the snapshots Lachlan had given me.

I fell backward on my bed, my legs dangling off. I closed my eyes.

A nagging memory floated to the front of my mind. Why was Magnolia's bracelet in Lachlan's room? He never mentioned that he knew her. He didn't let on that she had ever been in his room before. But she had to have been at some point, or had she given it to him? No, that couldn't be it.

It belonged to her mom before Mags started wearing it.

I swept my hair from beneath my head.

The journal. Did I miss a clue?

Leaning over the bed, I grabbed it and splayed out both the folder and the journal next to each other.

With a steady stomach, I examined the gruesome pictures of Magnolia and the other women post-mortem.

I stood up and locked my door. In the white space at the bottom of each snapshot, a murdered girl's name was typed in black. Magnolia had been the last victim of the Creekside Killer, but who had been his first?

I grabbed my laptop. I remembered a site where a journalist had documented the murdered and missing women from Brenham. Magnolia had been the youngest to turn up dead. The manner of her death didn't fit the pattern, but it was close enough as far as the small town police were concerned.

I reordered the snapshots to match the timeline from the site until my bed looked like a slideshow of death. Mags was found in a creek, just like the others, and she nearly had the same visual appearance. Purple discolored strangulation marks displayed around each girl's neck—except Magnolia's. They all had blonde hair and blue eyes, like Mags. But something was missing from the documentary. Every photo showed a dingy brown ribbon tied around the girl's neck, as if the killer tried to hide what he'd done. But there wasn't a ribbon around Magnolia's and no marks either.

I squinted, examining the photo and the detail of the fabric. I felt like I'd seen the paisley pattern before, but I couldn't remember where.

Reading over the website, I stared at the timeline. Last year, the murders began in May with the discovery of two bodies in a creek. Another body was found beneath a bridge in October, but it was thought to be a suicide at first. After that, a college student fitting a similar description was reported missing. This year—two more female bodies were discovered in May. In July, Magnolia was killed. Four bodies last year, three bodies this year.

With it being fall, a part of me wondered if we were closing in on the time when another girl would either disappear or wash up murdered. Was that why Magnolia haunted me? Maybe she wanted me to stop the murderer from killing anyone else.

"Why me?" I'm only seventeen—one-hundred and twelve pounds sopping wet after a rainy football game. What could I do? I couldn't stop a killer even if I found out who he was.

Queasy, I pushed the photos away and opened the journal. I flipped through the pages until I saw bold streaks of blue.

Friday, April 7

It's midnight and I'm headed out. Mom and I always ate at Halo's when I was little. I can't get her out of my head. Halo's makes the best BLT, our favorite. Eating there will be like eating with her.

Halo's. It was a diner in an older part of town. I flipped to the next page, but it was empty. The rest of the pages too. Magnolia appeared, Kaylee growled, and I dropped the journal. The pages flipped closed.

She disappeared.

Was she trying to get my attention? If she'd look less like a walking corpse, it would help. Steadying my breath, I reached for one of the documents in the manila folder. Halo's had been scribbled in the notes for two of the other girls. One victim had been a waitress at the diner. Was there a connection?

I leaned back on my pillow with Magnolia's journal, staring at the name of the diner. Halo's was a sketchy place at night. A place known to be dangerous because of robberies and murders during drug deals gone bad. Had Magnolia got caught up in something when she went there alone?

μ

The field was full of football players practicing as I walked up to the fence. Chris spotted me. The guys were taking a water break, and he jogged over toward me on the track.

"Hey, babe." He breathed heavily and held his helmet in the crook of his arm. Sweat poured down his face. My nerves tingled. He always looked hot all sweaty. "Come to see me practice?" Ginormous shoulder pads blocked my view behind him.

"Yep, why else?" I smiled. Not moving, I searched for any movements beneath the bleachers. I wanted to talk to Lachlan.

The coach blew his whistle. As Chris turned, sweat flung from his hair and across my cheek. "I'll pick you up at six. Got to go!"

"Wait, what?" I said, wiping the nastiness off my nose. I didn't want his sweat *on* me. *Nice for looking at, not for touching.*

"It's Wednesday!" he yelled over his shoulder, hustling off to the field.

Crap. I'd completely forgotten. A few football friends and their girlfriends went out for pizza every Wednesday. I'd completely forgotten and didn't feel like going. Especially if it meant pretending to be happy with half of my old squad sitting around the table.

I hurried beneath the bleachers.

"Lachlan?" I whispered.

I could hear the shriek of the coach's whistle from behind the stands.

"Lachlan?"

A flat voice came up from behind me. "What is it?"

I spun around.

Lachlan didn't smile or wink or do anything that mimicked happiness.

I pulled out the twenty dollars and slapped it in his palm. "Here." He smiled and turned to leave.

"No. Stop. I didn't text you for *that*. I need to ask you something."

His eyebrows arched. "Now what?"

"Did you know Magnolia?"

"Course," he said casually with a slight shrug of his shoulders.

"Not like that. I know you knew her, but did you *know* her. Like has she ever been in your room before?"

He broke eye contact and stuffed the money in his wallet.

"Well?" I asked again.

"Why do you want to know?"

"Answer the question." He was hiding something, but I didn't know what.

"Maybe."

That wasn't the answer I was looking for. "Yes or no?"

"Yes."

I shook my head. "You don't think that information was pertinent?"

"Pertinent?" His eyebrow quirked.

I huffed. "Tell me why."

He gave in to my not-going-anywhere attitude, and relaxed. "We were into the same things."

My stomach dropped. "I knew it. Was she buying drugs from you?"

His face wrinkled in disgust. "Drugs?" He rubbed his neck. "That's what you think of me? If she took something, it wasn't from me."

I contemplated his answer. I never thought of Magnolia as a drug user, but I also didn't think she'd accidentally lose her bracelet under Lachlan's bed either.

"What about her bracelet?"

He scratched his neck and avoided my eyes. "What are you talking about?"

"I saw it under your bed."

His biceps flexed as he re-tied his hair behind his head. "Didn't know it was there."

Was he telling the truth? Why else would her bracelet be there? "Were you sleeping with her?" Heat flushed my cheeks, the words tumbled out. But it would make sense if her bracelet was in his room, jewelry tends to fall off when two people are rolling around. And Lachlan had a *really* good body.

He narrowed his eyes. "Uh, no." The vein in his neck begin to show and he crossed his arms. "What's with the twenty-one questions?"

I didn't know him well enough to know if he was hiding something. What if he had something to do with her murder? He'd definitely lie then. I wasn't sure if I could trust him.

"I gave you what you asked for already."

"The folder," I said, not mentioning anything about the journal. "Halo's Diner. You know of it?"

He shrugged "Doesn't everyone?"

"Before Magnolia died, I thought I heard her mention the place." The lie flew out without even having to think. "And then last night, when I examined the snapshots, the same diner was scribbled in one of the notes. Do you think the two have anything in common?"

He exhaled a heavy breath. "Maybe you should go to Halo's then. I hear they have great prime rib."

I burst into laughter, fearful of the idea. "No way."

He crossed his arms. "That doesn't surprise me. I guess you'll never know why she went there."

"What doesn't surprise you?"

"Queen Sonora doesn't take risks. I bet merely talking to me makes you nervous." He raised his palms at our surroundings. "You asked me to meet you here, beneath the bleachers, rather than being seen with me at school."

"We *are* at school."

"This doesn't count," he replied, gesturing at the bleachers.

Refusing to continue our conversation, I turned around. I needed to go to Halo's, but I didn't really want to.

"It's not that scary. The unknown is always scarier than reality," he said from behind.

I turned back. "That's poetic nonsense."

"When's the last time you've been to Halo's?" he asked.

I had an old memory of my Mawmaw and Pawpaw taking me there when I was younger when Mawmaw was alive—and when Pawpaw didn't live in a psychiatric hospital. They hadn't lived too far from there at the time. A famous Seeburg jukebox sat in the corner of the diner. Pawpaw gave me money to play Mawmaw's favorite song, *A Sunday Kind of Love* by Etta James, over and over again. But now, the diner gave me the willies.

I didn't want to go to Halo's, but if I did, I needed to wait until Friday. The same weekday Magnolia had gone.

FOURTEEN

"That one," I said to Rosa, pointing to the gown with a beaded bust and flowy burgundy bottom. Fall Fling was only a week away.

"Is Chris upset that you didn't go for pizza Wednesday night?" She grabbed the dress off the rack.

"Maybe." I yawned. "It's been two days and he hasn't brought it up yet."

"You can do better than him," Rosa murmured before closing the curtain of the dressing room.

Better than Chris? I thought.

A minute later, she extended her leg out, exposing a silky knee first. In one swift motion, she stepped out with a smile and twirled around, swinging her arms out to the side.

"I don't know why you're buying a dress, you don't even have a date yet."

She stopped spinning. The dress swished in motion around her ankles. "I'm working on it," she said with a prowess tone.

"That's what I'm worried about." What was she up to? Who was she up to?

She placed her hands on her hips. "I found the perfect person to make Tyler jealous."

I tilted my head to the left. "Who?"

"It's a secret for now." She turned to face the mirrors and pulled outward at the fabric of the skirt.

I crossed my arms, annoyed that she didn't want to reveal his name. "We don't keep secrets from each other."

Releasing her skirt, she dropped her arms to her sides and looked at me in the reflection of the mirror. "Do you think I haven't noticed you're hiding something?

I swallowed. "What are you talking about?" I had driven by Halo's under the safety of daylight, and it didn't seem so bad. I planned to go by Halo's later tonight. My heart raced faster simply thinking of it.

She strutted over to a line of dresses and plucked a royal-blue gown from between two dresses. "This would look *perfect* on you." She hung the hanger off her finger.

"Try it on for me." She lowered her head and playfully pouted her lips.

I breathed out. "Fine." I wasn't as excited about the Fall Fling anymore.

With a deep inhale, I grabbed the gown from her hand.

The dressing room was tiny, barely enough room to step back and look at the mirror on the wall. As I undressed, Rosa slipped in through the edge of the curtain. "Geez Rosa, I don't have it on yet." I tugged the material upward over my belly.

She reached forward and helped me snug it on. "See, it's gorgeous!" she said.

Rosa threw the curtain open and motioned for me to come out.

The three-sided mirror reflected the gorgeous royal blue gown. My legs were exposed below the thigh as the material sprung from my waist and puffed around to the back.

A saleswoman with dark skin and vibrant teeth approached from behind. "I love it," she said to me. "You?"

Rosa's eager smile reminded me that buying a dress was pointless if I wasn't sure about attending the dance anymore. Who wants to celebrate and dance when Magnolia could choose to make an appearance … at any opportune time? It took the fun out of fun. "It's pretty. But I can't buy it today."

The sales lady scratched her head and rolled her eyes, probably assuming I was playing dress-up, never planning to buy anything in the first place. I guess she was sort of right.

"Well if you want to put it on hold for the week, we can do that for you." Her fingers braided over at her waist, waiting for my response. She didn't give up easily.

I shook my head. "Sorry." I sauntered into the dressing room, Rosa didn't follow.

My phone beeped with a text message, and I bent down to my purse.

The screen blackened before I had a chance to read who the message was from. I slapped the phone against my palm for the zillionth time, but it didn't blink on. Cursing the stupid device, I tossed it back in my purse.

When I came out, Rosa searched through more dresses. With a wink, she tried on another while I waited in the chair across from the mirrors. The saleswoman eyed me from her pedestal behind the counter. I stared back at her with the same look. She finally averted her attention, focusing on another customer who entered the store.

I uncrossed my legs. "Rosa, hurry up, will you?"

She came out with her normal attire on. "The dress?"

"Didn't fit." She grinned and held the burgundy one up. "I'm getting it," she said as she scrunched her shoulders toward the ceiling with excitement.

For once in a long while, I had a girl's day—with Rosa—and almost hadn't thought about Magnolia. Nor had been interrupted by her.

Was she finally giving me room to breathe?

In the back of my mind, a part of me knew that no matter how much better I felt, that would never be the case. Not right now at least. A piece of my soul would be held hostage until I found Magnolia's killer. Only then could I have my life back.

If I welched on the deal, I bet Magnolia would return with a vengeance.

Rosa removed a credit card from her purse and handed it to me. "Will you pay for it for me? I see something else I want to look at."

The card hovered in her hand. "Sure." I thinly smiled. In the same moment that I celebrated our girls' day, I also felt like her servant. She had this uncanny ability to make me feel inferior. But once we had become friends, she had always been there for me, like a true friend.

"So are you buying a dress?" the sales lady stated as I approached the counter.

I wasn't in the mood to argue. *It's not my dress.* I smiled and nodded.

As we moseyed out the store, Rosa asked. "You coming next Friday night?" I'd nearly forgotten about the football game taking place the night before Fall Fling. School had been out today, and my internal clock was off.

Attending the game would be a little difficult—cheering from the stands, watching the cheerleaders. Sitting on the bench would be even worse, I refused to do that.

"You have to come." Her jet-black hair contrasted her rosy lips as she begged.

"I don't know, Rosa."

"Don't tell me you're gonna let Coach Gold ruin everything. I know rah-rah-ing is your life, but now you're free from the stress. Enjoy it!"

I shrugged. "Maybe."

"What would Chris say if you didn't see him play?"

"Didn't you say I could do better than him?"

She rolled her eyes.

"Fine, I'll be there."

"Great!" she chirped. "Wouldn't be the same without you." Then she slid her arm through mine.

μ

It was nearly midnight, and I was exhausted, but I had to go to Halo's. Sneaking out seemed like a good idea earlier, but now I wanted to crawl into bed. I snapped Magnolia's journal shut. She went to Halo's at midnight, on a Friday. I needed to do the same.

I grabbed my backpack and shoved my wallet, phone, and a pocket knife for protection inside; the knife belonged to Chris, he'd accidentally left it at my house weeks ago. Would I even know what to do with a knife? Probably not. But I had to bring *something*.

With the straps over my shoulders, I slid my bedroom window open. Windows and I were starting to become a thing.

I leaned through the opening, but halfway out, my shoulders hitched backward. Something on the backpack had snagged, halting me from moving forward.

I jerked back and forth and leaned down, maneuvering like an inchworm. Removing the backpack, I dropped it on the grass.

The old me would never have attempted to sneak out this way. But I never had a reason to before. Rosa was a pro and it didn't sound that hard. My door would stay locked. My parents thought I was studying since they all but forced me to stay inside after shopping.

A thrill rushed up my legs as my feet hit the grass.

Backing my car out was trickier. I had parked on the side of the house where my parents' room was located. I couldn't turn on the ignition without the possibility of alarming one of them. Hunching over with one hand on the wheel and my feet on the ground, I braced myself and leaned back with the car in neutral.

The wheels slowly gave into my demands. I didn't weigh very much, but my cheerleader legs were strong.

My arm jostled as the wheels glided over the edge of the driveway. "Stop, stop, stop," I panted. I spied the red fire hydrant in front of the house. The bumper was in line to hit it.

"Come on," I growled through clenched teeth, shoving against the steering wheel, trying to force the wheels to stop.

My feet slid against the pavement.

"Damn it, stop!"

At the last moment, I hopped through the driver's door, banging my knee against the unforgiving metal edge, and slammed my left foot on the brake. I clenched my eyes shut. A metallic tap sounded as the car jerked to a dead stop.

Holding my breath, I peered in the side mirror. No Old Faithful. I started the engine and stepped on the accelerator.

FIFTEEN

Bright orange cones blocked a road that the county had been working on forever. I turned, following a detour to Halo's on the outskirts of town. Older apartment complexes lined the street.

Entering a neighborhood, the light from street lamps hung close to the bulbs, barely illuminating the yards. Ginormous trees shadowed the road. I hadn't been in this area since my grandma passed away. Driving down the streets where I'd ridden my bike as a child brought back good memories. Repetitive rows of chain-link fences edged the sidewalks.

The county had let this part of town run down, allowing the crime rate to flourish. Trash piled high on the corners of people's driveways, some in the street. People who lived here had petitioned for better upkeep, but the county didn't care. Many people had left. Vacant shacks remained between deteriorating homes with boarded-up windows. Now, a highway was being built close by. I bet everything would be demolished sooner or later. Every good memory gone forever.

After a few more turns, the tip of the neon sign brightened the slate gray sky.

Driving closer, the sign outside the diner shone bright white. Half-working green bulbs punctuated the edges. A yellow circle sat in the center, resembling a halo. Very original.

I pulled into Halo's small parking lot. The outside shined with a coppery-like exterior, a grungy yellow trim curved around the roof. As soon as I opened my door, I wanted to flee inside. Was someone or *something* watching me? I looked around at the few clunkers in the old lot. Ginormous fissures lined the cement beneath their tires. Nobody was outside. My eyes trailed up to a large warehouse behind the diner, a place that shut down years ago. The hair lifted on the back of my neck. Its shadowy red brick spray-painted by white graffiti gave me the willies. I'd heard rumors of parties taking place inside. Three small, shattered windows dotted the top of the building. I doubted any parties happened. The warehouse seemed vacant, unused, and full of hepatitis C.

I shrugged my backpack on and locked my car.

Through the sparkling windows of the diner, two couples sat in separate booths.

A tiny silver bell jingled as I opened the door to walk inside.

A large old man behind the counter looked up. His eyes met mine. A thick unibrow scrunched his flat face together as he eyeballed me. A dingy white apron hugged his sweaty neck.

I took three steps forward, my shoes sticking to the black-and-white checkered tile. Ruby red stools sat empty in front. A stench of ancient cigarette smoke outlasted the thick fibers of the old booths. I swallowed hard. The customers had at least thirty hard years on me.

I breathed in the noxious mix of greasy food and day-old coffee. In the back, the fryer hissed as something hit the oil. The far wall braced the vintage Seeburg jukebox that had seen better days. Three cracks crisscrossed the bottom half, as if an object had smashed into it. Dim bulbs shined on old black records. Did it still work? I reached into my backpack and grabbed a quarter from my purse.

The waitress with her hair in a bun strutted over to the counter and grabbed a plate piled high with onion rings. I walked to the jukebox and slid the quarter in. I pushed the button for the song that Pawpaw always asked me to play for Mawmaw. The tiny metal arm grabbed the black record and placed it on the player.

A Sunday Kind of Love strummed on. A comfortable warmth washed over me. I turned around. To my left was an open booth, and I sunk into it. As I hunched over the table, the waitress walked up with an off-white menu in her hands. She handed it to me. "Know what you want?" she asked.

Dried specs of food speckled both sides of the menu, like crusty braille. On the bust of her shirt was a nametag with *Shirley* scrolled in black. Large gold hoops hung from her ears.

"Um." I paused, looking at the options. The font was blurry like the same menu had been used for decades. "A BLT, and do you have any milkshakes?"

She used a pen from her hair and pointed at the bottom of the menu. "Three kinds: strawberry, vanilla, and chocolate."

"I'll take a strawberry."

Her lips pressed into a thin smile. "Anything else?"

She looked harmless, so why was I so nervous? Maybe it was the place. "Fries?" I said in a questionable tone. I hadn't come here for the food.

Her leathery hand reached for the menu. In a moment of hesitation, I didn't release it from my grip.

Her brows furrowed and she gave a slight tug. I let go. With a last annoyed glance, she spun around.

"Now what?" I asked myself.

As I waited for my food, I watched headlights drive past outside.

A clapping sound startled me. The waitress had placed a stainless steel cup on my table. A tall curvy glass filled with strawberry ice cream sat next to the cup. I peered inside at the rest of the pink milkshake, looking for bugs. This place didn't give me the cleanest vibe.

"Fries are almost done." She popped another bubble and handed me a straw, holding onto it a second longer before releasing it.

She stood, not turning around. "Uh, thank you?"

She popped another bubble before leaving.

I sipped and opened my backpack, pulling out my phone. The cold cream felt smooth on my throat. It tasted a lot better than I thought it would.

I scrolled through the photos until I found one of Magnolia from the year before her death—when she was happier. She had been in the middle of laughing when I took the picture. She never liked still-shots. That day was a Saturday and our small group ate in the park. Cooper and she were still dating at the time. He'd said something totally stupid, being his comedic self. Magnolia couldn't control the belly laughs that followed. That's when I captured the memory. Pure happiness radiated from her every angle. Magnolia's whole body smiled, from the tips of her manicured fingernails to the ends of her freshly-styled hair. She had an intoxicating aura that attracted anyone who had the lucky chance of being near her. The park was the last time I remembered her being truly, utterly happy.

A green plate of French fries clunked against my table, averting my attention. As the waitress turned to leave, I grabbed her wrist, stopping her. With the one devilish look from her, as if I committed a mortal sin, I released my grip.

She placed a hand on her hip. "What?" she said.

I raised my phone. "Do you know this girl?"

She let out a breath and rolled her eyes. "No."

I shoved the picture closer. "Please. Have you ever seen her before?"

She squinted and shook her head. "No."

"Are you sure?"

"Look Little Missy, I'm new. If you really want to know if she's been here before, ask Frank." She thumbed over her shoulder to the large man behind the counter.

I frowned. "Fine. Thanks."

Tapping my fingers against the tabletop, I sipped on more of the milkshake. Asking Shirley was one thing, walking up to the man who had a permanent scowl was another.

I finished my plate of fries and stalled as long as I could by slurping every bit of the milkshake.

I waited for the last customer to leave, but it took forever. My eyes felt heavy and I couldn't help myself. I fell asleep.

When I woke, heat rushed through my body from realizing exactly where I was. I grabbed my phone, an entire hour had passed. Drool covered my cheek.

I hadn't noticed the waitress standing next to me.

"You can't sleep here," she said, her hands flat on the table. "And you haven't paid."

Glancing around, I was the last one in the diner. I grabbed my stuff, scooched out of the booth, and moseyed toward the man behind the counter who was wiping it down.

"I need to pay," I uttered to him.

He cleared his throat and stuck his hand out. I swung my backpack around to my front and fished out a twenty, handing it to him.

He pressed a button, and the change-drawer thudded open. His eyes flickered between me and the money. His unibrow looked like a fluffy black caterpillar.

He closed the drawer with a thrust of his belly.

My voice wavered as I held out my phone. "Have you seen this girl here before?" I asked, a little high-pitched.

He shook his head and grunted.

I stuffed the change in my backpack.

"Can you take a closer look?"

He yanked my phone from my hand. I flinched, wondering if he intended to give it back.

"Yes," he muttered. "Months ago. A few times." His voice was scratchy like he'd smoked too many cigarettes.

I shifted back and forth on my feet, suddenly hopeful. "Really?"

He nodded and his unibrow did too. The dimple in his chin resembled a butt.

He handed my phone back and grabbed the dingy towel.

"Was she with anyone?"

He stopped.

"Well?"

He placed his hand out on the counter, palm-side up. "Want more info?"

I had a good guess of what he meant. He wanted money. What's with people always wanting money?

I fished out the ten that he'd given me moments earlier and slapped it in his palm.

"She was with someone, a guy. Shaggy hair, odd accent."

Accent? I stiffened. "Do you remember his name?" There was only one person I knew who had an accent, but that didn't mean much. It could've been someone else, couldn't it?

He shrugged his shoulders. "I have dozens of customers every day, how am I supposed to remember that?"

I wasn't giving up, I *needed* to know. I *had* to know. "Lachlan?" I asked.

Frank nodded. "Yeah, maybe."

"Do you know why they were here?"

Frank chuckled, his belly jiggled as he turned around. "Got things to do," he muttered over his shoulder, ending our conversation.

Had Magnolia led me to Halo's for this? Was Lachlan involved with her murder? Was he the Creekside Killer?

I refused to jump to that conclusion.

Lachlan hadn't denied that the two of them hung out. Maybe that's what happened here at the diner. They were simply grabbing a bite to eat … on this side of town.

If anyone would know how to get away with murder, it'd be the son of a detective. My heart beat faster. But Magnolia wasn't the only girl who was murdered. Lachlan didn't seem like the guy who would be killing one person, let alone a string of them.

He couldn't be involved, could he?

I shrugged my backpack around my shoulders and walked outside to my car. Unlocking the door, I sat inside, heavily thinking. I didn't want any of this to be true.

A rancid smell filled my nostrils, covering my throat like slime. The taste completely replaced the pleasant strawberry aftertaste from the milkshake.

In front of my hood stood Magnolia. My shoulders dropped. "Now's not the time." Her iridescent body swooped through the hood of my car, into my windshield—and passed through my body. An overwhelming puking sensation shot from my stomach. I fumbled for the handle. All but tossing myself to the hard ground, I splattered pink and white chunks all over the pavement.

Unable to speak, my head pounded. I grabbed my forehead.

I remained like that for minutes until finally, the clenching in my stomach stopped. Sweat covered my neck, dripping down my chest.

A sourness coated my tonsils.

"What was that for?" I said, catching my breath. I hadn't thought the hauntings could get worse, but I was wrong. This was definitely worse. Did she want me to stay? There was nothing else to find. The man already told me everything he knew.

I started the engine and wearily drove out of the parking lot.

Passing three stoplights, the detour sign waved in the breeze and the arrows pointed to the right. A car's headlights blinded me from my rearview mirror, so I moved it downward.

I veered right onto the dark road. My headlights the only lights brightening my path.

In the mirror, the car turned behind me. I drove forward at a slower speed. The last thing I needed was to get in a wreck in the middle of the night when my parents thought I was in bed.

I took a left, and the car behind me did too. Was it following me? I kept a steady pace down the street and took another right. From my side mirror, the vehicle went straight, not turning right. It wasn't following me. Relief sank through my arms. Then suddenly, the neon lights inside my car flickered and blinked off. I slapped the dashboard. "Wake up!"

My headlights shut off too.

Slowly, my car started rolling to a horrifying stop. In my rearview, the outline of Magnolia's face materialized, faded and not as strong as before. I spun around, but she was gone.

SIXTEEN

I managed to turn the stiff steering wheel. My car jostled—completely dead—as the tires skidded against the curb.

Great, I thought. *Now what?*

I grabbed my phone. If I called my parents, they'd kill me and ground me until summertime. If I called Rosa, she'd ask more questions as to why I was out here in the first place, and then wonder why I didn't bring her along. And Chris, well, he wasn't too happy with me, and I didn't want to hash it out with him right now.

Nobody needed to know of my curse, of Magnolia's ghost. Not yet. Hopefully, not ever.

Which left only one person who wouldn't ask more questions—Lachlan.

I thumbed my contacts and scrolled to his name.

The second my phone pressed to my ear, a silence filled the void. No ringtone.

My phone had died too.

I was in the middle of a bad part of town, on a dark street with one barely-working street lamp, and my phone dead. I looked out the window at a condemned home with boards over the windows. Was anyone inside? Would they have a cell phone? I shook the idea off. No way was I going in there.

I should be in bed right now. Not here.

I turned my phone over, removed the black battery, and slapped it against my hand. Blowing hot breath on it, I rubbed the sides.

With trembling fingers, I clicked the battery back into place and held down the power button.

"Come on," I said, waving my phone in the air, as if the motion would help. Nothing. "Stupid phone." I threw it on the passenger seat and reached for my keys. Trying to restart my car, I turned the key and jammed my foot against the accelerator over and over. A soft clicking noise reverberated from under the hood. Crap. What did I know about cars? A big fat nothing. But something wasn't working right.

I remained in my seat with the doors locked. What should I do? No moon. Pitch black. Panic bubbled in my body. The only option left was to foot it back to the diner—alone—use their phone. It was over two miles away.

No way. Not at this time of night all alone. Grabbing the handle on the side of my seat, I reclined my chair and wrapped my arms around my shoulders.

Outside the window, the houses sat dark, empty, quiet. My eyes filled with tears.

So pathetic—crying. This was all my fault. Stuck on the side of the road in a bad neighborhood. I had no one to blame but ME.

With my cell in my hand, I closed my eyes, as if pretending to be tired would lull my nerves to sleep. Every molecule panicked with tiny explosions of fear. The beat of my heart slowly thumped in my ears. My legs shook. I crossed them and bashed my knee on the gear shift. "Ouch, damn it."

I checked the locks for the tenth time. Magnolia's freaky ghost. She put me in this position. I huffed and rubbed my knee. If she'd only leave me alone …

Headlights approached, lighting up the car's interior. I swallowed my fear. Should I jump out and ask for help? Flagging down a random stranger at this time of night?

I scrunched down farther into my seat, below the sight of the oncoming car. "Stay calm, Sonora."

The bright lights widened across the dashboard. I moved farther down.

The lights faded as the driver continued on, unaware of my predicament. Maybe I should try and walk it. Or run it. Would the waitress still be at the diner?

A knock on my window startled me. Horror stomped in my chest, and my lungs froze mid-breath.

Hesitantly, I turned my head. A girl in her mid-twenties stood outside the window, staring downward at me. She smiled casually.

"Need directions?" her voice muffled through the glass.

A thin cross on a gold chain with a pink stone glimmered from around her neck.

I shook my head. "No. No. I'm fine. But *thank you.*" The last thing I wanted was to be rude. Maybe she'll turn around. I shook my head a little too much as I stated again, "I'm fine."

She didn't leave. "Honey, why are you sitting on the side of the road in a place like this? In the middle of the night?"

My shoulders drooped. She didn't look scary, but neither did the Creekside Killer I bet. I grabbed my phone from the seat next to me and held it up. "I'm not lost. My car won't work and my phone is dead. Do you have one I could borrow?"

Her eyebrows rose the moment she realized what had happened. "Your phone?" she asked in a softer voice. "You need to call somebody to come get you?"

I nodded, more grateful that she'd stopped.

With one finger, she pointed down the street. "Come with me, I know where there's one." My heart sunk into the pit of my stomach. She didn't have a phone. But everyone carried a cell, didn't they?

"It's okay. Think I'll wait," I replied.

Her head cocked to the side. "A pretty little thing sitting alone this time of night isn't good. Come with me, I have a place up the street from here."

Was she really trying to help me? I held down the power button on my phone again and tried the engine a third time.

Her hands rested on her hips. "I'm not waiting forever," she warned.

I grabbed my backpack and pulled the handle toward me, unlocking the door. It popped as it squeaked open. My feet touched the ground and I swallowed. I didn't want her to think I didn't trust her, but I didn't know her and where had she come from? Nobody else was outside.

I had a fifty-fifty shot she was telling me the truth. And if she wasn't? Well, I'd run like hell to the diner.

With heaviness in my stomach, I took a hesitant step onto the sidewalk, next to her.

She gestured for me to follow. "This way."

I locked my car and tried to breathe steadily.

"Honey, calm down. You're gonna make yourself pass out. What are you doing here anyway?"

I guess I hadn't hidden my fear as well as I thought. "I was eating at Halo's, and my car broke down."

She eyed me over her shoulder. "What's with little girls' cars breaking down?"

Her words caught my curiosity. "Other girls?"

She stepped over a gigantic crack in the sidewalk; I wouldn't have seen it if it wasn't for her. Dark shadows crawled every inch of our legs, the moonlight cut off by overgrown trees.

"Yep, you're the second one. Last time on my way home, another youngin', in the same spot."

Did I look that young? It wasn't like I was twelve or something. My pace slowed to a stop. "What color hair did she have?"

The girl raised a hand in the air, thinking as she walked farther away from me. "Uh, blonde."

"Do you remember her name?" I asked, catching up with her.

"Hmm, I can't remember." Her heels tapped the sidewalk next to me.

"Magnolia?" I blurted, halting all forward movement.

She spun around with a look of surprise. "Yeah. Yeah. Magnolia. That's what it was." She narrowed her beautiful eyes, eyelashes extra-long. "You a psychic? Because I don't need any of that mumbo-jumbo evil stuff."

I finally knew why my phone and car stopped working. I threw my hands in the air and wrapped them around her shoulders. She stiffened.

For whatever reason, Magnolia needed me to break down—right here in *this* spot. A hot wave of elation warmed me, realizing I was exactly where I needed to be. But I didn't know why.

A horrific notion swallowed my thrill of excitement. If this is the path Magnolia had been on—which may have contributed to her murder—I was on that same path.

I shrunk away from the girl, releasing her arms. She eyed me from the side as she turned around and picked up the pace a little faster than before.

Questions caught in my throat as I trailed behind her.

Walking in silence, I wasn't sure what to think or how to feel. Should I be happy? I'm closer to figuring out what happened to Magnolia. Part of me was scared to be on the direct path of something I didn't know. OR was this a simple coincidence?

"We're here," she said. Her hand reached forward and she raised a small u-hook to open a waist-high fence.

The gate swung shut, clanking as the side of the u-hook slammed against the metal pole.

"You coming?" she asked.

A numbness settled through my feet, I wiggled my toes. Without answering, I smiled and nodded.

I shoved the gate open with one swift push and she continued up the cracked path. Reassuring myself, I repeated inwardly that I was stronger than I thought and that I could do this. What's the worst that could happen?

Each step forward brought me closer to hyperventilating. I felt lightheaded and coughed. The worse thing that could happen is that I'm murdered and dumped in a creek.

She glanced at me.

The one-story home contained two large windows in the front. One window lit around the edges. A carport located on the left with three cars lined underneath. It reminded me of my Pawpaw's place.

Blocking the fear in the back of my mind kept me from crumbling. That, and the ground was completely covered in dirt, not one spec of grass. Hitting it would hurt and stain my clothes—one more thing for Mom to question about in the morning. *Because I'm going to survive, I'm not about to die. Tomorrow, this will all seem like a hilarious turn of supernatural events.*

As she was about to open the door, I reached my hand out. "Wait," I spurted, a scared tone hovered in my voice. My palm rested on her shoulder, and she looked down at my fingers as the waitress had earlier.

Her eyes widened.

I removed my hand, not wanting to scare her. I'd like to think that I could hold my own in an abandoned neighborhood, but I wasn't. Would I wake up from this nightmare soon? I squeezed my eyes shut and reopened them.

The girl stared at me with wide eyes, leaning away from me. "I'm not crazy."

"O-okay."

Walking into a stranger's house wasn't a bright idea. Was the house even hers? Did she live here? "I should go back to my car. This was a bad idea." My elbow trembled against my hip.

She suddenly laughed and shook her head, "Girl, you're weirder than weird." She smiled and waved me inside as she opened the door. "Don't stand out there alone, come use the phone."

Light washed over the porch from the open door.

Turning sideways, I spied the other yards. Across the street, a shadowy figure stood in the open doorway of a home with a hole in the roof.

A cold shiver ran over my arms.

I turned around. A strong scent of mildew wafted from inside, crawling from every inch of wallpaper. The faded walls were covered in tiny floral specs with missing strips, as if someone had torn random pieces off. It reminded me of something from the 90's, old and outdated.

I took my first step into the house. A handful of individuals strolled out of a hallway, one man playfully shoved another in his arm.

Three people were slumped on a couch.

The girl who had helped me walked into the kitchen area, disappearing around a corner. My steps quickened, not wanting to lose her. The wooden floors squeaked, and I stepped over a hole. As I rounded the corner, she placed a cordless receiver in my hand. The phone-set hung on the wall. "Here you go."

I nodded, holding back a cry.

"See, I don't bite."

"And them?" I motioned in the general vicinity of everyone else in the house.

A wide smile brightened her face, and she flicked her palm. "Them. They're harmless. Don't get me wrong, they ain't perfect, but they won't lay a hand on you as long as you don't lay one on them." She winked. "I have classes in the morning, so I'm headed to bed." She turned and left me by myself with two people at the table, playing cards. They weren't paying any attention to me.

I pulled out my cell from my backpack, and then it dawned on me. Lachlan's number was *in* it. *Crap.*

I closed my eyes and tried to remember his number.

The first three digits were easy, but the last four, the important four, were a blur. I dialed a random set I knew was in his, in some order or another.

After the first two attempts at calling, and an angry woman hanging up on me, I finally heard Lachlan's voice.

"Hello?" he said, clearing his throat. It was him, I was sure of it.

I turned sideways, away from the couple at the table, and cupped my hand over my mouth against the phone. "Lachlan?"

A few seconds later, he chimed in clearer. "Who is this?"

"Lachlan, it's me." My voice was breathy. Did I need to spell it out? "S-o-n-o-r-a."

A rumbling noise sounded through the earpiece. Did he drop his phone or fall out of bed? "Queen Sonora, this better be an emergency."

I rolled my eyes and moved my hand to speak. "It is. Can you please come get me? My car broke down."

"What? Where are you?"

"A couple miles from Halo's."

Suddenly he took on a more serious tone. "Halo's?"

"Look. Save the lecture. Can you help or not?" I wasn't in the mood to be chided by Lachlan, that was my parents' place. If I wanted that, I would've called them. "This was *your* idea."

His voice muffled to a distance. "Okay. Tell me exactly where you are."

Where? That was a good question. "Somewhere on Treehouse Lane. Give me a sec."

I placed the receiver down. The counter was cluttered with opened bags of chips. I looked around the corner for the girl, but she was nowhere. My shoulders sank. I cringed and faced the couple at the table. They hadn't noticed me yet, or so I assumed by the way they hadn't paid any attention to me.

"Excuse me?" I whispered.

They didn't stop talking.

"Hello," I said with a little more force.

The bald guy with his eyebrow pierced didn't look amused at my interrupting them. He wore a black leather jacket cut-off at the shoulders.

"Do you know the address here?"

He raised the pierced eyebrow and went back to his conversation.

With the receiver in hand, I marched outside and searched for the address of the house. Finally finding it behind a dead prickly bush, I couldn't see it clearly in the darkness. I raised the phone to illuminate the golden numbers with its glow. One digit was missing, and a faded outline of a four was in its place. "You there?" I asked.

"Yes."

"1647 Treehouse Lane."

"1647?"

"Yes."

"Alright, be there soon. Stay put."

Did he think I'd leave? "Fine."

SEVENTEEN

Outside, I crouched behind dead bushes that lined the edge of the house. Five minutes later, a pair of headlights approached from the left up to the street. I waited, not moving, not knowing if they belonged to Lachlan's car.

The car stopped in the middle of the street, and Lachlan stepped out.

My back relaxed.

As I moved, my hair snagged on the sharp grooves in the brick.

Reaching the path, I swung open the gate and ran to him and tossed my arms around his neck. "Thank you. Thank you. *Thank you.*" He wrapped his arms around me too.

The awkwardness of our bodies touching radiated. We released each other.

With my face inches from his, his eyes piqued with worry. "Let's get out of here," he said.

He didn't have to tell me twice. I climbed into his car, slumping into the passenger seat. I leaned toward him, away from the outside. Who would have thought a year ago that I'd be excited to see Lachlan, actually call him for rescue? *Damsel in distress. But I was no damsel. Definitely not.*

Driving away, I explained to Lachlan what had happened with my car.

With a lack of expression, Lachlan asked, "And it breaking down is odd because?"

"Because my car's never stopped working before."

"And you think that means?"

I paused. "Nothing. Fine, it's not odd." But it was. I still didn't know exactly why Magnolia had done it. Changing the subject, I had something to ask him, though, didn't want to.

My car within view, Lachlan wrenched over to the curb, nearly tapping my hood against his. He reached into the back seat and grabbed a blue and red cable with large metal clamps on each end. "Pop the hood."

"What?"

"Pop-the-hood." I'd never opened my hood before, never needed to.

The car was dark inside, and I couldn't figure out how to do it. I leaned out the driver's side. "Lachlan," I grumbled. "Don't make fun of me, but how do you open the hood?"

Lachlan smirked and walked over. He bent down next to my legs and found the lever instantly. His hair smelled of Irish Spring.

He attached the cables to my car's battery. "Turn your car on," he said. With his car running, I started my engine as instructed. I couldn't see his face over the open hood in front of my windshield and had to listen carefully.

My car sprung to life. The radio too.

"How did you know to do that?" I asked. I doubted most guys my age knew anything about cars, at least nothing more than what's shown in movies.

He let my car run a little longer before unclamping the cable and slamming his hood shut. He leaned back on his elbows with the cable cords in his hand.

I stepped out and closed my door, my car running still. "So what now?" I asked.

He shrugged. "Leave your engine running for a few more minutes."

I wasn't tired. Plus, I didn't want to drive home alone. "Can I sit with you for a bit?"

For the first time ever, Lachlan smiled without sarcasm. "Sure, why not. I'm awake anyway."

With my engine running, I locked my car and climbed into his.

I sighed. Treehouse Lane didn't feel as unsafe as it did an hour ago. So far, Lachlan hadn't asked for money in return for helping me—yet.

My knees bounced. "Why don't you and your dad get along?" *Wow, tactful Sonora.*

He fiddled with a Coke bottle between the seats before answering. "My mom left us when I was eight."

"She died?" I thought they were divorced or something—or at least that's what I had heard at school one time.

He shook his head. "No. She left, as in packed her bags and moseyed out the front door. She never came back." His voice didn't waver or crack. He opened the bottle and knocked back a swig.

"I'm sorry."

He swallowed. "It was a long time ago."

"So after she left, you and your dad?" My voice trailed off.

He raised his shoulders and stared out the windshield at nothing in particular. "We're just different. He's all straight and narrow, follow the rules, stay in the box. I'm not." He took another swig. "My stepmom's not so bad."

I nodded. Nothing like tripping through his bad memories. Why didn't I let it go? Not ready to tell Lachlan about my curse, I reached for my phone, buying time. I held the power button down. The screen flashed.

A few minutes went by, and I reached for the radio to turn it on.

Lachlan turned the volume up loud—too loud. I flinched.

"Thanks for helping me!" I yelled over the music. I was about to blurt something rude, but when my eyes locked with his, the vexed words clamped to the roof of my mouth.

I looked away, wishing I hadn't said anything at all. Why was I nervous? My heart sped with the rise and fall of anxious butterflies.

He turned the radio down. "I'm not an asshole, contrary to what you might think."

The way his eyes settled on mine made my belly flutter with knots.

A few seconds went by before I responded. "I don't think you're an *asshole*."

His face scrunched back to his neck. "Really?"

"Maybe a little opportunistic, but not an asshole." I paused. "If anything, I can be a bitch at times."

He smiled. "True."

I punched him in the arm for agreeing.

"Can I do something?" he asked.

"What?" I asked, confused.

"Can I kiss you?"

I froze, not replying.

A few seconds passed, and he leaned halfway over.

I should've protested, but in that moment, I didn't want to move. I had a boyfriend. But in the back of my head, flashes of Lachlan's gorgeous body came to. Along with something else deep in my chest. Did I have feelings for him?

His glossy eyes studied my reaction, and he leaned closer. "Can I kiss you?"

All other words escaped me, except, "Fine."

He leaned across the console. His fingers brushed my knee. My rapid breathing filled my brain with sound.

His fingers brushed my chin as they braided around the back of my head.

His warm palm slid down to my neck. He held my eyes.

Tingles shot down my arms, to the tips of my feet.

With the same hand, he pulled me closer—and I let him.

I opened my mouth to say something but only air escaped.

A freckle dotted below his right eye. A wisp of hair fell over his forehead as he lessened the distance more.

Our lips met. His mouth tasted warm and sweet of brown sugar … or Coke.

Our mouths moved in sync, harder, demanding, chasing waves of feeling. My hands found his cheeks, pulling him on top of me, wanting more of him. His skin softer than mine but with stubble on his cheeks.

As his upper body pressed against my mine, the back of my head smacked the window.

"*Ouch,*" I complained into his lips.

His fingers released. His lips too.

A heated lightness settled through my core. I opened my eyes as the weight of his body disappeared.

"Why'd you kiss me?" I asked, slowly taking in the scenery, gathering myself. I breathed him in one last time.

"I've wanted to do that for a while." he whispered. "Why'd you let me?"

I pushed him back, taking in the full context of the situation. "This can't happen." My words said one thing, but I was dying for more of him. What was wrong with me?

He gave me the same arrogant look he'd given in the cafeteria that day. "You shouldn't care what people think so much, Queen Sonora."

"Stop calling me that." I turned away, breaking the mood. "I'm out *here*, aren't I?" I went to Halo's, had taken a risk that I wouldn't have weeks ago.

"Yeah, and you called *me*. Why's that? Why is whenever you need something, you call me to meet in the dark somewhere."

"You know why." I paused. "But I'm with Chris and this"—I flittered a finger back and forth between us—"can't happen. You know that."

He grimaced. "Chris. That dickhead. Believe me, I know."

"What's that supposed to mean?"

He shook his head. "It means whatever you want it to mean." A pang grew from within; the thought of Chris finding out I'd kissed Lachlan twisted my gut. Did I still care for him? Could feelings for someone change that quickly? I had kissed Lachlan—and I liked it, which was something that certainly wouldn't have happened before.

Why did everything have to be so confusing? I dropped my head in my hands, and the question I had originally wanted to ask Lachlan flew to the forefront of my thoughts.

"Have you ever been to Halo's with Magnolia?" My voice faded as I spoke her name.

Lachlan leaned back and took a swig of Coke. "Yes." His answer was forced like he didn't want to tell me. But he *did* tell me.

"Anything else you want to share?"

"Not really."

"Come on, Lachlan. What were you and Magnolia doing at Halo's?" I paused before rushing the next question. "Did you kill her?"

He winced, spitting out a bit of Coke. "What? No."

"Then why were you with her at Halo's?"

He motioned to my car. "Get out and follow me."

My eyes circled around. "You want me to follow you?"

"That's what I said."

"Where are we going?"

"Take a chance for once and stop asking questions."

I had already taken a chance at Halo's and look where it got me. "Fine." I shoved open the door, the taste of his sugary lips on mine. I rubbed the connection off with the back of my hand—regretful doing so.

Lachlan was infuriatingly confusing. One minute I didn't trust him, the next, I was kissing him in his car. And the way he wedged himself beneath my skin. I never let anyone get to me the way he did. My feelings for him snuck up on me as I followed his car in the direction of Halo's.

Chris. Every girl wanted to be with him. But he was mine. Did I want to ruin that?

Lachlan Granger. What would it be like to walk down the hall on his arm, an outcast? How had this happened?

Halo's sign neared. Where was he headed?

As he turned on the road toward Halo's, he passed the diner and swung a left. I followed him as we parked at the vacant warehouse.

EIGHTEEN

The shadowy warehouse screamed terror, from the faded paint outlining tattered signs to the red brick tagged with graffiti. Absent of street lamps, my adrenaline spiked. I squeezed my keys, contemplating fleeing the creepy place. "Why are we here?" I asked, shutting my door. Spying the cars in the far corner of the lot, cars that *had* to belong to *someone*, I looked around. "Where is everyone?"

Knee-high blades of grass, sprucing from the decrepit lot, brushed against my knees. I reached down and rubbed the itchiness away.

"You wanted to know what Magnolia and I were doing, right?"

I nodded, my chest tightening. *Am I about to be murdered too?*

His jaw clenched in the darkness. "I ran into Magnolia at one of these parties, that's why we hung out."

When had Mags gone to parties in an abandoned warehouse? It was as if he were talking about a completely different girl. Not perfect, sweet-faced, Magnolia.

"I even picked her up when her car stopped, died once."

"Huh?" I asked, thrown by the admission.

"From the same house you were at."

He pivoted around and walked over to the only entrance on this side of the warehouse. He knocked three times on the door, paused, and then knocked two more times, paused, and then knocked once. A guy with a pink Mohawk opened the door.

I hadn't moved from my spot. Lachlan turned around and motioned for me to come with him.

A few feet inside, steps descended into a darker pit without a bottom in sight. I heard movement of something from inside. *Rats?* I stopped at the edge as Lachlan continued downward. "Come on," he said, his footsteps ringing against the tread. My shoulders tightened as I moved forward.

My hands glided over a long metal railing. The sound of pitter patter, of movement, deepened as we approached the end of the descending staircase. Lachlan opened a door into a large room with black spray paint obscuring the main windows. Dozens and dozens of people danced about. My eyes widened.

Vivid neon flashes beamed from a stage. The lights flickered back and forth through all the colors of the rainbow. I squinted and raised my hand as a beam pulsed over my eyes. If I had ever been susceptible to seizures, I'd have one now.

"Parties really *do* happen here," I said out loud, never thinking the rumors were true.

Lachlan grinned.

People wearing glow-in-the-dark bracelets bounced wildly, but there was no music. It was silent. Headphones covered the dancers' ears. Their footsteps patted against the cement floor as people moved and grooved.

The lights halted on fluorescent purple. In the center of the stage, a girl with large earrings that blinked neon pink and orange stepped behind a wide disc-jockey's desk. She reached downward.

"Stay right here," Lachlan said over his shoulder.

Short and tall bodies swayed, others jived to a different beat. Arms flailed and heads bobbed as they listened to music that only they could hear. I spotted two juniors from school but didn't know the couple's names; their matching alien shirts glowed beneath black lights.

I'd read about silent raves in magazines, but I'd never actually been to one. I watched a channel on YouTube once, that's as close as I'd ever come to experiencing it.

Lachlan returned, holding a pair of white headphones. The ends glowed around the edges. He placed a pair over my fingers.

"Put it on," he said.

My eyes moved over the crowd that silently boomed with life, each person in their own world. A world that I was about to become a part of. I tugged the headphones over my hair, snugging them into place on my ears. The moment I did, a blast of music shot to my core.

Lachlan grabbed my hand, wearing headphones too.

"Dance!" he mouthed. When he released my hand, he'd placed something small in my palm.

With the lights flashing about, it was hard to focus on what the small thing was. I brought it closer to my eyes, examining the tiny object with my forefinger. I couldn't figure out the color, but it was definitely a pill.

He leaned forward, pulling my headphones from one of my ears. "Stop worrying so much. It's organic." With two fingers, he placed a pill on his tongue.

He closed his mouth, his Adam's apple bobbed, and then he stuck his empty tongue back out.

I didn't know what to do. Take it or not? What if it messed with my mind more than Magnolia? Organic or not, what if the pill made me see crazier things?

Lachlan remained upright, not fallen over dead. I placed the pill on my tongue too, unsure if I should swallow. I closed my mouth, giving myself a second to think. A sweetness settled on my taste buds. Here goes nothing, I thought.

And I swallowed.

At first, I didn't feel any different.

But like an IV pumping medicine into a vein, a light sensation floated down my arms.

I couldn't contain myself, the intoxicating music filled my core. Fast. Carefree.

I pumped the air with my hands.

The rush thrilled each molecule of my existence, every tiny hair on my arms and the freckles on my skin alive as the rest of me.

Every muscle in my body vibrated with electric waves, my inhibitions swept away on a crimson tide.

My mind relaxed, giving way to the moment. This moment. A moment that nothing and no one could touch, not even a ghost.

I swung my head and moved to the music, completely forgetting the world.

My eyes wandered over to Lachlan, all two of him. Both Lachlans glanced back at me. Were our brains in sync? Could he hear my thoughts? My senses blurred off the charts.

μ

Ever been to a graveyard? The text read. An hour later I stood drenched in sweat. The rave drifted back into focus. I'd lost sight of Lachlan. Where had he gone? Who was I supposed to give the headphones too?

I cut through the undulating crowd and placed my headphones back on the DJ's stand.

Why had he texted me instead of asking me? Of course, I'd been to a graveyard.

The next text read, *For fun?* I chuckled, a little amused and a little creeped out at the same time. Beads of sweat dripped down my nose, dropping onto my phone. No, I haven't been to a graveyard, for fun. Why would I?

I made my way up the steps to the outside, counting them one by one to myself. I peered down at the text one last time before opening the large iron door and exiting the building.

Where was he? My wet shirt clung to my skin and my body felt cold against the breeze. It was dark, no streetlamps.

The moment the door clicked shut, reluctance wafted through me. Was I locked out? I turned around and yanked the handle, but the door didn't budge. I knocked the way Lachlan had, but nobody let me back in.

I jumped as a whistling sounded from the darkness, startling me. To my right, a shadowy figure leaned against the exterior wall with one foot.

I was the only other person outside.

Hugging myself, I didn't move or acknowledge his or her presence.

"Sonora," the familiar voice called from the shadows.

"Lachlan?"

Meandering from the darkness, Lachlan gave a bright smile, his skin gleaming. "Ever been to a graveyard at night?" he asked in a deep voice.

"I thought I was about to be mugged." I chuckled.

With his hands in the pockets of his black jeans, he walked closer. My heartbeat kept a steady pace between fear and excitement.

I was never "boy crazy" over anyone besides Chris before. Lachlan affected me in ways that I wasn't sure I liked.

My fingers clenched into fists, my nails making half-moon indentions in my palm. I gulped. "No. I definitely have not been to one at night, and never will."

He cocked his head to the side, and I knew I wasn't getting out of this easily. He dipped his forehead, motioning to his car.

"Now?" I asked. I looked at my phone; it was 5:22 AM. Dad would be up soon.

"Why not?" he retorted, removing his hands from his pockets and pulling his wavy hair back.

I didn't move, enthralled by the sexy tenor rumbling in his voice.

"Come on, Queen Sonora. It won't take long."

I grimaced, hating that he called me that. His triceps bulged from beneath the short sleeves of his black t-shirt. He was always wearing black. We matched if it wasn't for my tight blue jean shorts. A large part of me knew I should go home, but the liberated side of me said to go with Lachlan—wherever he wanted. Maybe the pill hadn't worn off like I thought. "I can't. If my parents haven't noticed me missing yet, they will."

He came closer. I removed my keys and stepped backward, away from him. He and I couldn't be a "thing." "This has been great, really. But I have to leave."

Lachlan halted and slid his hands into his pockets again. His sexy demeanor faded on the cusp of his grin. "Next time, then."

"Next time, what?"

"The graveyard."

I smiled. "I'm never stepping foot in a graveyard at night."

"Don't knock it until you try it."

NINETEEN

I blinked groggily at the alarm. Nine o'clock on a Saturday morning. *Ugh.*

According to Mom, only lazy people slept in. I sort of believed that mantra too, but my opinion had started to wane. Blah. I had somewhere to be.

If she didn't see me in the kitchen, she'd pounce in my room. I kicked off my covers.

A wicked headache throbbed between my temples. I wrinkled my nose. A strong acidic scent lingered. What was that? It didn't smell like Magnolia.

I sat up.

The odor burned my eyes. Is that what woke me? I covered my nose *again.*

Nail polish remover?

For half a heartbeat, the morning was like every other—besides the stink. I faintly remembered the rave … with Lachlan. When did I get home?

Something red caught my attention. On my mirror, hot pink lipstick scrolled out a warning. *My* lipstick. Is that the smell? The tube sat open, fully extended and mashed flat.

I froze. Who'd been in my room? Was I alone? My hands trembled.

Little pieces of pink clumps hung off the lipstick's edges, next to my car keys.

With tight shoulders, I jumped out of bed, tripping over Kaylee. In curvy long strokes, the words *Stop Looking!* on the mirror.

In the reflection, my closet door was open, but I liked to sleep with it closed. Why would it be open? My legs wobbled as though they'd give way any second. Staring at myself in the mirror, my hair was a gigantic tangle of craziness.

Black mascara streaked my cheeks, but I didn't remember crying. Had I blacked out? The same shorts and shirt hugged my skin, grungy from dry sweat. *Gross.*

I'd officially lost it. Or maybe it had been that little red pill. Was losing chunks of time a side effect?

Who wrote the freakish note on the mirror? Was it Lachlan? Had he followed me home? Did he bring me home? I held back a scream. If it wasn't him, then who?

I spun around, flung open my curtains, and pulled the blinds taut. Dim light seeped in, streaking my face. Kaylee jumped on my leg. Her nails dug into my thigh.

It was locked. I tugged on the sill in disbelief. It had been locked from the *inside*. I looked back at the mirror. Had I written it? I couldn't have. I wouldn't. I loved that lipstick.

Where's my car? Was it still at the warehouse?

I couldn't leave my room in these clothes with my face a mess, because Mom would question me a zillion times. I grabbed a half-empty water bottle from my nightstand and removed my shirt. Pouring water on it, I scrubbed my cheeks to get the mascara off, but it worked as well as erasing ink from a poster before a pep rally.

I changed into my pajamas, gave myself a once-over in the mirror. Faded streaks of black still on my cheeks. I peeked out my door.

My mom's and dad's voices echoed from the kitchen. The television chattered in the background.

I tiptoed to the front door, leaving Kaylee in the bedroom. The only window that faced the front of the house was the one in the dining room. But if I went in there, my mom would surely spot me.

Quietly, I unlocked the front door and opened it—*slowly*. I cringed, holding my breath. With the door trussed open, wide enough for me to slip through, I slithered out.

My car was in the driveway, exactly where I parked it every day.

My shoulders dropped. What was happening? Why couldn't I remember?

With stiff arms, I closed the door and zipped across the hallway back to my room.

The nail polish remover aroma was much stronger. *What is that?*

Searching, I spied a bucket on the floor in the dark corner of my closet.

I leaned in, covering my nose. The bitter scent originated from the bucket. Nail polish remover covered a pile of papers. Kaylee didn't come near.

I reached into the smudgy mess, not realizing what they were until I examined them closer. Liquid dripped from my fingertips into the bucket. A snapshot. The pics of evidence had been soiled; bluish ink bled into the liquid, mixing like a messy, marble fingernail polish. The snapshots were damaged beyond repair.

Below the mess sat Magnolia's journal—soaked pages ripped from the seams.

I grabbed a dirty towel from my laundry basket and carefully laid out each piece of paper. But it was no use. Everything was destroyed.

Who would do this?

I rushed out of my room, slamming my door behind me.

My mom sat curled up on the couch in her folly robe, reading her morning book. Beside her, my dad read the *Houston Chronicle*.

"Mom! Were you in my room?" I shouted.

A look of confusion filled her face. It wouldn't be the first time that she was caught snooping through my things.

"Sonora, don't yell at your mom," my dad snapped

"But dad, she was in my room! Never mind," I huffed, crossing my arms.

Mom brought a cup of coffee to her lips. She was calm, too calm, not annoyed or frightened by discovering photos of murdered girls in my room. "Sonora. Whatever it is, I haven't been in your room. I've been right here, all morning," she said. "What's with your hair?"

"I didn't sleep well."

"Hmm. Let me get your vitamin, seems like you need it." They wanted me to be *healthy*. "A healthy heart means a healthy mind."

My feet fidgeted. "Yes," I muttered, turning around.

Back in my room, I poured the bucket out my window and tried to salvage the evidence. But it was no use. Grabbing a trashcan, I tossed the ruined pictures and the journal inside, and tied the bag. What if I had missed a clue? What if I couldn't find the killer now because of it?

There was a knock on my door, and Kaylee barked. "Sonora, is something wrong?" Mom asked.

"Nothing Mom, I made a mistake. Sorry for yelling." The lipstick on my mirror was as pink as my blotchy skin. I rubbed my arms with nervousness. I didn't need her in here right now.

Seething on my bed, I spotted the friendship necklace Magnolia had given me on the floor. The half-a-heart locket sat open. After her death, I placed mine in my drawer, not wishing to be reminded of her every day. The police never recovered Magnolia's necklace, but it was around her neck each time I saw her at school.

I crept closer and leaned down. The chain was gathered in a glob on the carpet, in the middle of my room. As if someone had tossed it there or dropped it by accident.

What if whoever murdered Magnolia was after me too? What if they wanted me to *Stop Looking?* Had I been discovered snooping around?

My heart leaped into my throat.

I shut my window, locked it, and yanked my curtains closed. Kaylee's tail wagged at the door, wanting to be fed. If a stranger had been in my room, she would've barked or woken me somehow. Why hadn't she?

My heart raced, I rushed to the dining room and inched open the blinds to glance outside. Was I being watched? There weren't any cars on the street besides the usual ones.

Why would someone go through all the trouble of damaging the pics and journal, but not the necklace?

I went back to my room and contemplated calling Lachlan, telling him what had happened. Kaylee trotted in behind me and jumped onto the foot of my bed.

I pulled my phone out. My thumb hovered over the green *call* button. I still wasn't sure exactly how Lachlan played into all this. What if the intruder had been him? Maybe he knew the pill would make me unconscious, all so that he could get in my room and remove the evidence? The evidence that he'd given me in the first place. That didn't make sense. Maybe his father found out and demanded he destroy the pictures.

The only person I trusted completely was my older brother, Bram. We were so much alike, he a free spirit and me wanting to be free. When I was younger, I'd run to my brother's room for calmness, knowing that he could always make me laugh. I wished he was here now. He'd understand if I told him everything.

I tapped my *favorites* button and thumbed Bram's number.

The phone rang.

And rang.

After eight rings, his voicemail picked up. Did I want to leave a voicemail? I waited for the long greeting to finish, ready to leave a message.

But his voicemail was full. I didn't have the option. So I texted him, *call me.*

I swung my legs out of bed. My stomach growled and Kaylee huffed in response. She trailed my heels until I fed her.

"I'll cook some pancakes," I muttered to Kaylee, grabbing the box of mix out of the pantry. Mom stood in the center of the living room, no longer reading her book, but instead, faced the television. "Sorry for yelling at you earlier." She didn't react, her gaze fixed on the news.

"What's so interesting?" I sauntered around the counter and into the living room. That's when I saw a name scroll across the bottom, *David Ackerman*. Had I seen correctly? Unable to speak, my breathing quickened.

Mom's face paled. I snatched the remote from her hand and rewound the clip. She didn't protest. She remained standing there, frozen, her hand wavering in the air. My heart threatened to leap from its bloody cavity onto the floor. I gripped the remote, my knuckles whitening with fear.

I wished I hadn't pressed play. My ears pulsed with every rush of blood. Magnolia's father's body had been discovered in the house, an apparent suicide. He'd hung himself.

My eyes widened. I dropped the remote and it clonked against the rug.

"What?" I said, shocked. "Her dad?"

"I'm so sorry, honey." My mom's hand graced my back. I recoiled from her touch. She squeezed my shoulder and pulled me closer to her.

"But I was just there. The other day," I murmured.

"You were?"

I nodded, not looking away from the screen.

"Why would he do that? Why now? I mean, he's lasted *this* long…." My voice felt dry in my throat and my neck stiff. Goosebumps prickled my arms. Why? Why had he suddenly chosen suicide? He wasn't thinking clearly, his body malnourished and house a filthy mess, but if I had thought for a second he would've tried something like that, I wouldn't have left. I would've told someone. Was this my fault? Would he start haunting me too?

I darted into the kitchen, grabbed the milk from the refrigerator, and poured it into the mixing bowl.

Around and around my hand went, swirling the mixture at a pace matching the beat of the despair rushing through my veins.

Swish. Mix.

Swish, swish. Mix. None of this felt right. Someone had been in my room while I slept, and now, Mr. Ackerman was dead.

Swish. Mix.

Swish, swish. Mix. I turned on the gas stove and dropped spoonsful onto the pan.

Spreading butter on the pancakes, I finally sat down at the table.

Mom poured me a glass of orange juice and placed two vitamins on my placemat. "Sonora, say grace before you eat."

I grumbled softly, less concerned about praying for my food. "Heavenly Father, please bless these pancakes and take care of Mr. Ackerman. Amen. Where's Dad?" I popped the nasty-tasting vitamins in my mouth.

"In the shower." She paused. "You never told me you were at Mr. Ackerman's house," she said over her shoulder as she turned around, placing the pitcher on the island. Her eyes barely met mine as she walked back to the table.

She took a seat across from me, and picked up her knife and fork.

"No, I guess not."

Her brow wrinkled. Buying time and needing caffeine, I left the table and grabbed a Coke from the fridge. The Coke reminded me of Lachlan.

I sat back down and grabbed my fork, averting my attention at anything other than her. I didn't want to reveal the real reasons for being at Mr. Ackerman's house. Sticking a syrupy forkful in my mouth, I responded. "I only stopped by to see how he was doing."

"Don't speak with your mouth full, Sonora," she chided.

I grinned like a puffy-cheeked chipmunk, she wouldn't ask me to answer as long as I kept chewing.

"Well, if you visited him, then you would know what kind of state he was in. And I'm assuming it wasn't pretty. From what they said on the news, his house was full of trash. Dad said that he stopped appearing for his classes a few weeks ago." Mom shook her head sadly.

Magnolia's dad had been employed at the local community college along with my dad. With a shrug of my shoulders, I pretended to be unaware of anything that she said. Another forkful, I replied, "He didn't look very happy."

"Sonora, please cover your mouth. A lady doesn't chew with her mouth open." Even when wearing a robe, Mom's hair remained fixed and her makeup flawless. She looked like a life-size American Girl doll but much older and with kids.

"You're so predictable," I whispered.

Her head jerked up. "What did you say?"

Mom's life remained geared in the confines of what everyone else thought of her. I didn't wish to be that way anymore, but it was hard to break free from the suffocation of a small town.

I swallowed. "Don't you ever get tired of being so perfect all the time?" I couldn't believe the words that tumbled from my lips. It's one thing to think it to myself, it's another to say it aloud.

She lowered her fork. "Sonora. I'm not perfect."

A spurt of laughter escaped my mouth.

"No. Really. Nobody is," she said.

"But it doesn't stop you from trying," I replied. "Aren't you tired of the social game, all the expectations?" I knew I was. I was tired of *everything*. I wanted to sleep until the killer was caught so that my life would go back to normal. But did I want it to go back to the way it was? I wasn't sure anymore. But I knew I was tired of sneaking around and feared being haunted the rest of my life.

She took another bite, promptly closed her mouth, and swallowed. She grabbed her plate and stood up. "Thank you for making breakfast. Now get ready for the car wash."

TWENTY

Loud beachy music played in the background. My polka dotted bathing suit was soaked—my shorts too. It was a bit chilly out. I watched from a distance as Mom's BMW taillights flashed red while she braked before pulling out of the dealership's parking lot. She was the first customer at our car wash, raising money for the Athletics department at school. Cheerleaders practiced routines off to the side while football and basketball players chunked soapy sponges at them.

An old Firebird rolled in.

Crap! Lachlan.

He pulled forward, parking off to the side. My tired eyes followed him as he stepped out, wearing blue jean shorts and a black t-shirt. I'd never seen him in shorts before, let alone blue-jean shorts. His legs were super white, like ghostly white. I died with laughter.

"What's so funny?" Chris's eyes followed the subject of my amusement. "What is *he* doing here? This isn't his kind of gig."

Lachlan wasn't the type to help with any fundraisers, especially when it involved sunshine or washing cars. "Why would I know?" I replied.

Chris walked away, and disappeared into the crowd of peers with hoses and buckets. The sunshine didn't warm my skin as much as I wanted. Cooper and Angela stood off in the distance.

Lachlan walked toward me. I didn't know what to do. Run? Hide?

"Heard y'all needed volunteers," Lachlan said to me.

I squinted, not buying his answer. "Who told you that?" I asked.

We *did* need volunteers. The more people washing cars, the more money raised.

"Do you need help or not?" he muttered, appearing unamused.

I looked around before leaning in and asking, "How did I get home last night?" Angela watched us intently, but she wasn't close enough to overhear.

In an uncertain tone, he replied, "You drove yourself."

I smiled and nodded. "Never again will I take a pill that you give me. Or any pill in general." Had he heard Mr. Ackerman was dead? What if his death wasn't a suicide? What if he had figured out who her killer was, and was subsequently killed because of it?

He rubbed his neck. Standing in front of him, I wasn't ready to tell him what I'd found in my room. Would he even believe me?

"Qu— Sonora," he said, catching himself before finishing the *Queen*. "Are you okay?"

I winked. "Fine." Things were different between us now. "If you want to help, I can't stop you," I said.

Beside us, buckets splashed with suds.

A dually truck rolled in, cutting over the curb with its enormous tires. It was tall, mean, and covered in mud. Brown chunks dropped to the pavement, leaving a trail. The ground vibrated from its throaty exhaust.

Lachlan crossed in front of me and grabbed a wet sponge.

My feet were planted in place as I eyed him. Was he really sticking around?

The driver side window slid down. Maxwell Harper, a twenty-three-year-old who took five years to graduate high school, handed a few dollars to Jessica, the leader of the fundraiser. He winked at her and she giggled, stuffing the money into a tiny tin box.

Jessica spun around on the heels of her flip-flops, smiling with her eyes. Her cheeriness unwavering, she was born to fundraise. Giddiness sprung from her as she stated, "The truck isn't going to wash itself!"

Lachlan smacked a wet sponge on the tailgate, swirling the dark green exterior with suds. Chris joined next to him. My mouth went dry. I twisted a sponge in my hands, wondering what was about to transpire. This semester was unlike any other year. My life officially beyond out-of-whack.

"Sonora!" Jessica hollered, her happy fundraising face slipping. "Come on."

I began washing the rear window while watching Lachlan and Chris out the corner of my eye. From the looks of their fast action hands, it appeared they were in a race for who could wash faster.

Lachlan nudged my elbow.

"You're doing it wrong," he muttered, swiping left and right on the carriage. "Wax on, wax off."

Chris stared at us from feet away, hunching over and washing the hubcap of a wheel.

I lowered my arm. "Don't tell me how to wash a car."

He placed his fingers over mine and raised my hand upward. Tingles spread from where his fingers touched mine. My body temperature raised, warming me more than the sun.

"You're smearing dirt." He pressed down on my hand against the truck. "You need to *scrub* it."

I slipped my hand from beneath his and waved the sensation off. "I—I know what I'm doing. It's not rocket science." Heat flushed my cheeks.

He grinned, and my heart fluttered. "Just saying, you don't look like the car-washing type."

From behind, Chris shoved Lachlan forward; his shoulders jerked toward me. "What do you think you're doing?" Chris yelled.

Lachlan looked up, catching himself on the side of the truck. Students around us stopped washing and readied for a fight. Music continued in the background, *Shape of You* by Ed Sheeran.

All eyes were on them, and me. When I didn't say anything, Lachlan turned around and took a step toward Chris. Chris didn't move, feet in a wide stance, arms crossed over his broad chest. Lachlan was a few inches taller than him but lacked the stockiness. "Lay another hand on me, and you won't play football for the rest of the year," Lachlan said, voice unwavering.

"Is that a threat?" Chris asked.

Lachlan laughed once. His hands balled into fists at his sides. "It's a school fundraiser idiot. Everyone's watching."

A rose-breasted grosbeak landed beside me, on the roof of the truck, and squawked. Guess it wanted to watch the fight too.

"Chris, stop," I said, finally chiming in. My words felt like they had come from someone else, not me.

Chris's head tilted to the right, viewing me around Lachlan's shoulder. "What?"

"Lachlan's right," I replied.

"You're sticking up for him?"

"No, but do you want to ruin your last year of football. What about scouts?"

Chris's jaw clenched, through closed teeth, he growled at Lachlan, "You're lucky we're not alone." His eyes danced around at the crowd filled with other football players who had already positioned themselves into a wide circle as if to provide a barrier for the fight. In the distance, the coaches stopped talking and immediately ran toward us. Chris kicked a bucket. Soapy water slid everywhere. He glanced at me before turning around to leave. Cooper and Angela hurried after him.

What had I done?

Lachlan headed to his car.

"Lachlan," I said. "Don't leave."

He stopped and faced me sideways.

I took three steps closer to him. "Chris is a dumb jock, but what did you expect would happen when you came? You had to have known he'd be here."

His eyes met mine. "I didn't come for him. I came for you."

Air suddenly escaped my lungs and the smell of fish rushed at me in full force. I tried ignoring it, blocking my nose with the back of my hand. My legs wobbled, and

Magnolia flashed into view between us. The tip of my toes touched a bucket. I bent over and dipped my sponge into the bucket, and counted to ten. *Calm down. Get a grip.* Had she seen her dad on the "other side?" Didn't she have better things to do than haunt me now?

Without warning Lachlan, I flung soapy water toward him, straight through Magnolia. Mags didn't budge.

"What was that for?" Suds strung across Lachlan's face and fizzed in his hair. "You're gonna be sorry you did that!" He bent down stealthily and returned the favor by squirting a hose in my direction.

"Yikes!" I turned to run, from Mags. She rushed through my body, shoving me backward. I tripped and hit the ground, scratching my elbows. Puke inched upward. I swallowed it back down.

"Oops! Sorry." Lachlan reached a hand downward. I whipped my head about, but Mags had disappeared.

Inhaling and exhaling deeply, I wiped water from my face. Why did she *have* to do that? My stomach continued flopping.

I rubbed my eyes with the back of my free hand, grateful that she was gone.

Annoyance at Magnolia fluttered to the surface, but then came heaves of laughter as Lachlan helped me up. And for the second time, with Lachlan Granger, I couldn't contain *that* side of me. The side that wanted to be free and have fun in the moment.

A voice sounded from over my shoulder. "You two, get back to washing." Jessica pointed at three more vehicles pulling into line.

With a sexy side-smile, Lachlan said, "You heard the drill sergeant." He ducked down and slung soapy suds at my stomach, but I dodged his attempt and grabbed the bucket, pouring water over his head. Other kids watched, and Chris violently rolled his shoulders, staring at Lachlan from ten feet away as he slowly washed a different vehicle.

Jessica marched over. "You two, stop it. Get to work!"

Lachlan and I chuckled as she turned around.

We started washing the truck again and raced to see who could scrub faster. Around and around and over where others had already washed. Faster and faster. He went one way and I went the other. Until finally, a hose squirted over the hood, soaking both of us.

With every new vehicle, we repeated the process. Occasionally, we tossed sponges at each other with disapproving, narrowed eyes from Jessica.

Chris stalked by a few times. I didn't have the guts to look at him.

After three hours, the cars stopped coming. The music quieted. "Way to go, Cubs!" Jessica yelled into her megaphone. "We raised three thousand dollars!"

Completely drenched, I held a towel around my shoulders. Chris didn't attempt to approach me, and I watched him leave with Cooper and Angela. Lachlan followed me to my car.

"Guess I'll see you later," I said to Lachlan.

He nodded. "Yeah, guess."

I bit my lip and opened my car door. The awkward feeling when a couple finishes a first date—that's how I felt right now. Confused and unsure, but strangely hopeful. There was somewhere I needed to be and didn't want Lachlan coming with. I still didn't one-hundred-percent trust him. What if he had been the one who destroyed the pictures? I was missing a huge piece of the puzzle, and I didn't know how big it was.

I turned and placed a towel on my tan seat and sat down. Lachlan backed up so I could shut the door. Rolling the window down, he turned around. "Bye," I said, breathing a sigh of relief when he didn't ask what I was up to.

Slowly pulling forward, I turned out of the lot.

Compelled by pure determination to figure out the truth about Magnolia's dad, I headed to her house.

TWENTY-ONE

Yellow caution tape wrapped around the trees in the yard, warning people to keep out. But there weren't any cops or other people outside. The driveway was empty. Was anyone inside?

Not wanting to draw attention, I circled the cul-de-sac and parked down the street. "Okay, Magnolia. I'm helping," I said out loud.

My clammy hands gripped the caution tape. My wet shirt clung to my stomach, cold.

I rang the doorbell.

Nothing. I shoved my ear against the wooden grooves, listening. No sounds. No voices.

I jiggled the doorknob. Locked.

Leaning back and peering around at the yard, there were still no cops. But what about neighbors? *Had anyone seen me?* Dipping beneath the caution tape again, I quickly crept around back.

By way of pure luck, the back door was unlocked. I slid it open an inch. Silence echoed from inside.

Stepping over the threshold, the living room loomed secluded. The stillness was thick. My fingers found a light switch. The utilities hadn't been turned off yet.

"Magnolia?" I said into the open. "If there's something you need to show me, now is the time." I paused. "D-id your dad kill himself?"

A loud sound hummed from the ceiling. A fan dangled, halfway ripped from the ceiling. The shaft jutted from its joint, as if it had been yanked downward. The blades angled imperfectly like jagged tips from a well-used rake. Something heavy had weighted on the fan. I gulped. A body? Ice prickled up my spine. I wrapped my arms around my shoulders.

Below the fan remained a wooden chair, toppled on its side as if it had been pushed out of the way in a hurry. Oddly, the fan still rotated. The blades contorted while gradually circling low-speed. The humming sound turned into an awful screech.

I stood, horrified at the scene, at the *moment* of his death. It was as if I could picture him. The noose tied around his neck. Where was the rope? With a hand over my heart, I couldn't contain the thought of his body dangling from the fan. "Dear God, may he find peace."

Had he felt any pain? I winced, feeling sick to my stomach.

I didn't want to think of it. But like passing a car wreck, I couldn't look away. And I couldn't stop my brain from suggesting details that I never wanted to think about again.

A noise from the kitchen startled me, and I jumped. My arms fell to my sides, fists ready to defend myself.

Something thudded again.

I turned around and tip-toed toward the kitchen. Five chairs sat tucked beneath the table; the matching sixth chair was on its side in the living room. I swear I could *feel* Mr. Ackerman removing the chair from the empty spot I had walked past, like a time-warp, the past and present colliding.

Another *thud.* I yelped.

My attention turned to the refrigerator. I exhaled a nervous giggle. The automatic ice filler. Ours made the same noise at home whenever ice fell into the storage bin. That had to have been the noise.

The second my shoulders relaxed, a clamor knocked oxygen back into my lungs. My chest expanded with fear. This time, the noise came from the living room. It sounded like something had shattered. I wanted to run away, dart out the back door, and never come back.

"This is a bad idea, Sonora," I said, sounding like Mom.

My hands trembled at my sides. The temperature dropped and clouds of cold breath puffed from my dry lips.

Goosebumps raced from my ankles, up my neck. "Magnolia?" I whispered, not knowing why I was whispering, nobody was here but me. At least not in the physical sense.

I inched closer to the table and rounded the corner of the counter, holding onto the back of a chair for support. I leaned over, peering into the place that I didn't really want to go: the living room.

The fan creaked, and my eyes widened. "Magnolia?"

Blood hammered through my veins.

Seconds later, she still hadn't appeared. To the left, I spotted the origin of the shatter. A window had cracked. Large spider web-like lines branched out from the center, splitting the window from side-to-side as if an errant baseball had struck it. But there was no ball.

"What are you trying to show me?" My voice fell weak.

Mustering up courage, I shouted, "Show me!"

I crept into the living room, closer to the window. Below, tiny pieces of glass flecked from the crack, landing on the wooden seal that lined the bottom. I scanned the ground, searching for whatever it was she wanted me to find.

The floor was gross, covered in dust and dirt clumps. To the right was the fireplace, edged by large blocks of beige stone and topped with a mahogany mantel.

Ouch! I was wearing flip-flops, and a piece of glass wedged between my toes.

On top of the mantel were dusty pictures of Magnolia's family, before her mom died. I slid my finger across a photo, leaving a clean finger-trail in the dust.

The entire family was dead now.

My eyes fell from the mantel to the floor. The fireplace had been used at some point. Black ash charred the inside among broken pieces of logs. I hadn't noticed the faint smell of burnt wood before, but now I did.

I leaned over, stooping my head inside the fireplace, wondering. I poked a singed log, and it fell apart. Beneath it, I saw what looked like a shiny chain covered in dark, powdery soot.

Timidly, I reached my hand inside, and pinched the chain, pulling it from the broken log. The chain left black smut smeared over my hands. I knew exactly what it was without needing to clean it. Still, I darted to the kitchen sink and flipped on the tap, hastily squirting soap in my hands.

The fire-damaged chain coiled in my palm. I rubbed soap and water all over it. Dirty suds fell, swirling down the drain.

I used my shirt to dry it, leaving charcoal stains behind. I raised the chain, dangling the necklace in front of my eyes.

Tears rolled down my cheeks. It was Magnolia's necklace, the one that we had given each other. It was the other half of the *best friends*, the shape of half-a-heart.

"But why?" I whispered. "Why is it in the fireplace?"

I reached for my neck.

A thought passed over me, and my heart sank deeper into my spine. What if I had washed a piece of evidence that contained the killer's fingerprints? If Lachlan was right, and Magnolia had known her killer, he *could* have touched it. Why else would Magnolia have wanted me to find it?

Outside, the beep of a car-alarm sounded. Someone was here. I ran over and flipped off the lights. I whipped my head to the door. Should I exit out the back or out Magnolia's room?

The front door jiggled.

Stuffing the necklace in my pocket, I dashed across the living room as I heard the front door creak open.

Down the hall, I quietly turned the knob and entered Magnolia's room.

Voices came from the living room. Police? Maybe relatives or someone cleaning the place.

It wouldn't take long for whoever it was to observe the broken window, and then start looking for the intruder. Me.

I stood in the place where I had spent so many hours growing up. Where Magnolia and I'd had countless conversations and fell asleep to the top song of the week. A ball of sadness settled in my gut and I reached into my pocket, clutching my fingers around her necklace. Then I opened the window and crawled out, sprinting to the street.

The ride home was heavy. All I could think about was the necklace. How had it gotten there? Who torched it in the fireplace? I had been a terrible friend to Magnolia at the end, and she didn't deserve that. I hadn't known how to deal with the grief of her mother. I was never good at the whole emotional thing. I never knew what to say. Mags seemed depressed all the time and didn't say more than two words when I *did* try to talk to her. Eventually, I and the group gave up. And then she dropped off the cheerleading squad. If she hadn't died, she probably would've dropped out of school.

TWENTY-TWO

Standing on the outside of my body looking in, I watched a girl struggle to be free. The girl, the same girl from the other night who'd helped me when my car broke down.

My nightmare blurred into a new scene. Now, I sat in my car, in the back seat, watching myself in the front seat. Myself in the front talked to the girl through the window, stating that I didn't need her help.

I tried to talk from the back seat, but my words echoed into a void as if shouting into a canyon. To my left, a finger tapped the window. The same sound echoed. Where was the boundary between what I was experiencing and what I remembered?

As the driver's door swung open, my past self finally gave in to the girl's assistance.

My hand tingled. Glancing down, my fingers disintegrated in my lap. The sensation tickled up my arms until I reappeared in a different nightmare, a scene that I hadn't experienced before. No longer in a place of previous existence. This time in the woods, I stood off in the distance. Trees of all ages grew, literally erecting from the ground. I jumped out of the way, my feet almost split in half by a sprout.

Goosebumps painfully traveled up my spine. My ears burned. I wanted to leave. "Help!" I yelled, my voice rang into a thousand helps *until stillness consumed them.*

Everything dulled to black, and I woke to Kaylee growling in the shadows.

Pressing my palms to my bed, I sat up—quivering. "What was that?" Was I Magnolia? Had she been watching me in the back seat of my car that night?

The dream felt so real though. The taste of dirt mixed with copper settled on my lips. The line between real and not-real was blurrier than ever. It'd been a long time since I dreamed of anything besides Magnolia's death. Why had that girl struggled to be free?

Grabbing my phone, I checked the time. A message from Rosa blinked: *Got something to tell me? Lachlan?*

Great, how long could I keep him a secret? How much did she know?

I text back: *Nothing. Why?*

A minute later she replied: *Carwash?*

She must've heard about him being there. *Yeah, he helped at the carwash. Couldn't exactly send him away.* I left out the part about Chris nearly pummeling him—except Lachlan would've fought back if Chris hadn't stopped—like the last time they'd fought in the eighth grade. Surprised they didn't break each other's noses again.

Waiting for Rosa to reply, my phone rang with a god-awful chime. My heart skipped a beat, and the phone fumbled from my grasp. When had I changed my ringtone? A deep growl reverberated from Kaylee's throat.

Patting Kaylee, I reached for my phone. Maybe it was my brother finally calling me back.

The screen read: RESTRICTED.

The caller was anonymous. I raised the phone to my ear. "Hello?"

Kaylee snarled.

On the other end of the phone, heavy panting breathed into my ear. My hands shook. The phone tapped against the side of my face with uneasiness.

"What do you want?" I said.

The breathing on the other end quickened, panting faster.

"Please, I don't know anything," I pleaded.

The breathing sounded further away like I lost connection. I pressed the phone harder against my ear, listening closer.

The next moment, a scream resonated so loudly that my eardrum pulsed. It was Magnolia's voice. "Don't do this! Please! Don't let me go!" she shrieked louder and louder. I threw my phone down, and it bounced off the comforter onto the carpet.

First, the shattered window, and now this. Was she getting stronger? Would she ever leave me alone?

TWENTY-THREE

The cafeteria smelled like pizza. Chris refused to sit across from me, but instead, sat four seats down. A dullness settled inside my chest.

"Why does he keep looking at you?" Rosa asked, nodding at Lachlan and not touching her salad. She was trying to lose weight by skipping big carbs.

Angela and Cooper sat off to the side, whispering something. I thought they were fighting, but about what, I didn't know. Even though I sat with the group, I felt isolated.

I shrugged my shoulders.

On the other side of the cafeteria, Lachlan ate lunch with two other emos dressed in all black with black hair. I hesitated to look at him, not ready to acknowledge whatever was happening between us. Earlier, I had caught myself walking toward him in the hall but then turned around a second later.

Rosa slapped the table, snapping my attention back to reality. "What are you doing tonight?" she asked all smiles.

"Probably staying home. School night." Angela glanced over at me with a blank look. Being a school night didn't seem to matter anymore. I could always sneak out of my room. This new Sonora who breaks rules and colors outside the good-girl lines had its advantages. But it was also stressful on my emotional psyche. I rubbed my temples.

"My parents are headed out of town," Rosa added.

"Have plans with Tyler?" I guessed, wondering if she'd won him back by now. Her eyes wavered with hesitation.

Cooper and Angela huddled together, swooning and whispering. Maybe they hadn't been fighting after all. I still didn't like Angela though.

"Nooooo," Rosa said, rolling her eyes. Her word was drawn out like she hinted at something I was supposed to know. "Check your phone." She beamed.

Curious, I grabbed it. The text read: *Annual Stump Party in the woods!* She had missed it last year, being new and all.

Rosa squealed.

I squealed too, and Chris turned toward me. "What?" I laughed. "I almost forgot about the Stump Party tonight."

"Are you going?" Chris asked.

I nodded casually, unsure of how to respond. Last year, we went to the party together, but now, I wasn't so sure.

"What kind of question is that? Yes!" Rosa said. She jumped up and down like a little kid with her hands in the air. She didn't care who saw her. Rosa spun around doing a jig that only *she* could pull off. I looked over my shoulder at Lachlan, hoping to see him glance in my direction. Would he be at the Stump?

Rosa plopped down in her seat and grabbed her uneaten salad, standing up. "Have to be in Mr. Westerfeld's class five minutes early." Her voice deepened. "Apparently, we need to discuss my grades."

That didn't sound good.

"Whatever. I have to stay home until my parents leave, so meet you there. Okay?" she added.

Breaking into the cafeteria noise, a phone beeped at our table. And then another did too, until the entire cafeteria was one large room of echoing beeps and rings. The kind of ring that alerts if there's a tornado in the area, or severe storm.

My body shivered, I hated that alert sound.

My eyes fell to my phone. The alert wasn't what I had thought: *Creekside Killer in Custody.*

I couldn't believe it. I rubbed my eyes and shook my head. Was this a joke? I grabbed Cooper's phone from his hands. It read the same. The Creekside Killer had been caught.

In a burst of excitement, I pumped my hands in the air and screamed, "Yes!" Nobody paid any attention to me over all the clattering voices; I wasn't the only one elated.

Did this mean my life would go back to normal now?

My excitement waned. The only reason Lachlan and I were *working* together was to find Magnolia's killer. And now the killer had been found.

I looked over to the table that he'd been sitting at, but he was already gone.

I stuffed my lunch back in my small red bag.

"Where are you going?" Chris asked, standing in front of me.

It was hard to look Chris in the eyes, I didn't enjoy hurting him. "Nowhere important. Bathroom." I clipped the lunch bag closed and grabbed my backpack. "Can we talk about this later?"

His lips pressed together and his jawline tightened. He walked away without answering.

Leaving the cafeteria, I headed over to the bleachers.

A cool breeze whipped in and around the giant metal structure. I rubbed my sweaty palms together. Why was I nervous? I'd talked to Lachlan. Kissed him.

I interrupted two students groping each other. They immediately ran off once I encroached on their private make-out session. The girl tripped, scurrying out.

"Lachlan?" I walked forward.

Was he here? He wasn't the type to hide in the shadows all creepy-like. Oh wait a minute, yes he was.

"Lachlan?"

I searched all the way to the back of the bleachers, but he wasn't there.

Defeated, I headed to class.

μ

At home, Mom slipped an apron over her head. "I'm so thankful the cops caught that man today." She shook her head, contemplating the news. "After all this time. Magnolia's poor dad. If he were alive …."

"They haven't released his name yet," I added. "Maybe it's a she?" I was happier than anyone. I mean, Magnolia could stop haunting me now. I'd be back on the squad in no time.

I paused at the thought. Did I want to return to the squad?

"Mom?" I asked, pressing my luck.

She opened the freezer and handed me a bag of frozen broccoli. I loathed touching frozen food, ice, anything cold.

"Hmm?" Her mind seemed elsewhere, probably focused on the serial killer. Who was he, or she?

"Can I go to a party tonight?" I spit out, ripping the Stump Band-Aid off. I had to ask her. If I waited late to sneak out, I might miss Lachlan, if he planned on going. I needed to leave early, which required telling the parental units. I stared at my phone, Lachlan hadn't texted back.

Mom scratched her neck.

I filled a pot with water, being extra helpful, and placed it on the stove. "All my homework's done. I *really* want to go. Please." She didn't have to worry about my safety anymore, the killer no longer a threat. "I promise to be back by eleven, which is only an hour past curfew anyway...."

The microwave beeped.

I could see the wheels of control turning in her head. "Fine, Sonora," she said, her shoulders slumping. "But no later than eleven."

As we finished setting the table, my dad walked through the door. He enthusiastically kissed my mother on the cheek before the door closed behind him. "Did you hear the news?" he asked us.

She removed her apron and hung it on the hook behind the pantry. He disappeared into his room, and when he returned, he was holding something; I saw him slide a small navy box into his pocket, then smile at my mom who didn't notice.

We all took our seats around the table, and Dad said grace.

"How was work, dear?" she asked, reaching for the bowl of food.

"I got you something today."

My mom's eyes met his and she grinned. "You did?" After scooping rice and broccoli onto her plate, she placed the blue bowl back down.

He tilted his forehead. "Yes, but maybe I should return it." He winked.

"Let me guess," she said, placing her finger on her chin, thinking. "A spa day?" She smiled.

His demeanor drooped.

"Jewelry?"

His eyes perked up, and he wiggled his brows.

"Okay, earrings?" she guessed.

His eyes fell, and he made a pout with his lips.

She continued. "A necklace?"

His shoulders straightened.

He pushed the chair out with the backs of his legs and removed the navy box from his pocket. Then he walked over to my mom and placed it in her palm. "Happy anniversary," he said.

"It's not our anniversary," she mumbled.

"Well, not yet, but it will be next week."

Her fingers grasped the box. She took her time opening it, removing the small bow first.

Opening the box, she breathed in at the sight. "I love it," she said in a squeaky voice.

He plucked out the necklace and dangled it in front of her. His back faced me as he turned behind her and clasped it around her neck. As soon as I spied the necklace, I choked on a piece of meat. I beat my sternum with my fist, coughing. Grabbing my glass, I gulped a large amount of water.

Mom and Dad looked at me with bewilderment. Once they realized I didn't need the Heimlich maneuver, they returned their attention back to one another.

Mom's manicured fingers rested over her neck with adoration.

"I know you lost your cross a year ago," he added—a tone of pride in his voice.

"How did you remember that?" she asked, rhetorically.

He leaned over and gave her a kiss on the lips. My leg muscles tightened, my stomach too, I wanted to hurl. The shiny necklace was exactly like the one from around the neck of the girl—the one from my nightmare. Down to the little pink stone on the right side of the cross.

TWENTY-FOUR

"Wh-where did you get that?" I stuttered. My spoon trembled against the edge of my plate, Morse code for get-the-hell-out-of-there.

My question didn't seem to faze my father. "A man never reveals his secrets." He grabbed his silverware and placed his napkin in his lap.

My mom's face glowed, completely smitten by the thoughtful gesture. Though, I wasn't even sure the necklace was real gold. It looked too yellow.

The chandelier above the table brightened with each thump of my pulse.

What do I do? What does that mean? Either Magnolia found a way to torment me by somehow *encouraging* my dad to buy that necklace, or that necklace was the same one that girl wore the other night. *But that's ridiculous.* I rubbed my temples, feeling a headache approaching.

Magnolia was gone now. Her killer caught.

"Not even a hint?" I asked in a raspy voice. I placed a spoonful of rice in my mouth, forcing the mushy clump down my throat. I was no longer hungry.

"A quaint shop downtown," he answered. The casual memory jostled freely from his mouth.

"What shop?" I questioned further.

My dad's shoulders dropped and his face snapped to mine. Was there a trace of rage, or confusion, behind his eyes? I had my father's eyes. Hazel—not quite green or brown, but instead, remnants of both.

The hint vanished and his hazel eyes dropped, meeting mine. His voice was sincere. "Sweetheart, you've never been there before. It's a small boutique downtown, owned by a kind lady, Marie Vasquez. She helped me pick it out."

"Sonora, stop hounding your father. You're being rude," Mom said. My stomach heaved. This dinner was getting all too weird for me.

I swallowed and attempted to rectify the situation. "Sorry, only curious. It's a beautiful necklace." I gulped the last half of my water between two bites and left the table to fill it.

Breathe, Sonora. I squeezed the handle on the refrigerator door.

"Where's Chris these days?" Mom asked from the dining room, changing the subject.

These were my parents, they were good people. A little overbearing, but good people. And whatever was happening, I was sure there was an explanation. Or a ghostly one. Magnolia didn't have a reason to torture me anymore, so this had to be a coincidence.

Plus, I really wished to go to the Stump and didn't want my mom changing her mind.

Returning from the kitchen, I forced a smile at my father. "Uh, I don't know. He's sort of upset with me. But nothing I can't fix. Love you, Dad. Sorry." This whole Lachlan thing weighed on me.

Without inquiring further about my day, or asking about my grades, or my friends, he winked. A wink that meant everything was fine now.

After dinner, I went straight to my room.

Scrunching my pillow into a ball beneath my chin, I thumbed some music on and scrolled my phone.

I tapped Lachlan's number. I wanted to call him so bad and tell him. Tell him *what* exactly? Besides, the killer was caught. Wasn't he? There was no reason to talk to Lachlan anymore.

I decided against it and grabbed my makeup bag. If I planned on going to the Stump, I needed to add more eyeliner. Thick eyeliner always made me appear older. A Stump Party always called for more makeup. Lipstick too. I definitely needed a nice layer of pink lipstick. Not red, red was too bold.

Besides Rosa would probably wear red. I didn't want her to think I copied her.

Spritzing on Ralph Lauren perfume, I checked my appearance. Perfect. I opened my door. Hoping my parents weren't nearby, I scooted out. I didn't want to give my mom a chance to stop me with disapprovals of my makeup. I tiptoed through the kitchen to the outside and texted her once I reached my car and had driven safely down the street.

Then I called Rosa. "Hey, you there?" I asked when she picked up.

"Actually, I have a surprise for you." Those words made my stomach turn.

"A surprise?"

"Thank me when you get there, okay? And don't chicken out. Promise me."

What was she up to and why? "Rosa, tell me you're still coming."

She didn't respond.

"Rosa?"

"Guess you'll find out when you get there," she squealed.

"I *really* hate surprises, Rosa." Repeating her name in every statement was my small way of letting her know I wasn't happy. Surprises were kept for the type of people who didn't care what happened. I liked to know what was coming next so that I could be properly prepared. And my life was going back to normal now. No surprises.

I sort of didn't trust her. I mean, I trusted Rosa with 99.99% of my secrets, except for the rather big one of me having seen Magnolia's ghost. I didn't fully trust her when it came to having my best *interest at heart*. She always thought of herself first, put me second, and yet somehow, we remained best friends. Any time I thought about not being her friend, I became lonely and bored. For better or worse, we were two peas in the same high school pod.

"Stop being gloomy and thank me later. Byeee."

Driving down a dirt path, in the middle of nowhere, people parked along the edges of dirt. Vehicles blocked other vehicles from moving. I had arrived.

The piece of land was located on the outer edge of town, and consisted of acres and acres next to Lake Somerville, complete with a cozy lake house that rested in the back of the property. I'd only been to this place once before, at the same party last year.

After I finally found a spot, my phone beeped with a new message. Pulling it from my purse, it was a message from Rosa: *Have fun!*

What the heck?

I stepped out of my car. *Not cool!* I texted back. Headlights of cars pulled up behind me and parked off to the side. Jessica from cheerleading waved.

There was no wind tonight, the air humid and stale but not chilly yet. Unpredictable Texas weather. I should've put my hair up. Why didn't I bring a ponytail holder? Halfway closer to the party noise, my hair clung to my neck. I unzipped my purse and found a pencil. Using the pencil, I twisted my locks into a messy up-do.

Hordes of students from class traipsed down the dirt road, heading toward the noise. An uneasiness settled over my arms, and I crossed them. Right now would've been a great time to have Rosa by my side. Two girls wore green sweaters that hung off their shoulder in a fashionable way. I pulled at my shirt, trying to imitate theirs. If not for the pencil in my hair, I wouldn't look bad. What did Rosa have planned? This whole surprise thing made me uncomfortable, but I started walking anyway.

The music roared in the distance.

I got closer, stepping over bushes and between trees.

"Hey," a familiar voice said off to my right.

I turned, my heart caught in my throat. "Hi, Chris." The favorite sky-blue shirt that he knew I liked, hugged his biceps. He cocked his head to the side.

"Did you really mean what you said? That you're sorry?" he started.

A clear plastic cup filled with beer wobbled in his hand. Normally, I'd grab some too, but after the pill the other night, I didn't want anything else messing with my head.

"What are you talking about?" I asked.

The smell of smoke drifted from the crackling bonfire.

He squinted at my response. "I could've swung by to pick you up. You didn't have to drive all the way out here alone." The way he talked was like everything between us was suddenly fine now.

Standing close to him, I realized my feelings for him were no longer there. In fact, being next to him didn't feel any different than talking to Cooper. I motioned with my forehead to the main part of the party. "I should go. Where's ... Rosa?" The only other person on my mind right now was Lachlan. I couldn't get him out of my head.

"Huh? What are you talking about?" Chris glanced at my last-minute up-do and bit his lip. "Why are you doing this to us?"

I slid the pencil out, letting my red hair fall around my shoulders.

"I can't explain it. I know you deserve a better explanation than that, but I can't give one right now. I promise we'll talk later, okay?"

He glared at me before chugging his beer and turning around.

As he stalked away, I tried to will my emotions for him back to the surface. But there weren't any, and I couldn't deny it. I needed to be true to myself, for once.

My phone vibrated against my ribs. I had almost missed it between the vibrations of my phone and the vibrations of the music.

The tiny screen lit my shirt as I clicked open the icon. Lachlan finally texted me back.

Magnolia wasn't killed by the CKiller, he texted.

TWENTY-FIVE

What? What did that mean?

I whipped my head left and right, and searched the crowd for him. I replied. *Where are you?* My vision blurred from rapid panic as I shook my head. With a weak grip, I dropped my phone.

Bending down for it, the screen lit up again. *Look for the light,* he replied.

Really?

I scanned the area, searching for whatever light he referred to. Finally, I spotted a bright flash coming from deep in the forest.

A shoulder brushed against my arm. I moved over, bumping into a tall brunette girl on my left. "Sorry," I said to her.

"Sonora." The guy who had brushed against me looked older than I remembered seeing him last. His face a bit longer, and he was much taller. But it was Tyler.

"Hi, what are you doing here?" I asked him, giving him a side-hug and a bit bemused by his presence. I didn't even know he knew about the Stump, but I guess word spread to surrounding schools.

"I've been looking for you," he said.

I laughed, weirded out a little. "Me?"

"Yes, the text said to meet you." He leaned in and pressed his wormy lips against mine. I pushed him back.

Rosa, I immediately thought. Wasn't he dating Rosa? *What was she up to?*

"Woah, Tyler." I stood on the tips of my toes, searching for the light—for Lachlan. I nodded to my left. "I can't deal with you right now." I stepped around him and headed toward the source of the flash. Why in the world had he thought it was okay to kiss me?

Lachlan sat on top of a log, leaning against a tree with his arms folded. And he was as alone as someone could get in a group of high school partiers. This wasn't his scene, and he was completely out of place.

"What do you mean she wasn't killed by him?" I asked, rushing closer with shaky limbs. My foot snagged on a root, and I tripped onto him.

My cheek slimmed into his. *Dang it!* I pushed off of his stomach, and he readjusted his back.

"I overheard my dad, the guy didn't confess to killing Magnolia."

I inhaled, forgetting to breathe. "That doesn't mean anything. Who is the guy?"

"I don't know his name, not yet. But he confessed to killing the others. Not Magnolia."

My legs weakened. Bright balls of light filtered into my vision. Was I about to faint? If *he* hadn't killed her, then who did? I thought back to the necklace that my dad had given my mom—the one I'd seen in my nightmare. Did that have anything to do with it?

"Have you heard anything else?"

"No," he replied, plucking a piece of grass from the ground.

The sparkly flames of the fire danced, and the music lowered. People began gathering around the campfire behind us. Large stumps had been spaced out in a circle.

As I watched, Angela sat on Cooper's lap.

Lachlan stood up from his position. "Let's go," he said, pointing toward the logs and stumps. He grabbed my hand, and I let him tug me forward. My head spun from the news as we joined the group. A few people remained in the tree line, making out and smoking joints.

Tyler approached from the side, but when he saw Lachlan, he backed away.

Ten feet away, the flames snapped in the breeze. I sat on a log, Lachlan remained standing. Sparks floated up to the sky as the heartbeat of the fire pulsed.

"So, who wants to tell the first story?" Angela asked, turning everyone's attention to her. Cooper leaned forward with a marshmallow on a long fork that had two prongs. The flames charred the whiteness of the marshmallow as it caught fire.

I stood up and marched over, snagging a marshmallow from the bag next to Angela.

Dipping the marshmallow over the sparks, it lit up. I liked mine to be covered completely in black. Blowing the flames out, I blew once to cool it and grabbed it with my teeth, enveloping the crispy puffball in one bite. Angela looked away.

Lachlan seemed amused and moved closer to me. "Scary story …" he said loudly.

"What about the legend of the Creekside Killer?" a random person asked.

I melted inside.

"I bet he's been killing for years," Chris added. He raised his hand, motioning for Cooper, all the while eyeing Lachlan. "Toss me two, bro."

"Ever heard of the Kingsbury Run Murders?" Cooper said.

Angela grinned. "Do tell."

Cooper brushed Angela's legs off his knees and leaned forward, resting on his elbows. His face glistened from the heat of the fire. Cooper reached for his phone and turned the music down further so we could all hear, and continued. "He was this killer who murdered a dozen or so people during the 1930s, in Ohio. Body parts turned up in riverbeds, similar to the Creekside Killer." In one gulp, he chugged the rest of his beer and stomped it, squashing the can against the ground.

I held off on drinking long enough, I needed one to get through this night. I turned to grab a beer from the keg, hoping the subject would change soon.

"I have a theory on the Creekside Killer," Angela chimed in.

She rose from her stump. "I think there are two murderers. Like when Jack the Ripper had partners."

I wasn't educated in the serial killer arena, especially myths. But I'd heard of Jack the Ripper, who hadn't? "What makes you say that?" The moment my words exited, I clenched the plastic cup, keeping my hands from trembling. Beer foamed over the sides.

Angela moseyed around the campfire, walking closer to me. "There're those that think Jack the Ripper wasn't a lone killer, but in fact, multiples. This way when a girl was murdered, the police couldn't narrow it to one person. And since the police were only looking for one Jack the Ripper, all the killers got away with the murders. And not just that, but the Ripper killed hookers and homeless women. Kind of like the Creekside Killer."

"Magnolia wasn't a hooker," Cooper corrected her quickly, rubbing his neck.

"I never said she was," Angela replied. "But we all know she went off the deep end before she died. Who knows what she did, or who she hung with. Or who she was doing."

Her innuendos made me angry. I wanted to shove her into the fire.

"Stop talking about her like that," I said. Chris's gaze snapped up to mine. "You don't have the right." I sipped my beer. My core fumed as hot as the flames. "For all we know, *you* killed her."

Angela faced me. When she took a step, I tossed my beer on her. Snickers tumbled from the circle. She reached down to grab her full cup off a stump, but Cooper halted her by the wrist. "This is pointless. No more talking about Mags, okay?" He paused. "Truce?"

I rolled my eyes at him. What did he see in her?

She backed down and sat next to him. "Only because I love you," she said. *Love?*

Over my shoulder, Lachlan pulled back his hair behind his ears. He walked over and whispered in my ear. "Ever been to a graveyard at night?"

Graveyard or Stump Party? "Suddenly, the graveyard doesn't seem so bad."

A smile slowly settled on his lips as he rubbed his palms together.

"Where did you have in mind?"

"It's a surprise. Come on." I'd had enough surprises for one night, but I'd allow one more. After all, I was beginning to trust Lachlan. Somehow, I knew he wouldn't hurt me.

Leaving the party, his Firebird wasn't parked too far away.

He revved the engine before spinning out. He thrust the gear stick and stepped on the gas more. "You're going to wreck on this dirt road," I said.

"Stop worrying so much," he replied. With one hand on the wheel, he headed back toward town and onto a paved road. A graveyard wasn't on my bucket list of items to do before I died, but I guess I could add it now.

His thumb tapped the wheel. Was he nervous? Lachlan, nervous? Either that or he was impatient.

He grabbed a bottle from between the seats, this time it was water instead of Coke.

He dipped it at me. "Want some?"

I shook my head. It was a germ thing, sharing a drink with anyone grossed me out.

He circled the wheel to the right onto Blue Bell Road, three blocks from the town square. The road stretched eight miles from the south end around to the north end. A few cemeteries and graveyards scattered off it, but more than nine remained in Brenham. Generations after generations had been buried here, headstones dating back to the 1800s. Which graveyard were we going to?

"I wonder who killed Magnolia," he said. He spun the wheels to the left onto Prairie Lea Street, down the road from the police station where his dad worked.

"Did you know your dad questioned me once?" I paused. "After discovering her body."

"What, why?"

My throat felt dry. "My number had been in her phone as the last person she called. I didn't answer that night. I didn't even hear my phone ring." I looked away, out the window.

"Well, my dad never believed that she'd been murdered by the Creekside Killer. Turns out, he was right."

"Who else would have done it? She didn't have enemies."

He pulled into Prairie Lee Graveyard. A paved trail led to the back of the cemetery, smooth under the tires. Lachlan took his time and parked next to the fence in the back.

Other than the lights at the very beginning of the entrance, it was dark. Without thinking about it before, it dawned on me where we were. My stomach tightened. Magnolia was buried here.

TWENTY-SIX

"Maybe you should take me home." I bit my lip as I remembered my car back at the Stump.

"You can't go home, not yet. Where's the fun in that?" he joked, turning the engine off.

The darkness outside enveloped the interior.

He stepped out and shut the door.

I sat alone in silence—*alone.*

I stared at the rows and rows of headstones. In middle school, my fifth-grade class had taken a field trip to this place. Who takes a bunch of kids on a field trip to a destination filled with dead people? I had been instructed to place a piece of paper over a headstone and rub it with a crayon. It was morbid.

Out the driver's side of the car, a tall fence obscured a thicket of woods filled with more shadows than the graveyard. Tall dogwoods blocked the moonlight.

I rubbed my arms with my hands, creating a safety barrier between me and the deathly gloom outside.

Lachlan scampered off, not waiting for me.

If I didn't get out, I'd be by myself longer than I ever wanted to be alone in a graveyard—at night. Chills ran up my fingers as I grabbed the cold handle. The door creaked open.

Crickets and bugs chirped in a high-pitched symphony.

Behind the normal woodsy scent, there was sort of an odor like a hospital. Of decay.

Is that what morgues smell like?

The rancid odor smelled like rotting eggs but much more intense. It had to be in my head. It *had* to be. Right?

Not wanting to spend another second alone, I slammed the door shut and sprinted after Lachlan.

Stupid! How did I end up here? Tonight was supposed to have been a quick trip to the party. But now, the night had turned into something I didn't like.

A cool breeze wafted up the hem of my shirt. I rubbed my arms.

When I caught up to him, Lachlan slowed his pace. He glanced over his shoulder and winked. Had he left me alone in his car on purpose? Was it his way of forcing me out? I'd given him exactly what he wanted.

I stuck my tongue out at him. His tricks were unamusing. Hanging with Lachlan was uncomfortable and thrilling, like the fluttery feeling before a cheerleading competition.

My feet patted the soft cut grass that tapered the center path as I followed him. Where was he headed? *Please don't go to Magnolia's grave.* I didn't dare glance in its direction.

"You know the story that haunts this place?" he asked.

Goosebumps flecked my neck. "No? But I have a feeling you're about to tell me," I joked, wishing he wouldn't. I didn't need any more reasons for nightmares.

How long would it be before Magnolia emerged to torment me? Or would my presence be an open invitation for other ghosts?

My eyes darted about. An eerie blue light cast over each headstone and a fog had settled. The entrance to the cemetery was only a speck in the distance. Hundreds of gravestones and mausoleums covered the vastness. To my right, polyester flowers rested in a holder on a grave, the petals too perfect to be real. An empty vase to my left toppled over and shattered. I flinched away. Neither Lachlan nor I had made it fall over. This couldn't be good.

Cement crosses dappled the tips of stones.

Mags was the only ghost that had ever haunted me, but what did that mean? Was she only the start?

Leaves covered the ground and crunched beneath each step.

"So what's the story?" I asked with my arms crossed, keeping warm,

He nudged my arm to the left and we exited the path. Great. Walking over dead people. Where else was there to walk? Corpses lay yards below our feet. I swallowed. This would surely get the dead's attention if we hadn't already. "Isn't there a path around here? Are we supposed to walk over these people?"

"They're dead. They don't care."

Lachlan stopped in front of a cracked headstone. Beside it was a large mausoleum, bigger than most. Thick bushes dotted the exterior. His gaze floated up to the name *Mallory* engraved beneath the rocky roof.

"Look over there." He pointed at the headstone buried closer to the mausoleum than any others.

The headstone was barely legible and marked with brown stains. It appeared to have been cracked many times and cemented back together with a sloppy spatula.

I squinted and read the name. "Amoret Mallory, 1868-1897." My eyes widened. "Why isn't she in there?" I pointed at the mausoleum.

"Well, legend has it she was a witch who died in childbirth." Hearing Lachlan say 'childbirth' made me snicker, and his eyes narrowed. He wasn't the *birth* talking type. Neither was I.

He cleared his throat, and I regained composure. "As I was saying, when she died, her family refused to let her remains rest with theirs."

I burst out into laughter and waved his nonsense off. "You have no idea what you're talking about. How would you even know that?"

He cocked his head and continued. "She can't find peace until her body is moved in there." He pointed at the large structure. "Her soul is trapped until she gets justice. So when a person messes with her headstone, they end up dying mysteriously. She terrorizes every trespasser to their death."

I took a step back. "You're full of it."

I had enough ghosts on my plate. I didn't need a dead witch on my back, too.

He shoved his hands in his pockets. Lifting a single eyebrow, he said, "I'll prove it."

My amusement switched to nervous laughter. "What?" I shook my head. "No. Come on, let's go."

"You don't believe me?" He gestured toward the headstone with his elbow. "I'm going to push it over."

I jutted my hand out, grabbing his arm. "Don't."

He grinned slyly, inches from toppling it with his foot. "Believe me now?"

I dropped my hand. "I won't admit that. But *if* you're right, which I don't think you are. Not in the slightest. But *if* you are, then do you really want"—I glanced back at the headstone—"Amoret to attach herself to you?"

His voice lowered. "Do you really think she will?"

"Lachlan Granger, you are the most bizarre person. You know that?"

Without pause, he marched off, heading to another spot in a hurry.

"Hey, where are you going?" I hollered, not caring if anyone heard me. There was nobody out here but us. With one glance back at the cracked headstone, I gave it a wide berth and scurried after him.

A gust of wind whipped through the graveyard, shaking branches of trees. Leaves floated to the ground, tangling in my hair like unavoidable cobwebs.

Lachlan was clear across the yard. "Slow down!"

When I finally reached him, I halted feet away.

He stood in front of Magnolia's headstone. With a pounding in my chest, I spun back around. I changed my mind; staying in the car alone was better than standing on top of Magnolia's corpse.

Not ten steps into my retreat, my head pounded with intensity as if I'd been hit by a metal crowbar. Pain shot over my neck and coiled down my back.

TWENTY-SEVEN

My right palm slapped a gravestone as I fell. I slammed to the ground, hitting my knees.

A taste of a hundred pennies coated my mouth like fish mucus. I lurched forward, retching. The smell of singed hair filled my nostrils. I spat, trying to rid the awful bitterness.

Lachlan's footsteps closed in; I heard him before I saw him, his steps echoing in the void of my brain.

He bent over, grabbing my shoulders. A look of horror spread across his face. "Sonora!" his voice echoed.

My body felt detached, like I'd become trapped in a distant part of my mind. I reached up to touch the back of my throbbing head. I removed my hand, expecting blood. But there wasn't any. As quick as the pain had appeared, my headache began subsiding. My hearing blurred back to reality.

I clutched handfuls of grass, pieces of green embedded in my fists and beneath my nails.

My head snapped up.

In my line of sight, Magnolia's bare toes squirmed, covered in dirt. Her bloody grime-filled nails wiggled like spider legs, crawling toward me.

I punched the empty air, whipping my hand through her celestial form. Pieces of grass fell from my fingers, snagging on her translucent feet.

"Sonora, what's wrong?" Lachlan's voice melted in. The distance faded away and reality bled through. The headache drained through my piping veins. I quivered beneath the notion that I needed to tell him everything.

With a concerned face, he helped me sit up. I didn't have the strength to make it to his car, my body depleted of energy. My heavy arms weighted down by my even heavier hands. It took all of me not to fall over.

"Lachlan," I panted. "There's something I need to tell you."

"No, there's something I need to tell you. I was closer to Magnolia than I said"—

"Stop."

He didn't budge.

"Lachlan, sit." I swallowed, absorbing energy back into my one brave bone that wanted to tell him. My other bones vehemently warned against it.

My eyes flitted back and forth between him and Magnolia's grave. The cursive script on her headstone read, *Daughter, friend, and angel.* Someone should add *ghost* to the list. Her mom's grave next to hers, and an empty spot on the other side, probably for her dad.

Lachlan plopped down, facing me with his arms loosely around his knees. Strands of curly hair had broken free and hung over his forehead as he stared with wide eyes. It didn't take a genius to know I had something serious to say.

He waited.

Magnolia stood next to me. His left knee brushed through her right calf. Had he felt her? Could he feel her? By his unwavering stance, I assumed not.

Like an oven, an intense heat began radiating from her form.

Beads of sweat ran down my forehead.

I raised my right hand to touch her shin but curled my fingers before making contact.

"God, what's that smell?" Lachlan said, covering his nose. He looked around for the source. "Rotten fish."

For once, her smell was the last thing I noticed, like a dead raccoon on the side of the road. Maybe becoming used to her stench was a side-effect from having dealt with this for so long.

"You know how you asked why I wanted to find Magnolia's killer?"

He nodded, dropping his hand and scrunching his nose.

I peered back at her grave. Focusing on Lachlan again, I weighed his response. Would he think I was officially insane? I continued. "Well, she's sort of been haunting me."

His eyes wavered and his chin scrunched to his neck. "Haunting?"

I nodded. "Haunting. As in she's standing next to me right now. As in she just threw me to the ground. As in she didn't let me sleep until I agreed to find her killer. As in the source of the disgusting fishy, dead smell."

Lachlan took a deep breath, and his grip unlocked from around his knees. Looking down at the ground, he re-tied his hair behind his head. Was he stalling?

His eyes circled the graveyard, as if searching for her celestial form.

"She's right here." I pointed beside me.

Out the corner of his eyes, his gaze slowly slid to mine.

For the first time, a fiery redness shimmered off Magnolia and dulled to a pinkish sunset. As always, her hair draped over her shoulders. Drenched material clung to her pasty skin.

Lachlan bit his lip as if he didn't know what to believe.

"Can you see her?" I asked. An ounce of hope hugged the surface above the madness I vomited.

He shook his head side-to-side. "I should grab the EMF meter from my trunk."

"An EMF reader?"

"Haven't you ever watched those ghost hunter shows? It detects changes in temperature and electromagnetic energy when spirits are around."

"You have one?"

"No." He smiled. "I was only joking."

My shoulders sank. "Lachlan."

His grin faded to a stony expression.

"I'm not lying to you," I assured him.

His mouth opened. "That much I figured."

What? "Uh, you *figured* I was being haunted by Magnolia?"

"No." He took a second before replying. "That you don't believe you're lying."

I let out a sigh. He thought I was crazy. "It's not like that. I swear to you. She's right here." I pointed to her feet, not wishing to look her in the eyes.

He rubbed his neck, like he was processing the information.

"Believe me." I wanted to beg him, grip his arm and plead for him to believe me. But I feared touching Lachlan would make him run. He didn't run from anything though. "I know what I sound like. What I'm telling you is the truth."

I leaned forward. My arms loosened, not feeling as heavy anymore.

He cocked his head. "I won't admit that I think Magnolia's haunting you. But I believe *you* think she is. And if it's real to you"—he paused—"then who am I to say otherwise. I've heard of crazier things happening to a person when they lose someone close to them."

Was he talking about Magnolia, or his mom?

"And I know that the loss you experienced, well, it's a lot to handle. Like I said, Magnolia and I were closer than I let on. We were friends, and she was going through some hard stuff before she died."

He didn't believe me, but he didn't not-believe me either.

"I have something I've been keeping from you too," he said, changing the subject.

What else hadn't he told me?

Magnolia hovered, not leaving as if she waited for him to say something. She was too close. I scooted away from her.

Lachlan peered up at the sky before continuing.

"I think Magnolia was seeing someone. Before she died."

I slouched with disbelief. "What do you mean?"

"She *had* someone on the side. Someone that she said she couldn't tell me about. Whoever that person is may be the one who murdered her."

"Did you tell your dad?" I thought back to what Angela had told me, about the text that Cooper received: *I'm sorry.* Maybe that's what Magnolia was sorry about.

He nodded. "It didn't lead anywhere. She never actually said anything to me. It was a hunch, a sixth sense or something. When we hung out, her mind was always elsewhere. I'd ask her directly, and she'd blow me off."

"Lachlan Granger, the boy with a sixth sense who doesn't believe in ghosts." I sat there. Why hadn't Mags told me about this other person, whoever it was? Or maybe she *had* tried to tell me; I never answered my phone. Thinking of her made me sad. Lachlan had been there for her when I wasn't. I should've been there. I looked up at her, looking at me. She didn't flicker or move.

A couple of times she'd left voicemails I deleted before ever listening to them. "I was such a horrible friend," I said to her. During those times, when she was alive, I didn't know how to be around her. It hurt to be around her. The crash that took her mom was too much, too much for me. I had never experienced a loss of that size until then.

"We should go," Lachlan said, grabbing my hand.

I pulled away, not wanting to be touched. I moved sideways, away from him, and crossed my arms. "This can't happen. You and I." Why did I say that? Dread filled my arms.

"What about you and me, scares you so bad?" Lachlan replied. He stood up, not giving me another glance and walked away with force.

I didn't want to think about her anymore, I wanted none of this. "Go away!" I yelled at Magnolia. "I can't do this anymore." Her ghostly form shimmered and disappeared. The pain of everything grew into a knotted ball of guilt and regret and sadness. A rage from deep within bubbled. I clenched handfuls of grass next to my legs.

Lachlan's back blurred as he walked farther away.

My vision closed in. My breathing labored.

My mind retreated to a safe corner. A familiar corner, like a scent sucking me back to a time in my childhood where life was simpler. When my only responsibility had been to have fun.

Approaching Lachlan in the car, I creaked open the passenger door. He didn't say two words to me as we drove back to my car.

TWENTY-EIGHT

The next morning, I was too tired for school, but I didn't have a choice. The serial killer business bounced around my thoughts, as I turned on the faucet in my bathroom. Water from the shower nozzle beat against the tub.

I sat on top of the toilet, waiting for the water to warm. My left palm was sore from where I had smacked it against the headstone last night. Rubbing it with my fingers, my hand burned.

Steam rose from inside the shower. I stepped over the edge of the tub and closed the paisley printed curtain. The hot water rushed down my hair and over my face, shaking me awake.

I reached for the shampoo and shut my eyes. As soap rinsed from my hair, my back began stinging. I arched forward, away from the water. *Ouch.* Why did my back hurt? After getting all the soap off me, I grabbed my towel from the wrack.

Stepping out, I moved to the mirror and wiped the moisture off. My back hurt worse out in the air. Four fresh scratch marks, a few inches long, crisscrossed the right side of my lower back, above my hip. Did Magnolia do this to me? When?

I dressed carefully and ambled into the kitchen. Every move and stretch pulled the scratches, making them burn. I gritted my teeth.

Grabbing a plate of pancakes from the island, my mom faced away as she hovered over the stove. Next to the sink, a bill from St. Joseph Psychiatric Hospital sat lopsided against the travertine backsplash. The morning news played in the background.

"Morning, Sonora." She smiled. Around her neck was the necklace my father had gifted her—I flinched. Something was different. *It* looked different. "How was the party?"

I peered closer at her necklace. It was a cross, but the pink stone no longer adorned it. Had I been seeing things last night? Had Magnolia made me see something that wasn't really there? Was that possible?

Narrowing my eyes, I did my best to hide my reaction. "Morning." I couldn't trust my own vision anymore, my own memory. "Who gave you that?"

"What?" she asked, placing another pancake on my plate.

I pointed at her neck. My back ached from the scratch marks, and I adjusted my shoulders.

She palmed it, confused. "Your—dad," she replied slowly.

I plopped into my seat, bracing myself on the edge of the table.

"How was the party?" she asked again.

My vision flittered back, but my mind reeled.

Short and sweet responses were what she needed to hear. "Nice. Thanks for letting me go." I smiled. My eardrum pulsed with the rush of confusion. Cutting my pancakes, I took a bite, but my attention wavered between staring at my plate and glancing up at my mom's necklace.

"Wait," she said. "Did you work things out with Chris?"

I slumped farther into my chair. *Ouch.* "Not exactly." Goosebumps peppered my arms as Magnolia's odor hit me like a ton of fishy bricks. Behind Mom, Magnolia appeared *in* the counter, dripping ghostly water all over the granite. Her one bad eye rolled across her cheek and tapped the corner of the white hospital bill. My stomach recoiled.

Her eyeball tapped the bill again.

I hadn't seen my grandpa in a year. As far as I knew, my parents hadn't visited him either; dad and he didn't have the best relationship growing up. "Mom?" I muttered, my eyes fixed on Mags and the bill her veiny, goopy eye touched. "Can Pawpaw have visitors?" Maybe I should talk to him. What if he saw ghosts too? *Maybe this curse is genetic.* I licked my lips with cautious hope. Could he help me?

She stopped and turned slowly. "Why do you want to know?"

I shrugged my shoulders. "Just wondering if I could see him." Suddenly, Magnolia opened her mouth wider than humanly possible, and gnats swarmed out. The kitchen filled with hundreds of the black, flying bugs as they multiplied in number! My eyes widened and I fell from my chair onto the rug.

"Sonora, what's wrong with you?" Gnats circled Mom's head, but she didn't swat at them or move. *Can she see them?* They didn't enter the dining room but stayed solely in the kitchen.

"No-nothing." I inched back into my chair, unable to stop staring. Magnolia opened her mouth again. My clammy hands gripped my fork, ready to stab at the next thing to fly out of her. But instead, like a dark Texas tornado, the gnats swarmed back into her mouth, and she vanished; the bill on the counter slipped from its lopsided position, lying flat. My heart raced.

Mom squinted. "It's best that your grandfather focuses on getting better."

"Huh?" I asked, searching for leftover bugs, but there were none. "Oh yeah, Pawpaw. Best for whom?" *You stuck him away and pretend he doesn't exist—exactly what you will do to me.*

"If we visited him, it would only stir up emotions best left alone. Grandfather's in a good place, the nurses and doctors know what they're doing. Now, no more talk of him. Okay? You need to finish getting ready for school."

I shoved another bite in my mouth, concluding that I *had* to visit him. But that would mean stepping foot in the psychiatric hospital. No, I didn't want to do that. Definitely not.

TWENTY-NINE

After two more classes, I began to worry about Lachlan. He wasn't texting me, and I hadn't spotted him in the hallway either. Why wasn't he at school? My life had recently rotated to a fragile side of crazy. I needed to talk to him.

At lunch, I sat across from Rosa. Angela and Cooper kept their distance again and glanced at me oddly every once in a while.

"They have issues, leave them be," Rosa said, not eating again. Silver hooped earrings matched the bangles on her wrist.

"It isn't a diet if you starve yourself," I advised.

I scanned the cafeteria.

"Looking for Lachlan?" Rosa asked.

Tapping my foot against the ground, a second passed before I answered her with a head bob.

"I knew it," Rosa replied, chewing gum—five calories.

"What do you want me to say? Yes, I like him."

She frowned. "Sonora. It's Lachlan Granger. If you only learn one thing from me, let it be this. Lachlan's hot."

"What?" I stopped chewing, shocked by her confession. "Are you giving me your approval?"

The large loops dangling from her ears shook as she waved a finger in the air. "Yes. But don't forget, he's damaged goods."

And there it was, her way of getting inside my head. "Damaged goods?"

"He's like a lost puppy dog, needing a home. If you're prepared to give that to him, then I say go for it. And when it doesn't work out, come back to *me*."

She made me sick. I sucked on my cheek, contemplating shoving my sandwich into her mouth and forcing her to choke on the calories. "You know, Rosa, you're wrong. You're being a bitch, 'cause you don't want to lose your *loyal* best friend." My voice rose in volume. As conversations halted and people's attention focused on me, I felt exposed.

Angela's mouth dropped open.

Cooper leaned over. "Keep it down." He shushed with his hand, patting the empty space between us. He eyed me in a way that I didn't like. Suddenly, the smell of rotten fish lingered.

I leaned away from Cooper. Magnolia hovered on top of the table. I froze.

Cooper squinted at my reaction. "What's wrong?" he asked.

I swallowed another bite, trying to pretend like everything was fine. I reached for my bottle of water. My fingers lost grip, and my water tumbled, spilling everywhere, soaking my skirt.

In the seconds between spotting Magnolia and spilling my water, Rosa had left. Her seat was empty.

I looked beneath the table for her. How did she disappear so quickly?

"Coop, which way did Rosa go?"

I felt a *little* bad for jumping down her like I had. But my words were true. Sometimes honesty hurts, but Rosa and I needed to finish our conversation. She wouldn't put me beneath her anymore. The fact that she would assume a future breakup with a Lachlan, who I wasn't even dating, was beyond irritating.

Cooper grimaced. "Rosa who?"

I laughed wildly, feeling delirious. The room rocked back and forth.

"No really. Where'd Rosa go?" I asked.

Cooper's forehead scrunched. His eyes rotated to Angela who was ogling me. "I told you," she whispered to Cooper, loud enough for me to overhear.

"Shut up, Angela. Stay out of this," I spat.

Her posture stiffened and she pursed her lips.

"Look, Sonora." Cooper scooted closer so that nobody else could hear. Everyone at the table stared, so it didn't help much. "You should go to the nurse. I don't know who Rosa is. Call your mom, okay?" The tone of his voice was one that a teacher would use if talking to a child who had *issues*. His words twisted my heart. He'd never talked to me that way before.

"Why would you say that? I'm fine!"

I shoved him back, not understanding why he'd want to hurt me. I grabbed my purse and scuffed away. Everyone watched me leave. I clutched my purse tighter.

I large lump welled in my throat and I choked down a sob.

When I was far enough, I darted out the glass doors and ran across the street toward the bleachers.

Tripping on the curb, I flung my hands out to catch myself. My back ached, and now my knees throbbed too. With heaviness, I picked myself up. Tiny rocks from the track embedded in my palms, I brushed them off and straightened my skirt.

My body heaved as fat tears rolled down my cheeks and dropped to the ground. I couldn't take this anymore. I *needed* to talk to Lachlan.

I wiped my nose with the back of my hand and escaped beneath the bleachers, hoping to find him. My body hummed with heat from crying. Whatever small wind whooshed to bring relief, I couldn't feel it.

I covered my face and cried more. "Lachlan?" I asked through heaves and staggered forward. I fell to the ground and wrapped my arms around my knees, rocking back and forth. Tears soaked the collar of my blouse.

My head pounded.

With moist hands, I unlocked my phone. Lachlan still hadn't texted me. I thumbed to my *favorites*, searching for Rosa. I didn't want to apologize, but I needed a friend.

I scrolled up and down. Her name was missing.

Ready to snap, I rushed through my contacts. She wasn't there either.

I switched gears and searched for her number, instead of her name, but I couldn't find it.

Was this another illusion Magnolia was playing on me?

I flicked over to my recent texts between Rosa and me. They were missing. But I hadn't deleted hers, I never delete anything. There was a text there that I didn't recognize. It was to a contact named Tyler: *Come to the Stump tonight, I'll be there.*

Lightheaded, I dropped my phone and threw my hands behind me to stabilize my body.

I clawed at the twisting knot in my chest. I couldn't breathe. *This can't be happening.* My head throbbed; my body a knot of agony.

I ran into the stadium bathroom and hid in a stall. Minutes passed.

Why had Cooper said he didn't know Rosa? She'd been eating with us, hanging with us, for months. Hadn't she? I searched my memory. The first time we started hanging out at school was … My memories spun like a kaleidoscope, jostling, shifting in and around each other.

I'd met Rosa a few times before Magnolia's death, but we didn't start hanging out on a regular basis until after.

I braced myself against the stall wall to stand. Above my hand, the name *Crazy Janice* had been written in sharpie. Crazy Janice, the town psychic. Maybe she could help me? My knees ached from the cramped position they had been in. Wiping my face with my shirt, I pulled out a compact mirror and checked my eyes. They were swollen and puffy. I patted my cheeks with powder and reapplied my makeup.

Deciding to take as long as possible, I meandered from underneath the bleachers. The longer it took for me to get back to school, the more seconds my eyes had a chance to heal. I didn't want to return, more than likely I'd see Cooper or Angela in the halls.

My woozy mind created a dreamlike state. Passing the bleachers and walking across the track didn't fully penetrate my thoughts. I felt dangerously close to blacking out. Every inch of my skin crawled with tiny pinpricks. I rubbed my arms.

Holding onto the only rational thought—one of Lachlan, his face, his lips, his smell—my vision cleared. I needed to find Rosa. I *would* find Rosa. FIND Rosa!

I stubbed my bare foot. I was missing a shoe. Where'd it go? I turned around, scanning the trail, only to realize my red, Mary Jane shoe in my hand. I was holding it.

I wiggled my foot inside the shoe and kept walking.

For now, I needed to avoid Angela and Cooper, the only two people who knew I had asked about an invisible friend named Rosa. At least until I figured out what was happening. I had a plan. A small, teensy, no-good plan, but it was a plan—*Crazy Janice*. Maybe she could help me figure out who Rosa was. Did I make-believe her?

I stepped down from the curb and halted as a car rushed by, the tailwind blowing my hair. I scratched my elbow and looked both ways before moving forward. The full parking lot had given me a bright idea. What about Rosa's car? She drove a sunny yellow Prius and parked in spot 627. I always loved the color yellow, but my mom liked white the best—refined and elegant, so I drove a white Taurus.

It didn't take long to find spot 627.

Her car wasn't there.

Instead, in its place, was a green, beat-up Honda with dirt splattered above the wheels. A car Rosa would never be caught dead driving. For one, she hated the color green, and for two, there were dents all over it. Her car was spotless, in mint condition. Her car was an extension of her—vibrant and drawing lots of attention.

I thought about texting Chris. I needed to hear someone tell me I wasn't crazy! Would he take my call? But what if he called my mom. Could I trust him, could I trust anyone? I grabbed my head and squeezed my hair between my fingers.

No, I'd figure this out on my own.

From outside, the bell blared through the speakers.

Throwing open the glass doors, I rushed into the empty cafeteria and made a beeline to Calculus. The door was shut. When I opened it, all the students eyed me—my face flamed. Glancing at the teacher, I scurried to my desk.

Not halting his speech, the teacher bent over his desk to write something down.

I raised my hand.

"Sonora," the teacher replied with raised brows.

"Sorry, I'm late…" I winced. I didn't have an excuse. I could say I was in the nurse's office, but he'd probably check. Plus, I wasn't a huge fan of the nurse. Not that it mattered.

With a head nod, he scratched his forehead. "Maybe if you arrived on time, your grades would be better." Then he continued his lesson.

Everyone's beady little eyes followed me, I could *feel* them, but I didn't look.

The rest of class had ticked by. I walked through the halls like a ghost and passed my locker without stopping.

THIRTY

I was supposed to be in Coach Gold's office, which was really her empty Study Hall classroom. I made it in time before the tardy bell. But nobody was in the room but me, since I was the only cheerleader benched.

A void settled between my ears. I couldn't focus. I wanted to cry, but I couldn't. Tears rimmed the edges of my eyelids. I swallowed, letting them soak back in.

My numb body remained upright even though I wanted to fall over and curl up in a ball.

Unsure of why I hadn't thought of it before, I texted Rosa from memory. Even if I couldn't locate her contact in my phone, her number was permanently stamped in my brain.

Almost immediately, I got a reply. *Who is this?*

It's Sonora, duh.

Wrong number.

Holding back vile words, I typed. *This is Rosa, right?*

No. And I don't know who you are. Stop texting me!

"Sonora," a voice rang. Coach stood directly next to me, ogling my phone. She held out her hand. "I'll give it back at the end. You need to study, or do homework. That was the deal."

Unenthusiastically, I handed over the only thing that made me feel secure. She turned and left the classroom, heading back to practice I assumed.

Unable to text anyone, I stared at the dry-erase board, paying no attention to my backpack. My eyes clouded.

Before the bell rang, Coach returned my phone. "Here you go. Did you get some studying done?" she asked. I nodded, and then stuffed it in my purse and fled into the hallway.

I spotted Cooper and Angela. I halted. As soon as my brain caught up with my feet, I spun the other way around, deciding to take the long route to my car.

The bright sun blinded me as soon as my feet hit the pavement. I looked for Lachlan's spot, further up than mine but in the same row. He wasn't there. His spot was empty, not *his* muscle car or anyone else's car in his place.

Had I imagined him too? Did he exist? He *had* to. Angela, Cooper, and Chris all talked to him before.

Driving, my mind wondered, traveling anywhere but here. I turned right onto Blue Bell Road and then swung a left to Crazy Janice's. A white picket fence surrounded her tiny house. Above her doorway, a floral printed flag with the words *psychic* hung in the wind.

I stepped over old remnants of egg yolk splattered on her wooden porch.

Crazy Janice opened the door before I had a chance to knock. A plume of incense tumbled out behind her. A colorful chain dangled around her forehead like a gypsy. Her long gray hair draped over her shoulders, and eyeliner mapped the outside of her old, wrinkly eyes. "What can I do for you?" she asked.

"Um, I didn't know where else to go. Can you help me?" Asking the town psychic for help was my grand plan. If anyone would understand what I was going through, it would be Crazy Janice.

Her eyes narrowed, and she opened the door more. "Come in, child."

I walked past her.

The place was full of shadows, lit by flickering candles in various places. Sheer curtains covered the windows, coloring the walls shades of midnight blue and blood red. A long black feather hung in the corner.

"You've never been to a medium before, right?" She ushered me toward a circular table to the right.

I swallowed a shaky ball of fear and nodded. "I thought you were a psychic?"

"I'm a woman of many talents."

More flickering candles in red vases lit the smaller room, and the table carried a crystal ball. "Can you see my future in that thing?" I pointed at the table.

She chuckled and grabbed the ball, placing it on a shelf in the shadows. "No, that's just for looks."

"Oh." My shoulders dropped.

She stuck her palm out. "It'll be fifteen dollars for a reading, okay?"

I pulled the money from my purse and placed it in her hand. She opened a small box and stuffed the bills inside.

"Sit down, child." Her fingers tapped the back of a chair as she pulled it out for me.

"Do you know why I'm here?" I asked, sitting down. My legs bounced and my toes fidgeted.

Next to me, she halted. "Before we get started, do you have an item, something I could hold? It helps me focus."

"An item?" My heart pounded.

"Something from the deceased you're hoping to hear from."

Did I really want to hear from Magnolia? I wanted Crazy Janice to help me, tell me what was happening. Tell me where Rosa was.

I didn't have anything that belonged to Rosa, but I did have Magnolia's best friend's necklace. I pulled it from the zipper pocket in my purse and cautiously handed it over to Janice.

She closed her eyes and rubbed the locket between her fingers, much like a devout, God-fearing believer would do with beads.

My knees bounced beneath the table.

"My name is Sono—"

With closed eyes, she held up a hand. "I don't want your name, it's better if I know nothing about you. The reading is clearer that way." She dropped her hand and began rubbing the locket again. "You've lost someone dear to you."

You don't have to be a psychic to know that, I thought.

"M—her name starts with an M." She opened her eyes. "This necklace, she threw it in the fireplace. She was angry at herself."

Crazy Janice closed her eyes again. The killer didn't throw it in there? My legs stiffened.

"She says you know who killed her," Crazy Janice said.

"What? But I don't—" My insides quivered.

"—Shush. I need to concentrate, child," she interrupted. "M says you have the wrong person."

"I already know that."

"Can you tell me who killed you?" Crazy Janice asked into the open space between us.

"Yes, please tell me," I said to the space.

"A bridge?" she paused. "She says she fell from a bridge."

"But her body was—"

"—no details. Quiet, child." The old lady breathed in deeply. "Someone else is stepping forward. A male."

Was it Mr. Ackerman? My knees stopped bouncing.

"He's young." She squinted and rubbed the chain. "He loves you, and he misses you."

"You must be talking to the wrong ghost?"

She opened her eyes and dropped her hand, halting the process. "I know what I'm doing."

"Somehow, I doubt that. It's time for me to leave." If she was no longer talking to Magnolia, then she wasn't helping me. Maybe all this was for show, and she wasn't a real psychic.

"You still have five minutes left," she warned.

I scooched my chair back and stood. "No, really, I should leave. Can I have her necklace back?"

She reached across the table. The chain hung from her hand like a pendulum.

When I stuck my hand out, she grabbed my wrist. Her eyes closed. "Something dark lies within you, around you. Until you pluck it out, you'll never move on," she muttered.

Her grip tightened. I yanked my hand away, scared to ask what she meant. "Can I please have that necklace now?" My lungs constricted.

"If you don't resist this darkness, this demon, she'll overtake you. Your actions will no longer be your actions.

You must find the light." The whites of her eyes widened, and she leaned forward.

She grabbed my forearm and closed her eyes. I wanted to pull away but didn't. Goosebumps prickled up my trembling arms.

"She becomes stronger as you become weaker. She wants to be seen." Crazy Janice released my arm. I stood there. Not moving. "Your back. She hurt you already."

"Magnolia?" I whispered.

The medium stepped back and placed the locket in my palm. "It was not the one who wore this." She opened her door. I ran down her porch and to my car as quickly as possible.

THIRTY-ONE

In my bedroom, I tossed my backpack and purse on the chair. I closed my eyes and sank into the comforter, drifting, mentally and physically exhausted.

A knock on my door halted me from falling asleep. "Are you okay?" My mom's voice muffled from the other side. She opened the door.

"I'm fine." I turned over and scooted back against the headboard.

She sat next to me. The mattress dipped toward her, causing me to readjust my back. The scratch marks didn't hurt as bad.

"I heard that a boy in your grade was in the hospital. Do you know him?"

Searching the corners of my brain for any rumors, I shook my head—not having a clue who she referred to.

"Detective Granger's son. Lakey or something," she answered, guessing the pronunciation.

My head pounded with fear. "Not Lakey," I corrected. "Lachlan. And what do you mean he was in the hospital. Which one? How?" I spoke so fast, my words rushed together.

She glanced up, tapping her lip as if remembering. "That's right, Lachlan."

I waved my hand in front of her face. "Mom. What happened?" I needed to know. Was this the male who the psychic had a connection with? Was he dead?

Mom brushed a piece of hair away from her face. "Well, something about a fight. Nothing serious, he was released this morning. I only know because a lady from the Club is friends with Lakey's mom."

You mean his stepmom, I corrected her in my head. My muscles relaxed, Lachlan was alive.

What if whoever killed Magnolia tried coming after Lachlan?

Fear burned through me. There was only one person left who could provide insight into what was happening to me. At least I hoped he could—my grandpa. Had he ever seen ghosts too? Was that why he was in the *place* he was at? I'd call Lachlan when I was on the road. Make sure he's okay.

"Mom, do you mind?" I pointed at my backpack. "I need to study at the library. I may be gone for a couple of hours."

She squinted. "What class?"

Without flinching, I replied, "World History."

She rubbed my shoulder. "Sonora. Do you know him?"

"Who?"

"Lakey."

"You mean Lachlan."

Her posture straightened. "Do you know him?"

I shook my head, not knowing why it mattered. "Maybe. We spoke a few times." I reached for my keys.

"When will you be back?" she asked, standing up from my bed.

"Not sure. But if I don't go, my grade will tank." The urge to visit Pawpaw overwhelmed the deep-seated fear I had of the psychiatric hospital. What if I visited him and someone overheard that I saw ghosts? What if I was committed too?

Cold fingers grabbed my arm. I flinched, thinking it was Magnolia. "I don't believe you. Tell me the truth. Where are you going?" Mom asked, pausing. Her fingers relaxed on my arm in the same place that Crazy Janice held an hour before.

I yanked from her grasp. "The library."

"I don't believe you. Sonora, if you don't talk to me, I can't help you."

"Mom, please trust me. There's nothing I'm hiding from you." She never seemed to care before, why would she care now? "I'm leaving, I'll be back soon."

Before she could question me about anything or anyone else, I grabbed the keys from my dresser. I was suddenly desperate to see Pawpaw.

Her voice sharpened and became more serious. "Sonora, you can't drive when you're like this."

I turned. "Like what?" I spat, annoyed. Where was this anger coming from? This was too much for me to handle.

She flicked her finger at me. "Like this. Like … like when … You know what I mean."

I flung my keys to the corner of my room, hoping she'd leave. "Fine! I won't go anywhere."

Presumably stunned at my outburst, she inched around me and closed the door. I locked it immediately.

With my skin on fire and my blood pulsing through my veins, I grabbed the edge of my wicker dresser and squeezed. Tiny pops from the wicker sounded beneath each finger. I wanted to hit something. I wanted to throw something at the mirror. My life was spiraling, and everything I had done to bring it back into alignment had failed.

"Granger is dirt," a familiar voice echoed from behind.

Whipping my eyes up to the mirror, Rosa stood behind my shoulder. "How did you—"

With a peppy smile, she jumped on my bed. "Like I said, Granger is dirt." She smacked her gum, her vibrant yellow gum.

My fingers released the wicker dresser, and I slowly turned around. Glancing at my door, the tiny knob remained locked. "How did you get in here? Where did you go at lunch?"

I made my way to the bed, cautiously sitting next to her.

Something was wrong, terribly wrong.

The sensation of puke slithered up my throat.

She shook her head and a laugh escaped. "Sonora." My name spilled from her lips in a belittling way. "You know that you're nothing without me, right?"

Taken off-guard, I recoiled. I had suspected how she thought of me every once in a while, but to hear it aloud was completely different. Why now? Where was this coming from? "I'm nothing?"

My fists shook beside my thighs.

She smiled and leaned back on her elbows. "Sonora. You're nothing, a zero, and nobody even likes you."

"What?" I shook my head. "Why are you being so cruel?"

"Do you ever wonder why nobody sits by you at lunch, except for your wimpy little friends, Cooper and Angelica?"

"It's Angela," I corrected. A smile widened on her face.

With a flip of her hand, she rolled over on her belly. She crossed her legs in the air, not a care in the world— except for suddenly letting me know how little she thought of me.

"Rosa, get out."

"I'm not going anywhere." She grinned. Her face twisted evilly and her eyes darkened.

"Fine. I don't care."

Fuming, I snatched my keys and phone off the carpet and stormed out of the room before Mom had a chance to stop me. I ran to my car and slammed the door.

Mom came running out the garage door, but I floored it, backing out of the driveway fast. She waved her hands for me to come back. I pulled out my phone and searched for the address of St. Joseph Psychiatric Hospital.

μ

Thirty minutes later, I rolled into the parking lot of the hospital. I called Lachlan three times, but he didn't answer. My phone rang. I flipped it over, hoping it was him. It was Mom. I texted *I'm fine* so she'd stop worrying. My phone rang again, and I turned the ringer off.

I scanned the two entrances into the hospital. Which wing was he in?

With a heavy sigh, I scurried down the sidewalk, focusing on the entrance to the left. An old man in a hospital gown sat in a wheelchair, smoking a cigarette.

Three other individuals, dressed in casual attire leaned against each other. A bench lined the flowerbeds. The individuals had glassy stares like they'd recently taken their meds.

I shuddered.

A gigantic rotating door centered between two normal doors. I zipped in, spinning the rotating door faster than I should. Inside was a waiting room with rows of windows. A little old woman with wrinkly skin sat to the right behind a glass barrier. With a shaky flat hand, she opened the window.

"Can you tell me what room Ben Stewart is in?"

A name tag hung from her shirt with St. Joseph's labeled across the center in shiny gold lettering. She tapped on the keyboard and grabbed her glasses as she squinted at the screen closer. With a delighted smile, she sat up and clasped her hands. "He's in room 243." She paused. "If you're here to visit, I need to see ID."

I zipped open my purse and handed her my license. She wrote my number down and scanned the computer again. "You're on the list."

"What list?"

"The list of people that's allowed to visit," she replied.

I found that surprising but didn't argue. She pointed at the elevators across the hall located behind a giant door with iron bars.

"That's it?" I asked.

A buzzer sounded, unlocking the door. She motioned for me to enter.

I swallowed and grabbed hold of the handle, opening the door. Was I really prepared to do this? Too late to wonder.

I walked inside. The door closed and the buzzer sounded—locking behind me. A fishy odor floated by.

The smell became stronger. I wanted to run.

I hurried inside the elevator as it opened, rushing past people exiting in white ward attire. With trembling fingers, I tapped the second-floor button. The elevator was slower than cold syrup on frozen pancakes. My mind reeled with the possibilities. What if I got trapped inside the psychiatric hospital? What if I could never leave? I tapped my foot against the floor, hugging myself tightly.

As soon as the doors started to slide open, I stuck my hands between them. Pushing outward, I tried to make them hurry open, my heart racing.

I passed a room on the right. Inside were tables where patients played cards.

At the end of the first hallway, a burgundy plate glued to the wall listed the room numbers 200-220.

The dank odor remained next to me, I couldn't get rid of it. I hurried forward hoping to lose Mags along the way.

The next hall on my right listed numbers 220-240. Almost there.

At the sight of two security guards, I halted.

They stopped their conversation and turned toward me. I looked down at my clothes, my civilian clothes. I wasn't a patient. They had to have known that, right? Their eyeballs meta-morphed into giant, beady alien-size eyeballs.

I squeezed my eyes shut and growled under my breath. "Sonora, get a grip on yourself!"

When I opened my eyes, the guards had gone back to chatting, not caring that I stood there. I belonged in this place. I was bound to end up here.

The slimy aroma grew stronger.

"Magnolia?" I whispered.

I inhaled and exhaled slowly, coaxing my fidgety body to calm. *I'm an ordinary person visiting an ordinary patient.* "People do this all the time," I whispered.

I tiptoed forward and located room 243.

The door to his room was closed.

Do I knock? Or do I walk in? I didn't want to dawdle outside for too long.

With a heavy hand, I squeezed the cold handle and thrust the bulky door open. Cold air from inside wafted over my arms. I shivered.

Was he alone, or did he have a roommate?

Listening for voices from inside, I let the door close by itself. A small hallway blocked my view into his room. A bathroom was on my left.

I tiptoed, not hearing anyone. It was silent.

"Pawpaw?" The word felt odd on my lips. I hadn't spoken to him in a year. Was he here?

The foot of his bed came into view first, white hospital blankets draped over the edges. When I rounded the corner, there he was. His eyes were closed, and he had a gash across his saggy cheek and big nose. My back stiffened. The wound had been sewn with stitches. A thick gray beard covered half his face. The hairs in his mustache stained a permanent shade of caramel. If not for the gashes, he appeared normal. "What happened to you?" I thought out loud.

His chest rose as he slept.

One burgundy chair with wooden arms had been positioned diagonally next to his bed. I sunk into the chair.

His face was peaceful. I didn't want to wake him, but I *had* to.

"I don't have much time," I whispered. "Can you please help me?"

I swallowed.

His eyes didn't budge.

I placed my hand on his frail shoulder and shook it.

THIRTY-TWO

His eyes opened. I'd nearly forgotten how blue they were. The moment he saw me, a smile spread across his face, his teeth withered with gaps.

"Hi." I paused. "Do you remember me? I'm—"

"My granddaughter." He coughed, clearing his voice. "Of course I remember you."

His voice sounded as frail as his body.

He sat up, sliding his legs from underneath the white covers and swinging them over the bed. Wearing a striped pajama gown, he grabbed his glasses off the side table and placed them on.

"You're bigger. Guess that's what happens when I live my days in a crazy home."

I flinched at the word. "You're not *crazy*, Pawpaw." Aged spots dotted the corners of his forehead.

He laughed. "It's a joke. Indeed I'm not."

I relaxed—a little.

"Is it my birthday? What's today's date?"

I grinned. "October 25th."

"Nope. Not my birthday. What brings you?" He leaned closer. "Surely, your father doesn't know you're here." He chuckled and coughed again. His breath smelled sweet and bitter, like puppy breath.

I shook my head. "You know my parents. They definitely don't." I looked around the room once more for Magnolia but didn't find her. "I *needed* to see you."

He inhaled deeply, struggling for air. "That glass of water." He pointed at the white Styrofoam cup that had been sitting next to his glasses and a framed picture of Mawmaw.

"Pawpaw." I handed him the cup. "What happened to your face?"

He sipped.

"My face?" he asked, his eyes absent of answers. "Oh, these." He motioned toward his cheek. "I tripped. Nothing I can't handle, I'm fine now."

I swallowed. He didn't look fine. "I have to ask you something." I paused. Unsure if I could continue. Speaking aloud about Magnolia, for the second time, made everything too real. Not only that, but I wasn't sure who Rosa was. Was she a ghost?

My best friend disappeared and reappeared like magic—Rosa. She had been in my room without ever entering the door. I'd known her for a long while, she was my friend. Wasn't she? None of it made any sense.

I thought back, trying to remember if I'd ever seen Cooper or Chris talk to her—like actually talk to her. Every time we'd hung out as a group, did they ever acknowledge her?

With a little more resolve, not much, but enough to inch my courage odometer forward, I asked, "Pawpaw, why are you in this place?"

He smiled warmly and handed me the white cup back. "Here?" He gestured to the room. "The crazy home?"

There was that word again. Now more than ever, I didn't want to hear it, because I may be c—y myself.

"Yes." I nodded. "What happened?"

I placed his cup on the table.

He gripped the side of his bed, either out of comfort or for support. "When your Mawmaw died, I was in a rough place. She always made sure I took my medication.

The pills, they're important, you know?" His eyes glazed over and he stopped speaking.

"Pawpaw?"

He coughed, coming back to the conversation. "But after her death, I didn't want to live anymore. I stopped taking my meds on purpose at first," he blinked a few times before continuing. "Your dad may have told you I wasn't returning calls, wouldn't answer the door. I don't remember much of those weeks. I had a manic episode, a bad one."

My dad had never mentioned specific details about his father, or what exactly led to putting him in this place. It was a closed subject. I never understood why my parents didn't invite him to live with us. I mean, why put him here? No matter how bad their relationship had been, Pawpaw was still his father.

"Is that why they admitted you, because you tried to"—I was terrified to say the words—"*kill yourself?*"

"Your dad didn't put me in here." He coughed. "I did."

My mouth dropped. "W—what?"

"It's for the best. And honestly, I quite like it. They give me meds when I need them, and I don't have to live alone. I hate being alone. I never want to be alone again." He stared off into the distance.

I turned behind to see what he stared at. Was he looking at Magnolia, could he see her too? Was she here? Or …

"Pawpaw, do you see Mawmaw's ghost?" With the word *ghost*, the smell of Magnolia thickened.

He began laughing and coughing. "No, but I wish I could."

Was that an admission to having seen Mawmaw at one time or another? "Have you ever seen her ghost?"

He tugged his ear and narrowed his eyes. "If I ever saw her, I'd consider myself lucky, like she was a beautiful guardian angel watching over me." His knobby fingers squeezed my hand.

"Have you ever seen ghosts before?"

"Why are you asking about ghosts?" He coughed.

"Because I've seen a few myself. I need to know if I'm *not in my right mind*, if it's a genetically related curse?" Am I normal?

Pawpaw cleared his throat and exhaled a shaky breath. His thick brown eyebrows scrunched together. He replied, "Once. But it was a long time ago."

I covered my mouth, surprised by his response. My legs buckled from relief.

His bony fingers released my hand.

"How? Who was he, or her?"

He cleared his throat again. "I don't like talking about it."

I grabbed his brittle hand and warmed it between mine. "I *need* to know."

"Your parents wouldn't like me planting ideas in your head. The kind of ideas, memories a person doesn't share …"

A painful lump rose in my throat, I was mentally tired of the charade. All I wanted was help.

"But since you're the only one to visit me, I'll share it this once with you."

Warm tingles filled my limbs, I was finally about to find out the answer to all of this.

"For a month after WWII ended, the spirit of a fellow soldier followed me everywhere."

"Soldier? Why?"

He nodded. "It was a buddy of mine, someone that was caught in friendly fire, from my own Johnson rifle."

"Were you responsible for his death?" My grandpa had killed someone?

"His and enemies', but he was my friend." He cried silently and his fingers trembled in my hands.

"How did you get him to stop haunting you?"

"I didn't. One day, he just stopped."

My shoulders sank, unsure of what to make of his confession. At least I wasn't completely insane. Pawpaw had been haunted once, and now the same thing was happening to me.

He removed his hand from mine and cleared his throat once more. "You're afraid of ending up like me."

That's not what I was afraid of. Okay, it was. I wouldn't find living here as luxurious as he did. Maybe that makes me a bad person for thinking so, but I can't end up in a place like this. I had a future, I want to go to college, have a boyfriend. Date … Lachlan. But lest I forget, Magnolia might never leave me alone.

My hands dropped to my sides.

"Mental illness isn't something to be afraid of. Under the right medication, my life is as ordinary as yours or anyone else's."

I didn't want to talk about mental illness. That wasn't why I was here. Or was it? He leaned away and lay back down. His eyes focused on the white popcorn ceiling above.

One thing's for sure, Magnolia *had* to be real. Kaylee reacted to her when she was near, that wasn't in my head. Mom, my therapist, Lachlan, they all smelled her disgusting fish odor. That was a fact. Pawpaw accidentally killed his friend.

But me, what had I done to Magnolia? Had I accidentally killed her somehow? No. I would've remembered something like that. Right?

"Why are you haunting me, Mags?" I muttered, running my fingers through my hair and squeezing my head.

"You know why." A girl's voice echoed from over my shoulder.

I tensed, knowing who the voice belonged to—Rosa. I turned around. She loitered in the shadowy corner, picking at her mustard colored nails.

There was no way that she was a ghost, she wasn't opaque like Magnolia. And she didn't look dead. She was Rosa—she was alive. But how did she enter the room without being heard? Was she on the list? Did she have access?

"How did you get in here?" I asked, unafraid.

She winked at me. "Sonora, you know how I got in here. Because of you." Her head dipped to the side, and she rolled her eyes.

My heartbeat thrashed in my ears. My body quivered. I shook my head, blinking rapidly. "What do you mean? I didn't let you in." I rushed to the window, searching the hundreds of vehicles for her car.

"*What* are you doing?" Pawpaw asked.

Rosa's car hadn't been at school. "Where's your car? Where were you today?" I asked, hyperventilating.

"Who are you talking to?" Pawpaw's voice muffled in the distance, as if I was underwater, suffocating from terror. "I don't have a car. I haven't driven in years," his distant voice added.

I grabbed my chest. I couldn't breathe.

My eyes slid over to Rosa, studying her.

I inched closer, she didn't move. My fingers trembled as I reached for her hand, I needed to touch her.

Snatching her wrist, I yanked her over to Pawpaw. "This is Rosa. Do you see her?"

He squinted, looking in the direction I motioned. "I don't see anyone."

I dropped Rosa's wrists, and my arms shook as I backed away from her.

"Remember, Sonora," she said.

"Remember what?"

"*Remember!*"

The room tilted. My gaze clouded as I searched the corners of my mind, rummaging for clarity, dizzy.

Spotting a small trashcan in Pawpaw's room, I ran over and puked.

Footsteps approached from behind. "Sonora," Rosa said. "You can't do this alone. That's why I'm here. You need to *remember.*"

I shrugged away from her.

"Do what alone?" I stuttered, wiping my mouth with the back of my hand.

She sighed.

I blinked faster.

My eyes widened, not knowing what she was talking about, not *wanting* to know. I didn't want to know. I wanted my normal life back. I turned and yelled. "Go away!"

Not missing a beat—not gasping in horror—she answered. "I'm afraid I can't do that. You see, I'm *you*. You and I are the same."

My eyes danced around the room. My body tingled with uncertainty. She was crazy. Rosa had officially chewed too much gum, and the chemicals had gone to her brain.

"That's not possible. What you're saying is insane. You're not me." I shook my head.

At any moment, my heart felt like it might fly from my body.

She laughed and rolled her eyes. Rosa walked over and sat on the bed—next to Pawpaw. He seemed freaked out by my reaction of talking to an invisible person. *I* had scared *him*.

She patted his lumpy leg closest to her and winked back at me.

"Did you feel that?" I asked him.

"Feel what?" His eyes were as wide as mine.

Not wanting to argue with her in front of him, I simply asked her, "Why?"

She jumped up with giddiness. "Good, I can see you're coming around. Actually, I can *feel* it." She paused.

"For the same reason you *killed* Magnolia—self-preservation. You would've died too if you hadn't released her."

Breath shot from my lungs. I fell backward, my back slammed against the wall. My fingernails clawed the paint as I tried to steady myself.

"I killed Magnolia?" My voice rose.

She shushed me with a wave of her hand and shook her head. "As I've been trying to tell you, *we* did. When your brother died, it sent you into a tailspin of sorts. You lost your high-school grip with reality. You were all gloomy, like *all* the time." Her lips pouted. "Depressed. If it hadn't been for me, you wouldn't have lasted this long."

I wanted to run out the doors, scream to the cops that a murderer was in the room. But the murderer was me. I'd be alerting them to me! This couldn't be happening.

"My brother's not dead," I spat. I pulled my phone from my pocket and frantically dialed his number. It rang and rang and rang until his voicemail picked up. Instead of allowing me to leave a message—one that I was in desperate need to leave—a robotic voice answered stating it was full!

"That doesn't prove anything. His phone still works. Bram's alive. I would know if my own brother died." I paused. "Wait, did you kill him too?"

"Bram *is* dead," Pawpaw croaked.

"What?" I replied, not wanting to believe him. The word *dead* felt like a million stabs to my heart.

She rolled her eyes and popped a bright yellow bubble between her teeth. "I would never hurt our family. That's why I came to your rescue in the first place. I'll prove it. Type your brother's name into the search engine, see what appears."

My phone glitched, an overwhelming pain shot to the center of my soul.

Behind the bed, on the opposite end, Magnolia's ghost flashed into view.

Pawpaw waved a veiny hand in front of his nose. "What's that smell?"

Luckily, my phone continued working. I typed my brother's name. Within seconds, multiple articles opened. *Bram Stewart was tragically killed when a distracted driver ran a red light, hitting multiple cars.* The article continued with more details of the accident. It was the same accident that had killed Magnolia's mom.

"No," I sucked in a breath. The date of the article was January 1st—from the *current* year. A tidal wave of panic knocked the life out of me. My legs went numb. I crumbled to the ground.

"This can't be true," I murmured.

I pressed the back button.

The next article was an obituary, stating who my brother had been survived by: *Mr. and Mrs. Stewart, and his sister, Sonora.*

Thick tears swelled, tumbling down my cheeks. "But—but—how?" I stuttered.

Had my brother died in the car wreck? Was he the young male soul the psychic had told me about? And Rosa, was she the darkness I needed to pluck?

"You went to his funeral," Rosa said.

My head shot up. "I didn't!" I said. "I would remember that!"

"No, you pretend that you didn't, to deal with the pain of losing him." Rosa glanced over her shoulder nonchalantly at Magnolia's grotesque ghostly form. "Seeing Magnolia is an unfortunate side effect of killing her, I guess. I mean, our brain has been whacked since your brother died."

"You can see her?" I inhaled, horrified.

She scrunched her shoulders. "I already explained. I. Am. You."

"But …" I mumbled, not wanting to believe her.

"This will be easier if you can accept what you did or let me take over. This going back-and-forth thing, allowing me to take over only some of the time, isn't working for me."

Without waiting another minute, I rushed past Pawpaw, out of the room. Away from Rosa.

Running to the elevator and exiting the hospital's doors was a blur as I raced to my car, stumbling every few feet.

A guy in a wheelchair gaped as I flew past.

I stumbled down the sidewalk, tripping and scratching my palms.

Reaching my car, I yanked the door open.

The outside noise expanded. I couldn't catch my breath. The sound of mufflers and tires amplified, the sounds of crickets scraped my eardrums, everything was too loud. I needed to get away!

I grabbed the wheel, digging my nails into the leather. *Sonora, you can do this. Rosa is insane. She's not you. I'm not her. This is all a big mistake.*

My wheezing slowed to a pant. It had to be. It had to be.

I clenched my eyelids shut, trying to stop the stinging. My eyes hurt when I closed them, and they hurt when I opened them.

One by one, I opened each lid.

Turning the rearview mirror toward me, I checked my face and my bloodshot eyes.

What was I supposed to do? I whipped my head about, searching for Magnolia or Rosa, making sure neither of them was in my back seat. Was Magnolia aware of Rosa? How could Rosa see Magnolia? She never mentioned that she could before. Did my ghosts have conversations about me?

The sun was setting. The tip of it lay over the horizon, coloring the sky brilliant shades of pink and orange.

I drove out of the lot and turned on Main Street, not wanting to go home yet. Curly Coffee Creamery. Yes. Exactly what I needed. Magnolia and I loved to go to that coffee shop. They had the best pumpkin spice lattes during the holidays, and it was quiet. A place to decompress. I *really* needed to decompress.

Arriving, dozens of cars sat in the lot as I climbed out of the Taurus. The back of my shirt was damp from stress, my neck clammy.

THIRTY-THREE

A little bell atop the door rang upon entry into the coffee shop.

"Welcome to Curly's," a college-age guy said from behind the counter. His green apron made me think back to the car that had been parked in Rosa's spot at school. Fear prickled down my spine. I scanned the room. The shop was semi-full with patrons chatting, other people with laptops.

Hesitantly, I smiled and approached the counter.

"Can I have a pumpkin spice latte, *please*?" I asked, not seeing it available on the menu yet.

He entered my order without dispute. I suspected the employee noticed my terrible eyes and puffy face and felt sorry for me.

Stools lined the counter, and a television hung on the wall above a variety of coffee syrups. The news displayed on the screen with the caption scrolling across. I was tired of seeing the news. NO more news.

I took a seat and the pressure in my neck loosened.

The stool was well-oiled, and my body spun to the right. I locked my feet on a tarnished pole lining the bottom of the counter to stop from spinning. Plopping my arms in front, I rested my head and stared at the entrance. Moonlight gleamed through the windows. I closed my eyes as soft music strummed in the background.

After a few moments, a blanket of normalcy covered me.

A bell sounded, and my eyes shot open.

"Sonora," the boy behind the counter called. Spotting a small silver bell next to his hand, I was relieved. My order was ready.

I relaxed and sipped my steamy coffee. My gaze flittered back and forth from the large mirror on the wall to the TV displayed above. Minutes passed, turning to an hour. It was ten o'clock.

My phone beeped with messages from my mom, but I didn't read them and turned my phone over. I didn't want to hear or read anything from Mom right now. After three more beeps, I turned my phone off, wishing to disconnect completely.

"Do you want another?" the employee asked.

"Probably shouldn't." More caffeine would only heighten my nerves. "Could I have water?"

He nodded and returned five seconds later, placing a plastic cup filled with water in front of me.

One of the reasons Magnolia and I liked Curly's was its atmosphere that meshed a bar with a coffee shop. We were sophisticated, wannabe college girls when we came here—before her life spiraled out of control.

Before my life spiraled out of control, too.

Holding down the button, I turned my phone back on, finally ready to face reality—sort of.

I opened up the browsers. My brother's obituary loomed. How could this have happened? How could I not remember that he had died? I gritted my teeth through the pain of losing him, searching for small details of his funeral.

My eyes widened. I remembered something—an image of his portrait beside a closed casket. I shoved the water away. Goosebumps sprinkled my arms, enveloping my whole body. I lowered my face, unable to stop the silent tears that rolled off my cheeks onto my legs. Sniffling, I raised my chin, wishing to think of something else. Anything else.

The caption of breaking news caught my attention. A news alert flashed on the television screen. The face of the girl who had helped me that night. The alert was about her.

Wide-eyed and frightened, I read the caption rolling across the bottom of the screen. The girl's body had been discovered in a creek—a different creek than the one Magnolia had been found in.

Trembling, I sipped the ice water, letting it slither down my throat, coating my stomach with ice.

The Creekside Killer's latest victim before capture, read the caption. Then a picture of Angela's dad popped on the screen. *Coach Wilson, Creekside Killer.* My eyes widened. *He* was the killer? Angela seemed normal at school, she mustn't have known yet. Oh, my Gawd! Now I remembered where I'd seen the ribbon around the dead girl's necks. Angela's family's wreath on their door! Their fall decorations! A ribbon had been tied in a bow around the side, exactly like the one in the photos.

"What do you think happened?" a familiar voice sounded next to me.

Swallowing dread, I turned. Rosa sat on the stool beside me. Our legs touched.

She smiled. I didn't.

My face remained expressionless—frozen.

My heart raced. I averted my attention to the employee behind the counter. "Excuse me?" I waved him over. "Is there a girl sitting next to me?"

He rubbed his chin, seemingly confused. He took a step back and shook his head before walking away. Behind him, in the mirror, was Rosa's reflection—a toothy smile, popping her lemony gum. She grinned back.

"You're really me, aren't you?" I asked in a low, defeated voice.

She nodded once.

My gaze rose from our reflection, up to the news coverage. The girl had been found strangled and stabbed. The Creekside Killer—Mr. Wilson, head coach of the college basketball team—confessed to killing her. The manner of death exactly the same as the other girls—unlike Magnolia's.

I couldn't deny it any longer. Somehow, I had killed Magnolia, and somehow, I had blocked the memory of doing so—just like I'd blocked Bram's death. The realization of whom I was, what I had done, broke me. With Rosa floating around in my head. I couldn't cry anymore.

My fingers gripped the cold plastic cup. Water and ice spilled over the edge, seeping between my fingers. I released it and raised it to my lips, gulping what was left.

I didn't want to think anymore.

I didn't want to be alive anymore.

"Why—" I asked Rosa. If she was me, she'd know what I was referring to. No need to finish the sentence. In fact, no reason to speak aloud. All those times, hiding certain facts while we sat in my room, she already knew what I was thinking—what I was hiding.

Rosa began. "Magnolia had to die. But it was an accident. She called, wanting to meet up that night at the bridge."

I knew what bridge she meant. It was the same bridge Mags and I sat on numerous times growing up. We'd dangle our legs over the edge, talk about boys—talk about Chris and Cooper. The four of us, the perfect duo couple. That's where we came up with our name: The Royal Flushes.

Rosa continued. "She had something to confess." Rosa's voice darkened. "In a desperate attempt to get back at you for being a *dreadful* friend, Mags slept with Chris. She gave excuses, apologizing over and over and over again—" Rosa swirled her finger in the air while saying 'over'—"but you pushed her. You didn't mean for her to die. She tripped and fell, and you grabbed her hand before she went completely over the edge. As she dangled hundreds of feet above the river, your grip slipped. You were being pulled over too. We didn't have a choice, you, I *had* to let her go."

My lips felt puffy like they'd been numbed with Novocain. Her words, words that nobody else could hear, sank in. I was in a Sonora tunnel caving in on itself.

I had created my own nightmare—I had created Rosa. And now I remembered. "I needed you because I couldn't handle having my brother dead." Every time I was near Magnolia, it only reminded me of him. My body had felt like it was ripped in half at the thought of never talking to him again. The agonizing ache wouldn't leave, and I had retreated from my own life. And then I killed Magnolia ...

A satisfied smile spread across her face, as she nodded with a high chin. "The first time I met you was a month after the crash—a month after Bram's death," she said.

"I was depressed." Though, I had never named it that—*depression*. "I couldn't handle the overwhelming void his death left." It was like I had turned inside out, every piece of me exposed. Every little detail of my life scraped away, stripping happiness from my already too damaged soul. I'd tried to hang on, but the broken threads that had held me together stretched too thin and snapped.

And then I had begun hearing a voice, *crazy* thoughts.

"You wanted to kill yourself," she added.

I had been in my bathroom, about to end it all. "That day, I was going to cross the planes of existence and finally be with him, *my* brother." I was desperate to end the hurt. I couldn't take it. The pressure had consumed my thoughts every minute when I was awake. When I was asleep, I dreamed of him, only to wake up and realize *again* that he was never coming back. For God sake, his casket was closed due to his body being smashed beyond recognition. "I didn't even have the chance to hold his hand or see his face one last time. Magnolia—"

"It had to be done. You would've died too. It's basic survival instinct," Rosa said.

"But I didn't even call the police, call for help. I could've saved her," I said.

"You and I both know that's not true. The moment she slammed into the water, she was dead. Plus, it was night"— Rosa paused, maybe for dramatic effect, maybe not—"and your reputation would've been ruined. You would've always been known as the girl who murdered her best friend."

"But it was an accident!" I screamed. The guy behind the counter dropped a cup and looked at me. "What do you want?" I asked her, lowering my voice.

"I've taken over here and there when you needed me, and you need me now. Let me take over."

Is that why I couldn't remember coming home from the rave? Was Rosa the one who'd written on my mirror with lipstick?

Rosa nodded.

The picture of the girl's face on the news enlarged, encompassing the whole screen. My head ached. I wanted everything to stop.

"You have to give me permission, full permission. I need to know that I'll be you, full-time," she said.

I swallowed, not knowing whether I could handle being the one who murdered Magnolia. But maybe if I went to the cops, they'd believe it was an accident. But what if they didn't? All I wanted was to be a normal girl, with normal worries. I needed Lachlan now more than ever. But Rosa was all I had. "I'm yours," I mumbled.

Like a demon needing my acceptance, Rosa stood from her seat.

She grabbed my hand. Instantly, her existence slithered into mine.

Our reflection molded into one in the mirror.

I still looked like me. I *was* me. But Rosa was in control now.

For the first time, I willingly remained in the far reaches of my mind. I watched and felt myself—Rosa—asking for another cup of coffee. My life was like a movie, and I was in my safe confines, protected from the outside world, no longer hurting.

I can handle it from here. Don't worry, Sonora. I'll take care of you. Her thoughts were my thoughts.

With a flick of my hand, the employee sauntered over. I smiled and took out a piece of yellow gum from my purse. I handed him ten bucks and smacked my gum. "Keep the change."

With my shoulders back and my chin held high, I tossed the door open. The tiny bell rang—an angel got its wings. I laughed. The cool night air brushed my cheeks, and I breathed in a new beginning as I walked out to my car. Exciting plans were ahead.

THIRTY-FOUR

Friday afternoon. First stop—car wash. My car needed to glisten with perfection. Sonora didn't budge inside me, not even a little. She was weak and better off stored safely in a box.

Opening my car door with enthusiasm, I plopped my purse on the passenger seat.

With Sonora's reluctance to come back, it made it easier for me to stay. From here on out, *I* would be known as Sonora.

Fall Fling was tomorrow and the annual Fling football game tonight; I had a few last minute details to arrange.

I grabbed my phone. I had missed a few calls from Lachlan. I scrolled past the notifications and texted Chris, letting him know that we'd be going to the dance together. I knew he didn't have a date. *Fall Fling. You're with me.*

Rainbow suds twirled on my windows, and my car robotically moved forward on the wash's track. The soapy smell wafted through the vents. I breathed in the wicked scent with pure happiness.

Moments later, my phone beeped. *Okay, pick you up at 5.*

I shrieked with excitement. This would be fun, in an awful kind of way—fun for me, not for Chris. He had slept with my best friend, and *he* was the reason Magnolia had died. If he hadn't been a cheating sex-fiend, she'd still be alive.

μ

In my room, I decided to go all out for the game. I leaned forward, closer to my mirror. Sporting school colors, I dabbed some paint on my cheeks and added green glittery detail for fun.

I smoothed on some lipstick and mascara and pulled my hair up into a high ponytail. My shorts were ironed, and my top angled off my shoulders just right. Not in a whorey kind of way, but one that demanded attention and respect. Looking in the mirror with poised shoulders and perfect hair, I annoyingly reminded myself of my mom. I didn't like her, she was weak. Like Sonora.

Sonora stirred in protest.

"You are going to have fun tonight," I said to Sonora in my reflection.

A stabbing sensation rended my gut. I screamed and grabbed my dresser for support, staring in the mirror. "Settle down," I warned her. "You invited me in, and I'm staying."

A knock jolted my door. "Sonora?" Mom asked from the other side. My hands fell to my sides. To my relief, the pain dissipated.

"Yes, Mom," I panted.

"I thought I heard yelling." Her voice sounded shaky, questionable, and now wasn't the time to tell the truth. There would never be a time for that.

She jiggled the doorknob, but I had locked it. After a few quick breaths to calm myself, I leaned over, letting her in. I scowled and crossed my arms. "You did?"

She peered around the room.

A fake laugh vibrated from my lips. "Oh. Must've been my new ringtone." I motioned toward the phone on my dresser.

Not wanting to give her time to ponder, I said, "Really need to finish getting ready. The game starts in thirty minutes." *Leave, Mom.*

"Okay dear. But after yesterday, you had us worried." The tone of her voice meant she wasn't completely buying my story.

"I'm fine. Really."

With one more glance in my direction, she closed the door.

The weight in my chest lessened. I turned my head left and right, examining my makeup in the mirror, and then grabbed my keys.

I arrived at the game on time, the lot was already half full. I parked next to a sparkly red Mustang, figuring if I parked next to an amazing car, mine was less likely to get dinged. I angled the rearview mirror down and pursed my lips—like old times. Trying to hide the essence of Sonora that clung beneath my skin, I stepped out and headed toward the ticket line.

After paying the cashier, I moseyed underneath the bleachers to the student section. The band's drums and trumpets thundered all over the stadium as the game began. A football glided through the air to the quarterback—Chris.

I spotted Cooper in the stands. I was surprised he made an appearance, knowing that Angela's dad was the Creekside Killer. I shot my hand up at him, waving myself over.

As I climbed the bleachers, cheerleaders took formation for a new cheer. *Thank God I didn't have to be a stupid cheerleader anymore.* They're too friendly and rule-oriented for my taste.

Up the center of the walkway, I scooched in front of a row of people and finally made my way to Cooper. He threw his hands around his mouth and booed. I turned around. A player on our team strutted off the field, away from the referee.

"What did he do?" I'd missed whatever had happened.

"Chris grabbed 42's facemask—he got a penalty."

He leaned over. "How are you feeling?" he asked me.

"I'm fine, thanks for your concern. Where's Angela?" For once, I was curious about Angela. What does the daughter of a serial killer do on a Friday night? In a small town, *everyone* came to a football game.

He scratched his jaw. "The police station. Do you really think he killed all those girls?"

I nodded. *Except one.*

The football players moved back into position. I hollered into the air for our team, trying to get in the spirit more, but I was only here to *make good* with the group. I needed Chris and Cooper on my side in order for my plans to frame Chris to succeed. Without Cooper's approval, Chris might not attend the dance with me.

Forward to my left, I spotted the back of Lachlan's head. I'd know his wavy hair anywhere, and he was dreamy. It was as if I could smell his sweet body from all the way up here.

For the next hour, I found it hard to focus on the game and not on Lachlan. He wasn't even doing anything out of the ordinary, except for looking at me a few times. He faced the game as if interested and clapped when we made our first touchdown. Then he glanced back at me and crossed his arms dramatically, appearing bored.

I giggled. Seeing the art in his room clearly showed there were two sides to him. I wondered how much of him I didn't know about yet. Would he help me frame Chris for Magnolia's murder?

The air in my lungs became icy, and my chest constricted. I prepared myself for the visions, squeezing my fists. Magnolia was as strong as ever.

Seconds later, visions hadn't come, but my chest still felt tight. I opened my eyes.

Down below, Lachlan turned around. I averted my gaze that had lingered on him by default. Then suddenly, a profile of a girl that looked exactly like Magnolia—when she was alive—stepped down the bleachers and exited the stairs.

I jumped from my seat and dashed down the metal aisle. My steps made loud hollow thumps that scattered into the chaotic noise of the game. "Hey, where you going?" Cooper yelled from behind. Darting around the bottom row of people, I rushed down the stairs to find her.

Pushing through the spirited, green-wearing crowd, it was hard to find her. My eyes danced around over the people.

I rushed forward.

Beyond the stadium entrance, I saw her. A green sweater hugged her shoulders, contrasting the color of her long blonde hair. I pushed two kids apart, darting between them toward Mags. She didn't look like a ghost. She looked like a living, breathing girl.

By the time I reached the entrance, I was out of breath and had lost sight of her.

"Where are you?" I asked aloud.

A red-headed boy thumbed his shoulder. "Me?"

"Not *you*, moron."

I darted into the parking lot and saw her again. She climbed into an idling Bronco.

I rushed forward at a speed so fast that I almost lost footing.

The tinted windows were so dark that I couldn't peer inside. Reaching for the handle, I flung the passenger door open.

A girl screamed, jutting back from kissing a boy I didn't know. Blood rushed to my cheeks and I slammed the door closed, backing away. It wasn't Magnolia, but a girl eerily similar to her.

"Sonora?" a male's voice asked, startling me from my embarrassing episode. Why did I think attending the game would be okay? I needed to focus on tomorrow night. Rubbing my neck, I turned around.

Lachlan stood there.

"Oh, h-hey," I stuttered.

"You okay?" he asked. "I called you a lot."

I breathed in. "Yeah. Sorry. I'm fine."

His brows drew together. "I saw you run off. You looked worried."

I lowered my hand and took a step back. "Why do you care?" I needed him on my side, but I also needed the reassurance of how he felt about me.

Licking his lips, he appeared unsure. "Why wouldn't I?"

I licked my lips too and stepped toward him.

"I haven't heard from you since the Stump," he said.

I shook my head, angry at Sonora for not noticing Lachlan years sooner. He was nice. Beneath his hard exterior, he didn't care what others thought about him.

"Yeah. Sorry about that. I just, just needed to think," I replied.

His eyes drifted to the Bronco beside me. A massive guy stepped out of the driver's side. He had broad shoulders as if he'd been born with football pads. He was muscular and looked able to pummel anyone in his path. Coiled around his left forearm was a faded tattoo of a rattlesnake.

His eyes danced over to Lachlan's Venetian red shirt. The dude was an agitated bull in a Toro arena. Shit.

"Look, Gigantism. I thought I knew the girl in your car. My mistake," I said, rolling my eyes and waving him back into his vehicle.

"Run," Lachlan spurted.

I heard my feet hit the pavement before I realized I was running. Behind me, Lachlan followed, dashing beneath the grasp of Bull-man. "Where are we running?" I shouted over my shoulder.

"Anywhere!" Lachlan laughed. Did he find this amusing? His hair flapped against his head. I sprinted with everything I had.

Darting in and around vehicles as if dodging bullets, we finally made it back to the entrance. A cop patrolling the area eyed us suspiciously.

Bull-man's face peeked above a row of parked cars.

Lachlan and I leaned on the chain fence, gasping for air. Facing the stars, he panted in and out.

He leaned over, hands on his knees. He grinned up at me. "You sure know how to piss someone off."

I shook my head. "That was a total accident." I laughed. "That was hilarious." I straightened, letting go of the fence. He tied his hair behind his head.

"Lachlan."

He sat up, facing me. His face shined in the moonlight.

"I'm going with Chris to the Fall Fling."

His chin dropped. "Ouch," he said.

"It's not what you think though." I paused, needing to speak before he shut me out completely. "I think he may have had something to do with Magnolia's death."

His focus snapped to mine.

"There's only one way to prove it," I told him.

THIRTY-FIVE

"Sonora, your room is a mess." Mom said, picking up my clothes from the night before.

The doorbell rang. "That's Chris. Need to go." I grabbed my masquerade mask and rushed out of the room. My dress swished against my legs through the doorway.

"I want pictures!" Mom shrieked, following directly behind.

I opened the door. Chris stood on the doorstep, holding a pink corsage. A black limo parked against the curb. He'd gone all out, something I didn't expect.

Mom pushed by. "Come outside!" she motioned for us.

Chris and I moved into the evening light. I sighed. "Let her take her pictures. Commemorate the occasion," he whispered. Chris put his arm around me, and I recoiled before relaxing.

"What's wrong?" he asked.

"Nothing," I smiled. Sonora itched inside me, wanting out. I wouldn't let her change her mind. I had too much control, and I wasn't about to let go. It was her turn to be dormant.

Mom snapped four photos. I raised my hand. "That's enough," I said, a bit forced. Mom lowered the camera, and her forehead pinched together.

"We're going to be late," I said reasonably.

Not allowing her to hug me goodbye, I grabbed Chris's hand and pulled him toward the limo. Mom remained in the yard, staring at us as we climbed inside.

The back seats were full. Everyone inside the limo resembled elaborate sixteenth century guests, as if we were all from a grand Italian masquerade ball—the theme of the Fall Fling. A modern high-school throwback of *Interview with a Vampire*. Except nobody was a vampire, and Pitt and Cruise were absent. If I was one of the characters from the movie, I'd be the curly haired girl with a taste for blood.

Music roared through the speakers. Lights danced around the cabin, reminding me of the silent rave—and Lachlan. Sonora squirmed inside.

My knees rubbed against Chris's.

"Hey," I whispered to him through freshly painted lips. He smiled and grabbed my hand. A part of me cringed, the old dull part of me. But the new part, the vengeful part, wanted to get even.

I released Chris's hand and grabbed his face, leaning in, placing a big fat kiss on his unsuspecting lips. My insides twisted. Sonora fought. I smudged his lips with lipstick before coming up for air. I used my thumb to wipe it off.

All the girls in the car donned their masquerade masks except for me. Cooper's face held a solemn expression.

"C'mon Cooper. Cheer up!" I yelled over the music. Angela and he seemed to be off in their own little world. Angela slumped in the seat, solemn and not speaking much. I was surprised she even came, but it helped take the attention off of me. Everyone in the limo sat farther away from her like she was an unwanted China doll.

Cooper pointed out the window at a tall building in the distance, a spec above a thicket of trees. Angela practically sat on top of him as she peered in the direction that he motioned. I smacked my gum and rolled my eyes, but they didn't notice.

Another loud song chimed on, and the sunroof opened. Wind zipped in, ruffling perfectly coifed hair.

Cooper threaded his arm around Angela's waist, and she rested her head on his shoulder. *Yuck.*

I flipped off my high heels and wiggled my toes.

I stood up and poked my head out the sunroof, inhaling the fresh air. The sun dipped below the horizon. My red hair blew in the wind. Streams of lavender streaked the sky. This was freedom! The feeling I'd craved deep inside Sonora's psyche. After tonight, she'd never be able to clamp down on me again.

Oxygen blazed through my lungs and down my fingertips. I stretched my hands high above, not caring about the state of my hair. I was free. For the first time in a long while, I could be me, do *whatever* I wanted without the constraints. My restrained existence inside Sonora, not ever being seen, had stifled me. But now, everything was different.

Chris stared up at me through the sunroof.

"What are you doing?" he hollered.

Right now, I could kiss whoever I wanted, or not-kiss whoever I wanted. Not give a shit about what others thought. But I needed to wait until the night was over, then Lachlan and I could be together.

In the distance, the Majestic Hotel closed in, signaling me to get ready.

Lowering beneath the roof, my feet wobbled on the unstable cushion and I fell into Chris's lap. He winked. "Hey, baby." A sexy grin spread across his face as he cradled me. "Don't worry, I got you," he said.

"You bet you do."

I wanted to barf.

Sure that Cooper and Angela's eyes were on me, I smacked my lips against his one more time. "Love you," I said, swallowing with repulsion.

My volto mask presented the perfect amount of mystery. Shimmery gold painted the eyes, superimposed on the pearly white face. Unless you already knew what I was wearing, you'd have no idea it was me. I could spy, talk, or nod to whomever I wanted without the need to divulge my identity. I loved the mystery of it all.

My burgundy gown draped over my shoulders in slinky inch-thick straps, and a long slit ran up the side of my leg, exposing my thigh. Convincing Sonora to buy it hadn't been that difficult.

Glancing over, I caught Chris staring at my leg. "Later," I purred as I slipped on my heels and strapped my mask on. Chris's mask featured a funny beak with slanting eyes—a plague mask. Few could pull it off with such flirtatious appeal, but he did. And I despised him for it.

Out the window, we approached the parking lot.

The limo turned right a little too sharply, and I smooshed up against the shoulder of the girl next to me. From Chris's inside pocket, he removed a silver flask with the surname *Jenkins* engraved in the shiny metal. He took a swig.

As he lowered it, I grabbed the flask from his fingers.

The music played.

Pushing my mask up on my forehead, I grinned and took a swig before handing it back to him. He smiled.

The warm sensation of whiskey coated my throat and spread throughout my body. Sonora fluttered inside, sending shivers over my spine. My back jutted up and down as the limo drove over speed bumps. We pulled up to the entrance of the hotel's ballroom. I placed my hands on his cheeks and pressed my lips to his. He tasted of whiskey and lies.

"Another swig?" he asked. He gave it to me, and I gulped.

For a brief moment, I couldn't stop the flood of memories. When Magnolia had called me out of the blue that night—I answered for the first time in a long while. Losing my brother and her mother in the same car crash had meant we were linked. We were a part of a club that I never wished to be a part of—bound by death. If I had never answered my phone that night she wanted to meet, that night she confessed what she'd done with Chris, if I'd ignored her like all the other times, she'd still be alive. After Magnolia died, my soul had floated off course without a lighthouse to shine its way home.

I shook my head, flinging the depressing thoughts away. I was Rosa, and *I* was fine.

I threaded my fingers through Chris's. I longed for Lachlan.

The driver moseyed around the side and opened the doors, lifting his top hat at all of us inside.

Everyone piled out. "Ready?" Chris asked, completely enthused and oblivious, holding his elbow out for me to slide my hand through the nook of his arm.

I smiled sweetly and clenched my teeth. How many other girls had he slept with before Magnolia?

Cooper and Angela moved ahead of the group but stayed within shouting distance. They were far enough to feel like our friendship hung on by a single emotional thread.

Chris and I strutted forward, the golden couple.

From what I could tell, nobody else in the group had acted any different toward me.

Faint echoes of music from inside the hotel floated out the doors as they opened. Tonight would be epic. I didn't need luck, I was prepared. Tonight, I would frame Chris and put him in jail where he belonged. And then I would finally feel better, be free from all this foolish guilt.

The Fall Fling was being held at the same place as the fundraiser to find Magnolia's killer had been held. Tall vases with red roses and pink peonies decorated the edges of the colorful flowerbeds that held pictures of victims weeks before.

The glass doors whisked open, held by chaperones dressed in red vests and black capes. An older man bowed his head—giddy as the rest of us. "Welcome Ladies and Gents," he said, playing his masquerade greeting role well.

"You may acquire food and drinks inside." He flipped his hand gracefully toward the wooden doors, on the other side of the hall.

Dozens of colored lights lit the ballroom, turning the walls a shadowy collage of Mardi-Gras-ish colors. The room thundered with hundreds of students clustered around black tables lining the edges of the space.

Cooper and Angela melted into the crowd on the right, and Chris and I followed the rest of the group to the left. Looking back over my shoulder, I eyed them as they faded into the chaos. Good. Out of sight and out of the way.

Behind my mask, I searched the crowd. Where was Lachlan? For my plan to work, he had to show.

"Pictures first!" Chris shouted, bringing my attention back to the moment.

"Okay!" I replied, nodding, and scrunching my shoulders to my ears, faking excitement. With my purse slinked over my shoulder, we headed to the picture booth.

A thousand twinkling lights filled the ballroom ceiling. White and black checkerboard tiles covered the dance floor, matching the black tablecloths and white tulle bows on the back of each chair.

"Come on!" Chris pulled me around until we reached a line of students in gowns and tuxes waiting at the picture booth. With our fingers intertwined, he said, "What are you thinking?"

I grinned flatly. "Nothing. Just can't believe it's actually *dance* night. You know?" I smacked my gum.

With a nod of his head, he faced forward, joining in the group's conversation. He punched a guy in the shoulder, and they began chatting about Friday night's game, boring me completely.

The exterior of the large booth was painted with cartoonish masks, and a long heavy curtain blanketed the side. Six eager students pushed the curtain aside and giggled as they scurried out. A tinge of pot wafted off of them.

Chris squeezed my hand, pulling me forward beneath the mauve fabric into the booth.

A camera teetered in the far end. Splashes of greens and purples and golds splattered the festive backdrop.

I posed in my mask, with my hands on my hips, giving a superior stance. "Everyone freeze," I said. The girl next to me posed in mid-frozen position. The clock above the camera counted down from ten. None of us moved.

When a blinding light flashed, laughs filled the closet-like space. My phone vibrated against my ribs. While everyone exited, I unzipped my purse and followed them out.

I'd received a text message from Lachlan: *I'm here.*

The moment I read the message, Sonora woke up. She pulled and tugged at my insides. My head pounded. But I refused to let her grab ahold of me.

THIRTY-SIX

I leaned to the side, yanking Chris over, and whispered in his ear. "I'll be right back."

I kissed him with fervor, wanting to shove Sonora back into her snug corner. He nodded and gestured to come with.

I shook my head, kissing him on the nose for good measure. "I'll meet you downstairs," I said in my best sultry voice.

Across the dance floor and out the hall, I scurried to the bathrooms. With Sonora's persistence, I needed a moment to gather myself. The hallway wasn't much quieter than the ballroom, and it was thick with people, students, and teachers. Some hanging out, others walking to and fro. All wearing masks.

I pulled the lever, opening the door into the ladies restroom and slipped inside. At the row of sinks, I nervously breathed in and out. A girl from Chemistry finished washing her hands and looked at me weird. I brushed my fingers through my hair and straightened my dress, snugging it in the right places as the room emptied.

Bending over and glancing beneath the stalls, I spotted a pair of heels. I wasn't alone.

Shoving the mask on top of my head, I leaned on the edge around the sinks, not caring if they were wet. I squeezed the edge of the counter and stared at myself in the mirror. Blood rushed to my cheeks, and my forehead beaded with sweat. I wanted to splash my face with cold water but didn't.

Sonora, what are you going to do? I thought. I could feel her clawing her pretty little nails against the inside of my skin. In my reflection in the mirror, she stood behind me—a mirage that only I could see.

"A part of you wants this as much as I do," I mouthed under my breath, careful not to speak aloud.

I dabbed the sweat off, opened my purse, and placed two pills securely inside the edge of my bra.

"You have to make it through all of Fall Fling first," I mouthed to myself.

A metallic slide sounded, and a stall door opened. A woman exited, a lady much too old to be a student—a chaperone.

She raised her eyebrows at my presence and halted. A French twist held her hair taught. Her makeup was thick, filling in the wrinkles around her mouth and the edges of her eyes.

Three girls in puffy dresses entered, chatting and laughing and falling over each other.

I washed my hands and exited, not glancing a second time at them.

I didn't return Lachlan's text, I wanted him to search for me. I needed him around when Chris confessed to sleeping with Magnolia, giving Chris motive.

The hallway outside the bathroom was a few degrees cooler and it felt good on my clammy skin. A long gradual slope in the floor led back to the ballroom. The maroon patterned carpet was thin and outdated, and reminded me of the time Magnolia had haunted me at the fundraiser. Why hadn't she appeared tonight?

Back in the ballroom, I walked over to the drink station. A short table contained two gigantic glass bowls filled with colorful punch. Thick chunks of ice cream floated in the center. An orange cooler was labeled with the word, *water*.

"Can I help you?"

"Punch, please. One." I held up one finger and smiled.

A server in black-and-white attire served me a glass of pink foamy juice. I would've liked something stronger, but didn't exactly have anything to pour into my cup.

Sipping the sweet drink, I turned around and scanned the thick, shadowy crowd. Chris was somewhere, but I didn't know where. The frothiness of the drink slithered around my tongue, coating my throat.

A slow song, *Begin Again* by Taylor Swift, chimed on.

A few dozen people meandered off the dance floor. The thick chaos now a spotty clump of couples. I spotted Cooper and Angela on the far side of the floor.

A hand on the back of my arm startled me. Chris grabbed my waist and pulled me out onto the dance floor. In the middle, lights flashed green, yellow, red.

"Hey there," I murmured, dropping my eyelids in a flutter, pressing my lips to his ear.

I relaxed my hands around the back of his neck, and with my fingers, strummed the base of his hair. The short spikes on the nape of his neck tickled beneath my nails. We drifted toward Angela and Cooper.

Angela's unique dress crisscrossed her back, and even with the mask on, I knew it was her. Her head rested on his chest, her eyes closed. How does she show her face here? After what her father did? *The same way I did.*

Whatever. Didn't matter anyway.

Without pulling Chris, I leaned us to the left, moving a yard closer to Cooper and Angela.

My heart thumped. When the song faded, I released my grasp and nudged Chris's elbow. I moved the mask up to my forehead and mouthed, "Can we talk?"

"Are you tired? Sure," he smiled in a way that made me think he was in the mood to do more than talk.

A faster song picked up as we exited the dance floor. The bass thumped, vibrating the ground.

I pointed at the doors. Trying to speak over the song. "Want something to drink?"

He nodded.

For the second time, I headed to the drink station. Except this time, it was part of my plan. "Two punches," Chris told the waiter.

I waved my face with my hands. "It's hot in here. My feet are throbbing."

"Take off your shoes. No one cares." Chris turned around, looking over the ginormous dancing crowd.

I bent down to remove my shoes, slipped the pills Lachlan had given me from the tip of my bra and dropped them in his drink.

"Here you go!" I handed it to him. In thirty minutes, he'd be over. A laugh bubbled in my throat, but I remained calm.

He eyed me, raising his glass in a *cheers* fashion—and he drank all of it. "How about a refill?" he asked the waiter.

When he got his drink, I motioned toward the doors and he nodded. The loud ballroom didn't make it easy to talk.

When we approached the doors to the hallway, Chris reached out and pushed it open, holding it for me. I smiled beneath my mask. *Perfect.* When the door shut, muting the music, I moved my mask up.

"It's nice out here," he said, breathing in the cooler air. He wiped a sleeve over his face.

I began. "Chris. I know that we've had our problems, but I really hope you can forgive me. I was a Grade A bitch. And I don't want to be with anyone else but you."

He squared his shoulders to mine. "I feel the same way, babe." He removed his mask completely and held it in his hand.

My phone vibrated against my ribs again, but I ignored it. Masked people walked past as three chaperones remained at the doorway.

"Sonora. Cooper told me what happened the other day. Did you talk to someone yet?" I deduced he was referring to my outburst in the cafeteria.

"Whatever. Cooper's an ass. Everything's fine. Besides, I'm coming to terms with Bram's death and … Magnolia's." He winced at the sound of her name. I wanted to punch him, but that would be premature. "It's been a lot to handle. Don't know what else to say."

Words caught in his throat. "Yeah. For me too." His eyes graced the floor before peering back up. What did I see there? Guilt? Pain? Sorrow?

It doesn't matter. It doesn't matter.

I swallowed hard, and my chin came up. "Is there anything you want to say?" Would he tell me, would he confess?

He shook his head and avoided eye contact. "No … I love you."

"Me too."

Bastard. He had no effing clue I knew about his and Magnolia's little rendezvous.

I let his words sink in and stepped closer. He didn't flinch. Resting my fingers on the sleeve of his tux, his eyes fell on mine.

"We good?" I asked, wondering why the pills hadn't taken effect yet. Sonora squirmed inside, as if kicking and screaming against my head and ribs.

He smiled and pulled me in for a hug. I squeezed my arms around his back, locking my hands, breathing him in. For a moment, my soul softened—but only for a moment.

He stuck his elbow out, and I rested my hand through the nook of his arm. "Ready to go back in?"

"Sure," I said with a smile that hid the razor-sharp butterflies dancing in my gut.

He held the door open again, the music blared out into the hall, and we went back into the ballroom.

For the next few minutes, I felt free like I had in Curly's Coffee once Sonora granted me access. Freedom settled in my gut and Sonora quieted. Chris was about to pay for what he'd done. "A part of you wants it too," I whispered to Sonora. I inhaled deeply and smiled. A hand graced my shoulder. I spun around.

Lachlan. A Phantom of the Opera mask hugged the right side of his face, above matching attire.

He leaned in and whispered. "Can I talk to you?" A pang shot through my heart, a familiar pang. A pang that meant Sonora was fighting for control again. I looked back at Chris, but he didn't seem to have noticed Lachlan—yet.

"I'm sort of busy," I shouted, gesturing toward the dancing group. Chris would become a mushy mess soon.

Lachlan grabbed my forearm, moving his hand to mine. "Really?"

Chris stepped between us and pushed Lachlan back. "This again?" Chris asked, shoving Lachlan back another step. Lachlan removed his mask. Chaperones started coming our way. This needed to stop, we couldn't get kicked out. Not yet. But it *would* be helpful if Chris got angry in front of everyone—showing his *murderous* side.

Lachlan eyed me over Chris's shoulder, assessing the situation. Assessing me. Instead of pulling away, I smiled and placed my hand on Chris's shoulder. "Stop, Chris. It's okay. I'm here with you."

I stepped aside, pulling Lachlan with me. Chris glared at us. "Give me a few minutes, okay?" I said to Lachlan.

He pointed at the stairs in the distance, and I nodded. "Fifteen minutes!"

Lachlan backed off and disappeared into the crowd.

"I'd like to punch him good in the nose," Chris said behind clenched teeth.

"Chris, it'll be fine. Promise. I told him to leave me alone." I needed to assure him everything between us was good, I didn't want him storming off.

The thumping song faded. One of those lame line dancing songs came on, the kind that everyone pretends to hate but gets on the dance floor anyway. Chris didn't. With his hand on his stomach, he said, "I'll be right back."

I strolled to the refreshments table while watching Chris exit to the hall.

THIRTY-SEVEN

My nerves flashed through my veins at the steady increase of my heart. My eyes remained shut and I inhaled the faint aroma of sweat wafting off the dance floor. My phone buzzed again. I sighed and unzipped my purse.

Another text from Lachlan. *You coming?*

In a sec.

I stuffed my phone back in my purse, zipping it closed.

With a sulfuric taste on my tongue, I felt Magnolia's presence. But her power was doomed—the most she could do was make me sick, or cause my phone to fritz out. Or maybe she wanted Chris dead as much as I did? But what he had coming was much worse, jail. Someone had to pay for Magnolia's death, and it sure as hell wouldn't be me.

I slipped away toward the bathrooms.

I knocked on the men's room door. "Chris? Are you in there?" I pushed open the door. "Oops, sorry! Looking for Chris."

A guy washing his hands gestured toward the stall. I bent over, looking beneath the stalls.

There was only one set of shoes, and although most dress shoes looked the same, I had a good guess whom they belonged to.

"Chris?"

A muffled, caught-off-guard, voice replied. "Sooonora?"

I tapped the app on my phone to record our conversation and made sure my phone hung enough out of my purse to tape it as clear as possible. "I saw you earlier. You didn't look so good."

He didn't reply at first. I heard him fumble with the lock and he exited the stall.

I should be grossed out, and I was, a little. But mostly, I felt the rush of adrenaline. I felt alive! I was about to get him to confess.

As he washed his hands, I locked the bathroom door.

"What are you doing?" Chris asked, drying his hands, his pupils wider than normal.

"We need to talk." A rancid fishy smell filled the bathroom. Chris covered his nose.

"What is that smell?" His skin turned a greenish-pale.

I narrowed my eyes. "I know about you and Magnolia. How many other girls, Chris?" My words punctuated the air sharply.

He bounced back and forth on the balls of his feet. "I'm gonna be sick again." He ran to the stall door, but I blocked his way, retrieving a knife from my purse.

As soon as he saw the glimmer of my pocket knife, he backed up. It was *his* knife.

"Did you kill her, Chris?" I inched closer.

"Stop, Sonora."

"How many times did you sleep with her?"

He showed his palms, backing up farther. "Only once. I promise!" His expression went blank. "How did you know that? Why are there two of you?" He reached forward and his hand swatted through the air beside me.

I wouldn't let him change the subject. "Did you know how guilty she felt?"

Magnolia's ghost flickered in the corner of the bathroom. Was she watching?

He began stuttering. "I—I—I didn't think she had the chance to tell you yet, not before she died."

The truth was free now. He may not have killed her, but he confessed to what he did. And I knew *my* part in it all too.

I swallowed. "Is that why you killed her? To keep her quiet?" I accused.

He paced in circles, stumbling and grabbing at his hair. "What? No. I wouldn't have done that." Sweat trickled down the side of his face.

I held the serrated blade out farther, hoping to frighten him into confessing. "I. Don't. Believe. You."

His nostrils flared. He slammed his fist into the wall, leaving a dent in the sheetrock. A vein popped out of his forehead, and his eyes went cold. "I didn't kill her!"

He lunged for the knife in my hand.

Without meaning to, I stabbed him in the gut before either of us registered what had happened. Instead of fighting me, he halted mid-struggle and stumbled backward. The blade slid out of his stomach, still in my grasp.

He pressed his right hand against his gut. "Sonora! Help me!"

I held out my hands, covered in his blood.

Magnolia hovered in the corner. "Is this what you wanted?" I screamed. "Blood for blood?" She didn't speak.

Chris slumped against the sinks. My phone buzzed. Lachlan.

"Sonora, please," Chris gasped. His white shirt turned crimson.

I ignored his pleas and pressed the app button again, stopping my phone from recording further.

"Help me," Chris said, a horrified look on his face. He crumbled to the ground as blood soaked his shirt.

I wanted him to feel the hurt that I had felt. "Did you even care about Sonora?"

"Who?"

"Me!"

His eyes rolled and focused on my face. Blood flecked the corner of his mouth. His reply came out on a thready whisper. "Sonora, you're crazy."

There was that word. Crazy. I *hated* that word. I dove at him and drove the blade into his leg. He screamed. Sonora's voice echoed in my head, *Don't kill Chris! Don't!*

"Shut up!" I yelled back at her.

The bathroom door jostled. "Who's in there! Open this door! I gotta go, man!"

Chris gasped, "Help!"

But his scream was too weak, and whoever was on the other side stopped trying. "Guess they couldn't hear you over the music. Sucks to be you." Chris's eyes fluttered, his head wobbling on his shoulders.

My phone buzzed. Lachlan was *calling*.

I answered. "Lachlan, I need your help! Chris came at me with a knife! He's hurt. I'm in the boy's bathroom. Hurry!"

Chris's face paled. "I didn't attack you," he seethed, barely conscious. A pool of blood covered the floor beneath his leg.

"It was your knife. Who do you think the cops will believe?" I slashed my hand with the blade. The pain was exhilarating. Wiping off the handle of the knife, I kicked it beneath the sinks.

I bent over Chris's limp body. "This didn't exactly go as I planned, but it'll do."

A knock banged on the other side of the door. "Sonora!" It was Lachlan's voice.

The door clicked open. Magnolia hovered next to it. Did she unlock it? No, impossible. Someone had to have a key.

The door swung open. Lachlan shot through.

His eyes immediately fell to the floor. He halted in his tracks.

As his gaze found mine, a pang hit my heart and shattered it into tiny gelatin pieces. Sonora's strength increased. My neck stiffened.

"Lachlan," I gasped, blood dripping from my hand. I grabbed my chest and took a giant step to the counter. Sonora fought me, I could *feel* her inside as she battled for control. I looked up at my reflection, seeing—*her.* "No!" I yelled, not wanting to lose.

Lachlan ran to me, shoving napkins against the gash in my hand. "I need help. He killed Magnolia, and he tried to kill me!"

Behind him, Chris lay on the ground. With semi-closed eyes, Chris wheezed as he inhaled and exhaled.

His shirt was soaked red. Blood pooled beneath his knees.

My hands. My dress. Blood underneath my fingernails, filling the cracks in my skin. Sticky blood glued my fingers together. I giggled at the sight.

Blood.

A lot of *blood.*

My hands shook. My whole body trembled, from my bloody nails down to the tips of my toes.

"Sonora," Magnolia hissed. I looked up as her ghostly form rushed *through* me, pushing me out of the way. I bent over, the wind knocked from my lungs.

No, no, no!

Sonora gained control and I—Rosa—seeped slowly into the far corners of nothingness.

In the mirror, thin lines of icky maroon smeared across my cheek. My hair was a mess. I flipped the water on, frantically splashing my face and flushing the pain in my hand.

I furiously rubbed the blood from my right cheek. I rubbed so hard, it should've hurt. But it didn't. I felt numb. I was done hurting.

Moans echoed from behind.

"Sonora, you have to get help," Lachlan tugged my arm, pulling me away from the bloody boy on the floor. *Oh no, Chris!* I didn't mean for this to happen.

Swirling thoughts trapped my brain like a thick crowd in the hallway at school. I couldn't push through the thoughts. *What had I done?*

"I killed Magnolia," I whispered.

Magnolia moved across from me. Her dank, disgusting body lingered—between me and Lachlan.

"I killed Magnolia!" My voice boomed in the bathroom, echoing off the tile. I couldn't handle the guilt any longer.

I fell to the ground; the back of my head hit the edge of the sink on my way down. The world evaporated, blending light and dark, yellow and green.

Wailing filled the bathroom, a sound of pure anguish bouncing off the cold walls. It was coming from me.

I fell forward, slamming my palms onto the bathroom floor. "I killed Magnolia. I killed Magnolia. *I killed Magnolia!*" I sobbed.

Lachlan's eyes widened. Chris's eyes had closed. Was he dead too?

My eyes flickered between them—and Magnolia.

"I killed you," I said to her. "I'm so sorry. Can you forgive me?" I begged.

With those words, it was as if the walls that had held her back from moving on shattered. Her celestial dress stopped dripping.

Her face became whole, shining like the sun.

Her body became whole.

The tiny bloated lines in her skin that leaked with water disappeared. Her frame thinned; she looked as healthy as when she was alive.

I retreated further beneath the sinks, frightened.

Slowly, my gaze inched forward to her feet. Her polished nails. She was wearing the sandals that she loved.

Magnolia was still a ghost, but she no longer looked *dead—murdered—drowned.* Her dress wasn't torn, it was flowy. Her eyes, pretty and sparkly blue. Her skin, pearly perfect. Our friendship necklace glimmered around her neck. "Thank you, Sonora," she said to me.

"You can speak?" I said, shocked.

Her eyes fell to the ground and then back at me. "I forgive you, Sonora. Until you admitted what you did, I couldn't leave."

Hearing her speak, in that beautiful Magnolia voice, was as clear as the sunny day in the park.

"My death was fueled by the town's need to find the murderer. The way we died, the way everyone thought I had been murdered in the same way, it connected those girls to me. I tried to warn you about the other girl before he killed her too, but I failed. You were my only connection to the outside world, nobody else could see me." She peered over her shoulder into the distance. "I see my parents now. I have to go. It's time. Everything will be okay now."

Magnolia faded away. But unlike all the other times, this disappearing act felt final. A weight that had been strapped around me lifted, peeling layer by layer.

The clarity of what I had done to her, what I had done to Chris, rushed through me with a blinding force. I couldn't hide the truth, nor did I want to. I just wanted … nothing. I wanted nothing. I was nothing. Maybe I never would be.

I wanted the hauntings to stop. And now they had.

THIRTY-EIGHT

My wrists ached. The cuffs dug into my bones. Mr. Granger ducked the back of my head beneath the roof of his cop car. I let my head fall back on the seat, my weak muscles full of relief. It was finally over.

As I sat inside the car, Lachlan stared at me from the other side of the window.

Blood coated his hands and forearms. What did he think of me now? What did everyone think of me now?

Was he afraid of me? Would I ever see him again?

At the station, I wrote Mr. Granger a full confession. It was half a page. I had never planned on murdering anyone. My dad rushed through the doors, Mom by his side. Their fingers entangled in a mess of hopelessness. "Don't speak. Our lawyer is on his way," my dad said.

"I'm sorry, Dad. It's done." I didn't want to hide any longer.

"You need to put these on," Mr. Granger said, handing me a set of folded red clothes. "We need your dress for evidence."

In a separate room, a female officer remained at the door, not leaving me alone. I changed out of my dress and heels and climbed into the red shirt and pants. Using gloves, she picked up the fluffy gown and placed it in a large plastic bag.

The cop opened the door. "Follow me," she said flatly. As we exited the room, Mr. Granger stood feet away—with Lachlan beside him.

A single shot of hope zipped through me. "Why are you here?" I asked.

The officer squeezed my arm, forcing me further away from him. "We need to keep moving."

"Hold on," Mr. Granger said.

She released her fingers, and I rubbed my arm.

Mr. Granger stepped back, and Lachlan stepped forward, closing the distance between us. How did I get here? How had I never *noticed* Lachlan before these last couple of weeks? I hated myself for not loving him before. For being so high and mighty on my own stupid high-school pedestal. Gawd, I'd been an idiot!

I desperately wanted to rewind time. And I desperately wanted to see my brother.

Lachlan grabbed my hand. His warm fingers rested on mine. "Sonora," he said. His soft voice smooth on my ears.

I closed my eyes, wishing we were elsewhere. "Say it again. My name."

He squeezed my hands. "Sonora. Everything will be okay."

My eyes shot open and I shook my head. "No, it won't. We both know that."

Pain etched into the corners of his eyes. "Chris is in critical condition. But he's not dead."

"Is that supposed to make me feel better?" I didn't feel anything. Nothing.

He released my hand, but I didn't want him to let go. A smile tilted his lips. "You're underage, you won't go to prison. And if he doesn't die, then well, that's good. Right?"

I scrunched my shoulders. "Maybe. Why are you being so nice to me?"

"You're still you. The same girl from the rave, the same girl that climbed through my window and asked for help."

"That's enough, let's go," the officer said as she grabbed my elbow. My wrists pulled against each other, bound by the cuffs.

Lachlan leaned forward and wrapped his arms around me one last time. I inhaled the brief moment before being yanked away. For all that I had done, I'd make it right. Somehow. If Magnolia could find peace, so could I.

EPILOGUE

Psychiatric hospitals weren't so bad. I had one roommate, and six months left before I'd be released. I was lucky, Chris didn't die. In fact, he testified against locking me up. Magnolia's death was ruled an accident.

How ironic. If I'd only confessed when I remembered, would I be here now?

"You gonna use that?" Chandler asked, motioning toward my notepad. She was a paperholic and wanted a few pages. "Is he coming today?"

My room was twice the size of the one I had at home. Two beds and two desks and one large window. Sun gleamed through the blinds of our window, sending diagonal shadows along the room's eggshell walls.

Chandler's body shrunk back into her spine, a permanent Hunchback of Notre-Dame appearance. She never looked anyone in the eyes and had been living here much longer than me.

I opened my drawer to give her one of my pencils and a few pieces of paper. Next to the notepad were the newspaper clippings from my case. I refused to hide my past, 'confronting it was part of the healing process,'" Dr. Sylvia had said.

A picture of Chris in a wheelchair, healing from his wounds, sat front and center. Magnolia's school picture sat next to his on my dresser.

"Here," I said to Chandler, handing the supplies to her. The clock on the wall reminded me to hurry. "I don't want to be late. Lachlan's visiting today." THE END

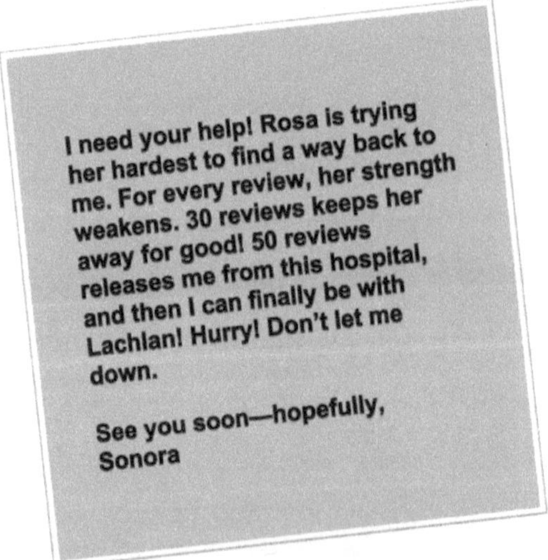

ABOUT THE AUTHOR

Dawn Husted grew up in central Texas, in Aggieland. She discovered her love of writing after graduating from Texas A&M University. She enjoys writing urban fantasy, science fiction, romance, and paranormal suspense.

She lives with her wild husband, two kids, one stray cat, and an Australian shepherd.

Visit www.DawnHusted.com.

Scythe of Darkness
Mia was looking forward to her senior year of high school.
But when a hot new student arrives, she's thrust into a
sinister world where grim reapers exist. Mia's life is about
to become more entangled with death than she ever
thought possible.

www.dawnhusted.com
Available as eBook and Paperback

Safe

What if the one place that's supposed to keep you safe is the one place that could kill you? After the world's nearly destroyed, an island is preserved for survivors. Eighteen-year-old Penelope Evans lives in the Colony along with hundreds of other islanders.

An impenetrable perimeter surrounds their homes and keeps everyone protected from the outside world. But when an unexpected meeting is scheduled, requesting all citizens, Penelope is on alert. This meeting springs a series of events that leaves her running for her life, leading further from normality and toward an epic truth. Can she survive inside a sealed perimeter?

www.dawnhusted.com
Available as eBook and Paperback